BACKLASH

Books by Rachel Dylan

CAPITAL INTRIGUE

End Game
Backlash

ATLANTA JUSTICE

Deadly Proof
Lone Witness
Breach of Trust

BACKLASH

RACHEL DYLAN

BETHANYHOUSE

a division of Baker Publishing Group
Minneapolis, Minnesota

© 2020 by Rachel Dylan

Published by Bethany House Publishers
11400 Hampshire Avenue South
Bloomington, Minnesota 55438
www.bethanyhouse.com

Bethany House Publishers is a division of
Baker Publishing Group, Grand Rapids, Michigan

Printed in the United States of America

ISBN 978-0-7642-3431-6 (trade paper)
ISBN 978-0-7642-3777-5 (casebound)

This is a work of fiction. Names, characters, incidents, and dialogues are products of the author's imagination and are not to be construed as real. Any resemblance to actual events or persons, living or dead, is entirely coincidental.

Cover design by Faceout Studio

Author is represented by the Nancy Yost Literary Agency.

20 21 22 23 24 25 26   7 6 5 4 3 2 1

To Daddy.
You're the reason I can write books filled with faith
and demonstrating the amazing love of God.
I miss you so much, but the gift of faith
and love you gave me will live
in my heart forever.

CHAPTER
ONE

The incessant knocking on her condo door made Layla Karam grumble as she threw off the covers. She had no idea who would be so insistent—especially at two in the morning. Over five years at the CIA had made her cautious, so she grabbed her gun from the nightstand and went to the door, ready for anything.

She looked through the peephole and let out a sigh of relief, then disarmed the alarm system to let in DEA Agent Cassandra Ruiz.

"Cass, what's going on?"

Cass's dark brown eyes were bloodshot, and she was shaking. "I should've shot him."

"Shot who?" The dread Layla had felt when she first heard the knocking returned.

"A man was in my house. I hesitated instead of pulling the trigger, and he got away."

"Have you called the police?"

Cass shook her head. "No, because I think it might be connected to our DEA op."

How could that be possible? "Come sit down, and let's go through this."

Layla led Cass into the living room and sat down with her on the couch. She'd never seen Cass frazzled, but right now the agent was a mess.

"Let's start at the beginning," Layla said. "Tell me the entire story. Take your time."

Cass took a deep breath. "I worked late. When I got home, I immediately noticed that someone had been rummaging through my house. Things were strewn everywhere. He was definitely looking for something. As I was surveying the damage, a man jumped me from behind. I was able to fight him off. I fired a warning shot, and he started running. I could've taken him out, but I didn't."

"Did you recognize him?" Layla had shaken off the cobwebs of sleep and was now fully awake.

"No." Cass's hands shook as she clasped them in front of her. "But he had Mejía tattoos on his arms."

The Mejía cartel was the most dangerous and brutal cartel in Honduras. The DEA had recently performed an operation in Honduras, and Layla had been brought on to the team to give her more field experience—something the Agency was pushing her hard on. "There's no way that could be a coincidence."

"Exactly. I'm sorry to barge in on you in the middle of the night, but since you're only a few minutes away, I thought I needed to warn you ASAP in case he decided to head here."

"You did the right thing. Have you noticed anything before tonight? Anything out of the ordinary?" Layla had, but she didn't think this was the time to bring it up. Cass was agitated enough, given her harrowing night.

"No. It's been business as usual since we got back stateside. Everyone at the DEA was satisfied with the outcome, even if we didn't get all the way to the top of the cartel."

"I assume you don't bring work materials home?" Layla had to put that out there.

"You know I don't. That would be against all security protocols."

"Could you have been mistaken about the tattoo? Could he have just been a thief?"

"None of my jewelry was taken."

"Electronics?" Layla questioned.

"He did take my tablet, but there won't be anything work related on it. But I'm pretty certain about the tattoo."

"We got a boatload of cash from the op. Maybe he thought you might have some of it."

Cass groaned. "If he was looking for confiscated money, then he had to think I'm a dirty agent."

Layla lifted her hands. "I'm just throwing out possibilities. I'm not saying that about you. But I'm wondering whether the cartel could have a reason to *think* that."

"I'm sorry, I'm just on edge. But no, I play by the book." Cass's voice became steadier.

Layla didn't know Cass *that* well, but she didn't have any reason to suspect she was playing both sides. Although, Layla had heard rumors that the DEA had their fair share of dirty agents. "Have you reported it to the DEA?"

"Not yet, but I will. I wanted to make sure you were safe first. I sent a quick text to Zane and Diaz to warn them, too, just in case."

Zane and Diaz were the other two members of the DEA

team Layla had been assigned to. "Whatever you need from me, just say the word."

"Can I crash on your couch for a few hours? I'd rather not go home until light."

"Of course."

"Thank you." Cass paused. "I can't help but think trouble followed us home from Honduras."

◆

Layla had woken early the next morning to find a kind note from Cass. She must have left right at the crack of dawn. They'd exchanged a couple of texts, and Cass had said she would call DEA, which Layla felt was the right move.

Now Layla weaved quickly through the Saturday crowd that had gathered for the fall street festival in Old Town Alexandria. Maybe she was being paranoid, but she couldn't shake the feeling that she was being followed. *Again.*

She'd kept that fact to herself last night. Cass had already seemed way too unsteady. But Layla wondered if there was something going on involving their joint mission. Could her suspected tail be connected to Cass's thief?

She glanced over her shoulder and didn't see anyone, but she kept moving as briskly as she could without running. Had working at the CIA made her this jumpy?

When she finally saw the smiling face of one of her best friends, Vivian Steele, she let out a breath.

"Why are you so flushed?" Viv asked.

"Walk with me." Layla grabbed her friend's arm.

"What's wrong?"

"I feel like I have a tail."

Viv frowned. "Are you working right now?"

Layla shook her head. "It could be that I'm just on edge, but all my instincts are telling me otherwise."

Viv was one of the few people who knew that Layla worked at the Agency. To the rest of the world, Layla was a State Department analyst.

Viv touched her shoulder. "I trust your instincts completely. Do you want to get out of here?"

Layla shook her head again. "There's no reason to be silly about this."

"Do you think you're under some type of surveillance?" Viv's hazel eyes widened.

Layla couldn't say for sure. "I don't know."

"Have you noticed anything before today?"

That was the thing. She had. "Lately I've felt like someone is watching me, but I haven't been able to substantiate that concern. And then, when I got off the Metro and started walking over, I thought I might have a tail."

Viv stopped and looked around for a minute, her eyes scanning the crowded streets. "I don't notice anything out of the ordinary, but it's pretty packed down here today."

Layla sighed. "I'm sorry. Forget I said anything. Let's eat. Izzy wanted to join us, too, but she'll be a little late. She said to go ahead and order hers." If their schedules allowed, they met for lunch each Saturday at their favorite restaurant, the Old Town Grille. They'd met Izzy Cole, an NCIS agent, a few months ago and had welcomed her into their friend group.

"You know you never have to apologize to me," Viv said. "Given the nature of what you do, you have every right to be concerned. Have you told anyone at work about this?"

"No." And she wouldn't. She was going to hold this tight to the vest. Viv only knew a piece of what Layla worked on because they'd been on a task force together, but there was a lot that Viv was in the dark about.

They entered Old Town Grille and met Ginny, the friendly hostess who greeted them every week. The short, older brunette smiled at them. "Girls, I'm so sorry. I know your favorite table is in the back right by the window, but a group of tourists came in, and they were insistent that they sit at that table. I've got you a great table on the other side of the restaurant, if that's okay?"

Viv gave Ginny a warm smile. "Of course. We understand that you can't hold our table for us. We'll have a great time regardless."

"That's right," Layla added. "You all are extra busy today."

Ginny led them to a table on the left side of the restaurant. "That's because we have the festival traffic, but I won't complain about being busy. I assume you don't need menus, but let me know if you want them."

Layla laughed. "You're right. We're way too predictable for menus."

"I'll send your server over."

Once they had placed their orders, Viv looked right at Layla. "I know you too well. Something is definitely up. Are you going to tell me what's really going on?"

"That's the thing, Viv. I don't know. I really don't. All I have is this sinking suspicion that someone is following me."

"I guess this goes without saying, but could it be connected to whatever you're working on right now?"

Layla had been asking herself the same thing. "I'm not sure."

"You can't talk to me about details, but is there anything you can share?"

Layla considered her options. Viv worked as an attorney

at the State Department, and the two of them had worked together before on highly sensitive classified projects. She knew she could trust Viv with her life, so she decided to open up in a high-level way. "I worked with DEA on a mission last month. One of the DEA agents came to see me in the middle of the night. A man had ransacked her house."

Viv twirled her straw in her soda. "So there could be a connection between someone watching you and what happened to her?"

Layla nodded. "Yeah. Or it's completely possible that I'm just being paranoid, or that there are two separate things going on."

"You need to be careful." Viv's tone had turned serious.

"I will, I promise, but let's stop talking about it and enjoy lunch. I'm sure everything will be fine."

Viv shifted in her seat. "Then is it safe to bring up the reunion and your last-minute excuse not to go?"

This topic was almost worse than the other. "My excuse was legit. I really did have a work emergency come up yesterday."

"Well, once you bailed, Bailey and I decided not to go either."

"You shouldn't have let me stop you."

Viv leaned forward. "You might have dodged the reunion, but that still doesn't resolve the larger issues you have with Hunter."

Layla groaned at her ex's name.

"Maybe it would be good to talk to him and finally get some closure."

"Closure," Layla muttered. "How much closure can you get from the love of your life cheating on you?" Her heart had been shattered into a million little pieces her third year of law school when she'd found out Hunter McCoy had been unfaithful.

"It's not just that he cheated on you. It's how it all went down."

"Are you talking about the fact that he chose a college girl who couldn't have been more different than me? Or the fact that he told me right in the midst of my interviews for the Agency?"

"Both," Viv said flatly. "I can still hear the pain in your voice over five years later. Facing him is just what you need to be able to move on. You can't pine over him forever. It's time to open yourself to new possibilities. It's been long enough."

If only. Layla had been convinced that Hunter was *the one*. She'd asked God so many times why. Why had she been so wrong? And how could Hunter have been so cruel? "I understand what you're saying, but dealing with feelings isn't always a rational exercise."

Viv patted her hand. "I'll be by your side. You don't have to go through this alone. You know that Bailey and I will always be there for you."

"Speaking of Bailey, she and Marco have been inseparable lately. I think they might be in it for the long haul."

Viv laughed. "That's an interesting way of putting it."

Layla was thrilled that Bailey had found someone. Even if it meant they now had to share her with Marco. Their friendship was strong enough for anything.

"Thanks for helping me take my mind off things," Layla said. "Even if it was by bringing up an equally difficult topic." She laughed.

"Anything for you." Viv smiled.

They'd been through a lot together, and Viv had become

like a sister to Layla. "Enough about me. How was your week?"

Before Viv could answer, a loud explosion rocked the restaurant, throwing Layla backward onto the ground. She took a deep breath as the air filled with acrid smoke, and then her world went black.

CHAPTER
TWO

NCIS Agent Izzy Cole was almost at the Old Town Grille when the explosion happened. Without hesitation, she started to run as fast as she could toward the billowing black smoke, her heart pounding.

"Call 911," she yelled to a few onlookers as she flashed her NCIS credentials.

As she made her way to the front of the building, a few flames were still burning, but she plowed forward. She had to find her friends. These women had welcomed her into their lives with open arms only months ago. She'd never had real girlfriends before, but now she didn't know how she could live without them.

Izzy stepped through the rubble and saw multiple injured people on the ground. She stopped to check the pulse of one young woman, and when there was nothing, she kept moving forward.

One man was conscious, his arm bleeding. She squatted beside him. "Put pressure on it. Help's on the way."

He nodded and did as she directed.

She scanned the restaurant and spotted two women under piles of debris to her left. Fearing the worst, she ran over and started pulling away the pieces of wood and rubble until she could see Viv's face. Her friend's hazel eyes flickered open.

"Viv, can you hear me?" Izzy asked.

Viv nodded.

"Are you hurt? Can you move everything?"

Viv still didn't speak but took a moment to flex her limbs and then tried to sit up. "Yeah, I think so. Layla. Where's Layla?" Her eyes widened.

Izzy feared shock was setting in. "Let me check. I think she's right over here."

Her pulse continued to thump loudly as she approached the person she believed was Layla. There was more debris on top of her, including a beam of wood that had probably come down from the ceiling. Izzy started to remove the debris and saw that Layla's eyes were shut. Bright blood was streaked through her long black hair. Her olive skin had lost a lot of its color. Checking for a pulse, Izzy let out a huge breath when she found one. Layla was unconscious, but she was alive.

Viv squatted beside her. "Oh no."

"She's alive. But we shouldn't move her until the paramedics get here. I don't know if she's suffered any head or neck trauma." Izzy turned toward Viv and saw that her eyes were dilated and she was shaking. "Just stay put, Viv. You don't need to be moving either."

Thankfully, the sound of sirens filled the air. After another minute, police and paramedics flooded the area. "We need help over here," Izzy yelled.

A few paramedics jogged over.

"She's not conscious. Possible head trauma, but I'm not sure." Izzy turned toward another EMT. "And please check her out too. I think she's in shock."

Viv was now sitting on the ground with her legs hugged tightly to her chest as she shivered.

Izzy took a step back to give them room to work and realized she was shaking. A stocky young officer from Alexandria PD approached her.

"Ma'am, I'm Officer Baker. Can I ask you some questions?"

She nodded. "I'm Special Agent Cole, NCIS."

"I didn't realize NCIS was working this."

"We're not. I was coming here to meet my friends for lunch." She pointed toward Layla and Viv.

"Ah. Can you tell me what you saw?"

"I was walking toward the restaurant and was about a block away when the explosion happened. I knew my friends were here, so I started running toward the scene. I helped a few people before I got back to this area."

"Did you see anyone fleeing the scene? Anything suspicious?"

Izzy shook her head. "No, sir. Nothing like that. I assume you're going to have the bomb squad come and take a look?"

"They're en route now. Anything else you saw that you think could be relevant?"

"No. You should know that both of those women are federal workers for the State Department."

Officer Baker jotted down a note. "Thank you. Appreciate your help here."

"Of course." Izzy took a deep breath and turned her attention back to her friends.

EMTs were helping Viv onto a gurney. Her face had lost all of its color.

"We're transporting them both to Alexandria Hospital," an EMT said.

"Can I ride with you?"

"No, but you can follow," he answered.

She flashed her credentials. "Please."

"Why didn't you say you were a Fed?" The EMT smiled.

Izzy watched them roll Layla toward the ambulance. Still unconscious. She pulled out her phone and sent a 911 text to Bailey and gave the hospital info. *Lord, please let her be okay.*

◆

Layla awoke feeling like her head was being squeezed in a vise. Her mouth was so dry, and she had no idea where she was. She took a breath, but it hurt to breathe deeply.

"You're awake," a soft voice said.

Layla's vision blurred but then came into focus. Izzy stood by her bedside. Where was she? She couldn't put her thoughts together clearly.

"What happened?" she croaked.

Izzy took her hand. "There was an explosion at the restaurant. You were knocked unconscious."

Layla gasped, sending shooting pain through her ribs as the memories roared back like a freight train. "Viv?"

"She's okay. They're treating her for shock, but she'll be fine. Bailey is with her now."

Layla closed her eyes for a moment but already had so many questions. "What are they saying was the source of the explosion?"

"They checked for a gas leak, but the bomb squad found an actual explosive device. What they'll try to figure out next is motive. They're running background checks on the owners and all employees."

A much more sinister explanation came to Layla's mind, but Izzy didn't know she was CIA. And she couldn't tell her. So she kept her mouth shut.

Bailey Ryan burst into the room. "You're awake!"

Seeing one of her best friends was almost too much for Layla as the tears started to well up.

"I'm going to check on Viv and let the two of you talk." Izzy excused herself, leaving Layla alone with Bailey.

"I'm so glad to see you," Layla said.

"I feel the same way."

"How is Viv?"

"Doing better. They're going to do some tests just to make sure she doesn't have any internal bleeding."

Layla's heart dropped. "Oh no."

"It's just precautionary. The doctor doesn't think so. They already did X-rays on you while you were out. They think you suffered a concussion. No fractures, but bruised ribs."

"It feels like it." Layla paused. "Before Izzy gets back, I want to tell you something."

"What is it?" Bailey glanced toward the door.

"I think I could've been the target."

Bailey's green eyes widened. "Work related?"

"Yeah. I've felt like someone has been watching me the past couple of weeks."

Bailey pulled up a chair and sat down. "So you think you're being tailed, and then this explosion. Sounds like bad news to me."

Layla nodded, and pain shot down her spine. "I wanted you to know about my suspicions in case anything happens to me. You should also know that we didn't sit in our normal seats today. Can you run down whether the people at our usual table are among the casualties?" She also needed to check on Cass and the other Honduras op team members to make sure nothing had happened to them.

Bailey squeezed her hand. "We'll figure this out. You helped me when I needed you, and I'll do the same for you. No questions asked. But right now, I'm going to insist that you get some rest. I'll find out what I can on the bombing details."

"We go there every week for lunch."

"I know," Bailey said softly. "It does make a convenient target." She stood. "But there's nothing you can do right now. Try to sleep a little, and we'll figure it out. I promise."

Layla closed her eyes but couldn't shake the suspicion that someone wanted her dead.

CHAPTER
THREE

Private investigator Hunter McCoy met Detective Elijah Hall from Alexandria PD at Hunter's office. They had been randomly paired together as freshman roommates at the University of Virginia and had been best friends ever since. They couldn't have been more different. Hunter, a scrawny kid from rural Virginia who tended to get into trouble, and Elijah, a city kid from the Bronx who studied hard and didn't have time for Hunter's nonsense. Hunter had learned many life lessons from Elijah, including expanding his way of thinking about the world. Growing up in rural Virginia had given him a limited perspective on life and people. Being friends with Elijah had opened his eyes, and he was a much better man for it.

Hunter had gotten a call from Elijah that they needed to talk about the restaurant bombing.

"Does Alexandria PD want to hire me?" As a private investigator, Hunter had done freelance work for them in the past.

"No. It's nothing like that." Elijah's dark brown eyes met his.

"What is it, man? It's not like you to beat around the bush."

Elijah took a breath. "I wanted to meet in person because there's something you need to know."

Hunter knew something was wrong but waited for Elijah to spit it out.

"One of the victims of the bombing today was Layla."

Dots danced before Hunter's eyes as a wave of nausea hit him. "Is she dead?"

Elijah placed a hand on his shoulder. "No, she made it, but she's at Alexandria Hospital."

"How badly is she hurt?"

"I'm not sure, but I thought you'd want to know."

Still in shock, Hunter stared at him. "Do you have any leads?"

"Nothing yet. Bomb squad is doing their thing. FBI got called in, too, because of the possible terrorist threat. So far two fatalities and lots of injured."

Hunter ran a hand through his hair.

Elijah moved a step closer to him. "Look. You need to go see her. I don't know how serious it is. And it's always been clear to me that you never stopped loving her."

Wasn't that the truth. "I'm probably the last person on this earth that she'd want to see."

"That was a long time ago. A lot has happened since then. I think she'd welcome a visit from you, especially given the circumstances."

"I'm not so sure about that, but you're right, I have to go.

Even if she kicks me out. I need to try." Hunter didn't know what he'd do without Elijah's friendship. He was more like a brother than a friend.

"Don't wait." Elijah stood. "I'm headed back to work. Hit me up and let me know how it went."

"Will do. And thanks again."

"Always."

Hunter watched Elijah leave and then tried to muster up the courage to drive to the hospital. Everything with Layla had ended so badly. They'd only crossed paths a couple of times since law school graduation, and those instances had barely been a quick and awkward hello.

But now his main concern was making sure she was all right. Had terrorists targeted the Old Town restaurant? Or was this something else entirely?

He wasn't law enforcement, but as someone who had a law degree and had been a PI for five years, working high-stakes cases, he couldn't help but want to get answers. Especially considering that whoever was behind this atrocity had hurt Layla. *His* Layla, even though he had zero right to think of her like that. He'd given that up a long time ago.

He had to push aside his fear and the past and get down to the hospital. If something happened to her and he didn't have the chance to try to make things right, he would never forgive himself.

A knock on the door of her hospital room awakened Layla from a light doze. Her boss, Brett King, stood in the hallway.

"Brett." She shifted in the bed.

"I came to check on you as soon as I got word that you

were on the list of victims." He walked into the room and sat down beside her bed. "How're you feeling?"

"Been better, but I'm alive. Not everyone at the restaurant was so fortunate." She still couldn't believe there had been a bombing. Her brain wasn't processing everything quickly enough, but a nagging voice in her head told her something was really off. "Has there been any chatter about it?"

He moved closer to her and shook his head. "No. Given that one of our own was injured, though, we will monitor the investigation closely. Did the Feds come to talk to you yet?"

"No, but I'm sure they will."

"I assume you'll keep your cover intact?"

"Of course." She couldn't believe he would even ask that.

Brett's shoulders slumped. "This is really bad timing, considering all you've gone through today, but there's something else I have to talk to you about, and unfortunately it can't wait."

Her heartbeat thumped. She didn't need more bad news. "What?"

Brett squinted his light blue eyes. "There's no easy way to say this, so I'll just come out and say it. Effective immediately, you're put on administrative leave."

"What?" she said loudly. "Why?" She never would have expected those words to come out of Brett's mouth. "You can't sideline me because of this. It wasn't my fault."

"The Inspector General's office is conducting a confidential investigation. I'm not privy to the details of the investigation, but I was ordered to put you on leave."

She felt like she'd just been pushed off a cliff. "I don't understand."

"I don't either. All I can tell you is that it definitely didn't come from me, but the direction was clear."

"Wait a minute. You're saying I'm the *subject* of an IG investigation?"

Brett shoved his hands in his pockets. "Yes."

"And it has nothing to do with the bombing."

"That's right."

None of this made sense, but she was now certain of one thing: All of these events couldn't be coincidences. But because of that, she couldn't trust a word Brett was saying either. And she couldn't talk to him about Cass yet. "I don't know how to respond."

"You don't have to say anything. And like I said, I hate that it had to come about during this episode. But, Layla, my hands are tied."

"The IG's office gave you the order?"

"Yes. It didn't come up through operational command."

She had to put something out there for Brett to consider. "Don't you find it a little odd, the timing of all this?"

"I was just given the order at the end of the day yesterday. I was going to wait until Monday morning when you came into the office, but then this happened, and it was better just to tell you. Your building access has been revoked pending the investigation, but you will continue to be paid. I guess that's the only silver lining." He paused. "Layla, if you've gotten into some type of trouble, it would be better to talk about it now."

It stung that Brett was truly concerned she could have done something wrong. "There's nothing to talk about, Brett. I'm clean."

He gave her a slight smile. "Good. Then hopefully this can be sorted out quickly, and we can get you back to work. You should hear from someone in the IG's office for an interview, but I'm not sure on timing. And the Agency requests that you don't leave the greater DC area until this gets sorted out and that you surrender your passport."

"What do they think, I'm some sort of flight risk?"

Brett lifted his hands. "I was told it was procedure."

That sounded crazy to her.

He patted the edge of the bed. "I've taken up enough of your time. I'll get out of here. Hope you start feeling better soon."

"Thanks." What else was she supposed to say? She watched him walk out of the room.

Someone had to be coming after her. She tried to rest as much as she could, but her brain was spinning.

When another knock came on her room door a couple of hours later, she hoped it would be a friendly face—and it was.

Scarlett Bell, her friend and mentor, walked into the room with a vase of bright pink tulips in hand. Scarlett knew her well. Layla loved everything pink.

Scarlett placed the vase on the table beside the bed. "Layla, what happened? Bailey called me and told me you were in the Old Town Grille when the bomb went off."

"I was there with Viv."

"Yes, Bailey mentioned that, but she said Viv was stable."

Layla nodded. "Yeah. She'll be fine. We were both very fortunate."

Scarlett tucked a strand of brown hair behind her ear. "I'll stop by and see Viv on my way out."

"Listen, Scarlett, I know you may think this is crazy, but I believe the bombing could be linked to the Honduras op." Layla was free to confide in Scarlett since she had been read into this DEA operation after the fact. Scarlett worked at State in the INL Bureau—basically the international narcotics division. She had been assigned to Layla two years ago as her interagency mentor. Fifteen years Layla's senior, Scarlett was a highly regarded government servant who had worked at DEA before State and had tons of field experience. The Agency had been urging Layla to get into the field more, and Scarlett was trying to guide her through that process.

"Why do you think that?"

"Cass's house was ransacked last night, and she believes her attacker was linked to the cartel."

Scarlett took her hand. "Layla, I know I'm the one who's always pushing you to take risks and get out there, but this is a highly dangerous situation. I didn't know what had happened to Cass, but after hearing that fact, I'm even more convinced that I have intel to explain why the cartel might be coming after the team."

Layla's pulse quickened. "What?"

"It was my understanding from the post-op briefing I got from DEA that the mission was a success, but there were some casualties on the cartel side."

Layla nodded. "All from self-defense, though. Completely legitimate use of force by our team." Even though she was just getting into fieldwork, she had been drilled hard on protocol and knew that they had dotted all their *I*'s and crossed all their *T*'s on the mission. She'd been impressed that no one in the DEA had wanted to cut any corners.

"I'm not questioning protocol."

"Then, what is it?"

Scarlett looked away. "One of the men killed was Roberto Mejía."

Layla's heart sank. "I assume he's related to Diego?"

"Roberto was Diego's little brother."

The full implication of Scarlett's revelation was coming into focus. "You're telling me that someone on our team killed the leader of the cartel's little brother?"

"Yeah, so now you potentially have Diego seeking payback."

"Have you told the others?"

"Not yet. Getting down here to see you was my top priority."

Layla was so glad that Scarlett was there. She'd been a guiding force in Layla's career. What started out as a professional mentoring relationship had become a valued friendship. "Brett just came to see me."

Scarlett's eyes lit up. "I'm glad he checked on you. Sometimes he's a bit dense with these things."

"He wasn't just inquiring about my well-being."

Scarlett raised an eyebrow. "What happened?"

"He told me that I've been put on administrative leave, pending an IG investigation."

The shock on Scarlett's face mirrored Layla's own emotions.

"So you didn't know anything about this?"

"Of course not. Why would you be investigated?"

That was the million-dollar question. "Brett claimed ignorance. Said it went up the chain and was out of his control, and that I'd be hearing from the IG's office soon."

Scarlett leaned closer to her. "Layla, this isn't good. IG investigations can put a blot on your record forever."

Layla sighed. "But what am I supposed to do about it?"

"Fight it. Hard." Scarlett's eyes sparked. "Do not roll over on this. Get legal counsel. Someone you trust and who has the requisite security clearances. I know you went to law school, but you shouldn't defend yourself."

29

Hearing how dire Scarlett made the situation sound only made Layla feel worse. "Okay."

Scarlett squeezed her hand. "I'm sorry. You've been through a hugely traumatic event today, but I want to make sure that you're covered so you can handle this investigation and get your record cleared. You are way too valuable to the Agency for them to mess around with something like this."

"What are you saying?"

"They must think they have something on you. You'll need to go back through your work and see if you cut any corners. Did anything that could cause red flags."

Layla already knew the answer to that. She played by the rules. Always. It was one of her qualities that she thought would hamper her ability to be an operations officer. Integrity meant something to her. "I understand."

"I'm sorry that I've made things worse for you, but I thought you needed to know about the cartel. You should watch your back. Rely on your training."

Even though Layla had never intended to be more than an analyst, she'd gone through training at the Farm because the CIA insisted. Now maybe that training was going to be put to good use. "I'll be on guard, believe me."

"Good. Because your life may depend on it."

◆

Hunter arrived at the hospital and, after pushing through some red tape, found out where Layla was. When he got to her room, he heard a female voice talking in hushed tones. Taking a deep breath, he knocked before peeking his head inside.

Hunter didn't recognize the tall, slender brunette with glasses by Layla's side. But his eyes immediately went to

Layla. Alive . . . she was alive. Yes, Elijah had told him that, but he had to confirm it with his own eyes.

Even though he could tell Layla was injured, she still looked gorgeous. Her long, wavy black hair flowed past her shoulders. When she made eye contact with him, neither of them said a word.

The woman walked over to him and stretched out her hand. "Scarlett Bell. You must be a friend of Layla's."

He took her hand. "Hunter McCoy."

As he said his name, he saw a flash of recognition in Scarlett's eyes. Unfortunately, she knew exactly who he was.

"I'll be back later to check on you. I'm going to see Viv." Scarlett leaned down and whispered something in Layla's ear before making her way to the door.

Hunter turned his attention to Layla and walked over to her bedside. "I know I don't have any right to be here, but when I heard you were injured in the attack, I had to come."

She didn't immediately respond, and an awkward silence filled the room. Would she tell him to hit the road? Or worse? He clenched his fists by his sides and hoped she would say something soon.

"How did you even know I was here?" she asked softly.

"Elijah works for Alexandria PD. He told me." He knew Layla would remember Elijah, given how much time she'd spent around him back when they were together.

More silence. This had probably been a bad idea, but there was no going back now. He stood in front of her, looking right into her dark brown eyes, and he was finding it hard to steady his breathing. There was something about her that cut to his core. And his decisions had ripped apart everything they'd had together.

"I've had quite a day," she whispered, almost like she was defeated. "But *you* really don't need to be here, Hunter."

He exhaled, not ready to give up. "What are the doctors saying?"

"I'll be okay. Concussion and some bumps and bruises, but it could've been much worse." Her voice started to shake.

It took every ounce of willpower in his body not to hold her and try to comfort her. Instead, he took a tentative step forward. "But you're alive, and that's what matters."

"Have you heard anything about the investigation?" she asked.

"Minimal. FBI is working a terrorism angle, and Alexandria PD and FBI are on the scene."

She bit her bottom lip.

He knew that was one of her tells. "Is there something you know?"

"No. I wish I did."

He'd known Layla well enough to see she wasn't telling him everything, but he wasn't in any position to push her.

He heard motion behind him and turned. Two men stood in the doorway. The taller one spoke.

"Ms. Karam, I'm Agent Blakely, and this is Agent Jones from the FBI. Can we ask you some questions?"

"Sure," Layla said.

That was Hunter's cue to leave. "I'll check on you later."

"That's not necessary," she said.

But there was no way he was just going to slip away, never to be heard from again.

Hunter walked out of the room and stood outside of the agents' line of sight, then pretended like he was looking at his phone while he listened to the conversation. He knew he shouldn't, but he needed to know she was okay.

Agent Blakely cleared his throat. "Let's start at the beginning. You were having lunch at the Old Town Grille?"

"Yes."

"Who were you with?"

"My friend Vivian Steele. Izzy Cole was going to meet us, but she was running late."

"Do you remember anything suspicious? Anything out of place?" Agent Jones asked.

"No. We were waiting for our food to arrive. Everything was very normal, like it usually is."

Hunter's gut was screaming that something was off. There was some reason that Layla was holding back, and he had no idea why.

Agent Jones cleared his throat. "And you work for the State Department?"

"Yes," she said without hesitation.

Hunter was one of a handful of people who knew State was just a cover for Layla.

"And your friend works there too, right?" Jones asked.

"Yes. We both do."

"Did you go to this restaurant often?"

"Every Saturday."

Hunter realized the importance of that tidbit.

"Do you know of any other Saturday regulars?" Blakely asked.

"Not like us. Not every Saturday," Layla responded.

"Is there anything you're working on right now that you feel could put you in danger?" Jones asked.

That was exactly what Hunter wanted to know.

"Not that I can think of."

"Exactly what do you do at State?" Blakely asked.

"I'm an analyst in the Bureau of Near Eastern Affairs."

Hunter moved closer to get a better look into the room.

Blakely jotted down some notes and then pulled a card out of his jacket. "If you think of anything else, please give me a call. We'll be following up as the investigation unfolds."

"Thank you."

Hunter scurried down the hall to avoid the agents, but he couldn't stop wondering what kind of trouble Layla was in.

CHAPTER
FOUR

That night, Izzy helped Layla into her condo. Bailey and Viv were there waiting.

"You didn't need to go to all of this trouble," Layla protested. "The doctor said I would be fine."

Izzy knew Layla didn't like all the fuss, but considering the circumstances, it was more than warranted. "We're doing this because we want to."

"Well, Viv needs some TLC too," Layla said.

Viv patted Layla's arm. "I didn't get hit in the head like you did."

It was nice how Izzy had become a part of the group. She was the youngest of them all, and she looked to each of the other women for advice and guidance. Now there was an opportunity for her to help in return, and she was going to do just that. "I'll start making dinner soon. You two just relax. Let Bailey and me handle everything."

Layla lifted her hand. "First, I need to talk to everyone. Please sit."

Izzy took a seat in one of the chairs.

"I've been placed on administrative leave," Layla said.

"Because of the bombing?" Izzy asked. "What about Viv? Have you too?"

Layla and Viv exchanged a glance, and something passed between them.

Izzy felt like the odd one out. "What am I missing?"

Layla shook her head. "It's just me. This has nothing to do with Viv. There's an internal investigation. I have no idea why I'm being investigated, and neither does my boss. But for now, I'm not going to be working until this is sorted out."

Izzy looked at Bailey, who also remained silent. "So this investigation doesn't have anything to do with the bombing?"

"They are acting like it's a totally separate thing," Layla said.

"And you're not so sure," Izzy guessed.

"Here's what I do know. I've felt like someone has been watching me for the past couple of weeks. Today, the restaurant I frequent every single Saturday like clockwork was the site of an explosion. And then, on top of that, I'm told that I'm being investigated by the IG's office. Does that seem right to any of you?"

Izzy bit the inside of her cheek as she tried to process this information. She didn't want to say it, but she thought Layla was hiding something. As she looked at the other two women in the room, she had the same sinking feeling. Since she didn't have the tight bonds built from years of trust like they did, she didn't think it was her place to interrogate Layla. Especially not after the day they'd had. She'd let it go for now, but she was determined to figure out why she was being kept in the dark.

"There's more," Viv said. "Bailey found out that the tourists sitting at our normal table were among the casualties."

Layla nodded. "That bomb was meant for me."

Silence filled the room for a minute.

"But why would you have been targeted? You're an analyst at State. Why try to take you out?" Izzy asked.

"I'm not sure," Layla responded.

"I've got another question," Bailey said. "How did you feel about seeing Hunter today?"

"What?" Viv asked loudly. "Hunter? When did you see him?"

Layla sighed. "He heard about me being hurt in the bombing and came to see me in the hospital."

"Wow," Viv muttered.

"Yeah, I ran into him on his way out," Bailey said. "He looked like he was starstruck to me."

"Who is Hunter?" Izzy was once again confused.

When Layla didn't immediately answer, Bailey spoke. "Hunter was Layla's boyfriend in law school. The relationship ended badly when Hunter cheated on her."

"Oh. I'm so sorry." Izzy still wasn't convinced that many good men existed in the world. She'd borne her fair share of heartache in that department. She was still in counseling regarding the assault that happened to her at the hands of a police sergeant.

"Yeah, I don't talk about it much, but Hunter really hurt me," Layla said quietly. "We haven't had much communication since we graduated from Georgetown."

Izzy hoped she wasn't overstepping, but she was concerned about her friend. "How was it today, then?"

There was so much sadness in Layla's eyes. "At first I was shocked. I couldn't really believe it was him. It was hard seeing him standing there. He said he had heard about the bombing and had to come see me."

"Word travels fast," Viv said.

"Especially if you're a PI," Bailey added.

This story just kept getting more interesting by the moment, but Izzy couldn't help but be angry at this Hunter guy, because he'd obviously caused Layla so much pain. The fact that he'd come to see her today made Izzy think there was even more to it. That seemed to be the theme of the day.

◆

After Izzy and Bailey went into the kitchen, Layla turned to Viv. "I hate lying to Izzy, but I think it's best. I shouldn't have even made the comment about me being a target. I was speaking too freely around her. I'll need to be more guarded going forward."

Viv nodded. "Yeah. Even if we've become super close with Izzy, that doesn't change the stringent requirements you face." She turned to face Layla on the couch. "You think this has to do with the DEA joint mission you told me about?"

"Given that this is the second incident involving the team, and some additional intel I got from Scarlett, yes."

"Scarlett came to see me too. She said she was worried about you but didn't want to get into all the details. There's more to all of this, isn't there?"

"Yes, but I'm telling you as much I can right now." It was for the best to keep some information to herself.

Viv gave an understanding nod. "If Scarlett is worried, then I'm worried. She doesn't scare easily. Her reputation at State is for being about as hard-nosed as one can be."

"Yeah. I'm fortunate to have her as a mentor—and a friend. It's good to have someone watch my back outside of the Agency." Layla was learning quickly that having people on your side meant everything.

"How many people were on your team?" Viv asked.

"Four, including me."

"Where does the IG investigation come into this?"

"I'm not sure. I know they were reviewing my actions associated with the WSI case and how I helped Bailey, but I was told pretty soon after that happened that I had followed protocol and that there were no further issues—especially when you consider the Agency's involvement in all of it. That was supposed to be a done deal."

"Maybe it isn't? And those impacted are calling in some favors to exact revenge?"

"But then, why would I be the only one in the crosshairs? What about Bailey and Marco and the rest of the NCIS team, including Izzy?"

Viv grabbed her hand. "The bombing was too close of a call. If there is someone out there who wants to hurt you, and if this was in any way connected to that, then you're in real danger. You need to figure out how you're going to protect yourself."

"I know."

"You could come stay with me," Viv offered.

"No way. I'm not bringing you into this any more than you already are. I have a state-of-the-art security system here, and I'm more than confident in my gun-handling skills."

Viv was quiet for a moment. "Maybe you should reach out to Hunter."

"You *cannot* be serious."

"He's a PI. Maybe he can help."

Layla tried to stay calm. "Even if I was to consider your suggestion, there are a million reasons why I shouldn't."

"Layla, I know you don't want to hear it, but I have to be in brutal-honesty mode right now. You've got multiple threats coming at you from all sides, and we can't be sure what the exact cause is."

"But then what? I reach out and what happens?"

"I don't have the answers, but a PI would be just the person to help you investigate—especially in relation to the IG review."

"You know it's a lot more difficult than me just picking up the phone and calling Hunter. There is so much history there. If you're right and I need someone, then I should find an investigator who can start with a blank slate. Be objective. Not bring all the baggage with him."

Viv's eyes narrowed. "Yeah, but you can't do that, because no one else can know what you do for a living. Hunter is one of the few people who already does know. That's a game changer."

"I can't go to him for help. There's no trust there anymore. I'll have to do this my way." Layla hugged Viv tightly. "But thank you, I don't know what I'd do without you."

On Sunday, DEA Agent Zane Carter walked out of an Alexandria sub shop and headed to his SUV. When someone grabbed his arm, he turned, ready for battle with his other fist reared back.

But he relaxed when he saw the woman in front of him. "Cass, you ought to be glad I didn't flatten you."

"I need to talk to you," Cass said with a shaky voice.

"What's wrong?"

"Let's get into your car."

"All right." He unlocked his vehicle with the key fob, and Cass jumped into the passenger seat. He'd worked with Cass for about four years, and he'd never seen her act like this. She was always so level-headed. Cool as a cucumber, regardless of the mission or danger they faced in the field.

For a split second, the unthinkable occurred to him. What if Cass was strung out on something? It wouldn't be the first time something like that had happened to even celebrated agents. But he quickly pushed that thought out of his mind and turned his attention back to her.

"Talk to me, Cass."

"Drive."

He did as she instructed.

"The cartel is out to kill our team."

"I know you're still shaken up about the break-in at your house, but we need to take things one step at a time and not jump to any conclusions." Cass had told him about the tattoos she'd identified on her attacker, but it had been dark, and she'd been fighting the man off, so he wasn't a hundred percent sure this was linked just yet.

"There's no jumping to conclusions. I'm sure you heard about the bombing in Old Town yesterday. Layla was there."

His stomach clenched. "She was? Are you sure?"

"Absolutely. I spoke to her a few minutes ago. She has some minor injuries but will be okay. She goes to that restaurant every Saturday for lunch. This was planned."

"You think this is a coordinated effort to take out our team?" Zane's mind went into overdrive.

"I do, because I'm not done updating you. Layla also talked to Scarlett Bell."

"What did she say?" Scarlett always had the best intel.

"Get this. Her contacts are telling her that the word on the street is that Roberto Mejía was killed during our operation."

Zane's grip tightened on the wheel. "Are you sure? Could it be the cartel feeding our sources misinformation?"

"Scarlett thinks it's solid intel, and it would explain the major backlash we're getting."

"Okay, I get the motive, but how would Diego know who to come after? We were extremely careful with cutting any video surveillance."

Cass shrugged. "I'm not sure. That's one of the many unknowns."

"We should go see Diaz and brief him on the latest developments." John Diaz was a seasoned DEA agent and the fourth member of their team.

"Glad we're on the same page. I'll punch his address into my GPS." Cass pulled her phone out of her jacket.

"He's in Arlington, right?" Zane asked.

"Yeah. Since it's Sunday, the traffic shouldn't be too bad. We can do it in fifteen minutes from here."

"How did you know where to find me?" Zane asked.

"You love that sub shop. I swung by your place first, and when you weren't there, I figured hitting up your favorite restaurant was a good plan. The coffee shop down the block was my next option."

"You know me pretty well, don't you, Cass?"

She gave him a little smile. "We've worked together for quite a while."

"We have, and we've done a lot of dangerous ops in multiple countries. What went south here?"

She shook her head. "I don't know. Do you really think we can trust anyone at the DEA or at Langley right now?"

He turned his attention back to the road. They couldn't take any chances at this point. "Based on what you're telling me, the only people we can trust are the four of us. How could the cartel have found out our team's identity? As long as that's an open question, we have to keep this circle tight."

"I called Mason and told him what happened to me, but he doesn't know about anything else, I don't think."

Mason Gray was their boss at the DEA. "We should let him know about Layla. If it was just one of us being targeted, we could envision some other explanation, but with both of you attacked within such a short time period, we have to operate under the assumption that it's all tied together."

"But you still don't trust Mason?"

"I don't want to think we can't, but we have to be cautious. Right now, though, we can't keep him iced out on the basic facts because we need his help. Did Layla think you were on the right track?"

"Yes, she was concerned. But it seemed like there was more going on that she didn't want to talk about."

Zane huffed. "Well, that's typical CIA. I wouldn't be surprised if the Agency messed this up somehow."

Cass was silent for a moment, clearly thinking. "Layla's not even a field officer—not by design anyway. She's an analyst who has done some limited fieldwork."

"Yeah, but she did well on the op." Zane glanced at her, wondering where she was going with this. "We had no issues with her performance."

"I'm not questioning her skill. I'm thinking that it's even more disturbing that someone could have found her out, given her lack of fieldwork. You and I are out there all the time. So is Diaz. That isn't the case with Layla." She turned and looked over her shoulder.

"You see anything?" he asked.

"All clear so far."

They rode in silence the rest of the way to Diaz's house, but even in the quiet, Zane knew the two of them were in work mode. This wasn't a leisurely weekend afternoon drive.

Cass looked down at her watch. "Diaz always goes to Sunday service, but it's almost two. He should be done by now."

"I talked to him late last night, and everything was good."

"Let's find out."

Zane stopped the car, and the two of them walked up the driveway and onto Diaz's front porch.

"Zane." Cass pointed to the front door, which was slightly open.

Zane pulled out his Glock, and Cass followed suit. "On me," Zane said.

He took the lead as he pushed open the front door all the way. Silence filled the air. He walked inside the foyer, which opened up into the living room. The place was a mess. Tables overturned, sofa cushions taken out, and everything was strewn around. Someone had been on the hunt.

They cleared the first floor room by room before heading upstairs.

"I don't hear anything. I don't think Diaz is home," Cass said.

"We need to check everything." He wasn't going to make any snap judgments.

When they got to the top of the stairs, he turned right and walked down the hallway and into the first room. The smell hit him. A smell he knew all too well. John Diaz lay in the middle of the bedroom floor in a pool of crimson blood. His throat cut. Zane muttered a curse.

Cass's eyes widened as she entered the room. "Oh no. We're too late."

They had to get the Feds in there ASAP. Zane pulled out his phone and scrolled through his contacts. He pushed the button and lifted the phone to his ear.

"Mason, it's Zane. We've got a major problem."

CHAPTER
FIVE

Sunday evening, Layla sat at her kitchen table, drinking a cup of tea and trying to stay focused on the task at hand. She had to keep fighting back the emotions that flooded through her from all that she'd gone through in the past forty-eight hours.

There was a loud knock on her door, and she jumped up from her seat. Picking up her side arm, she walked to the door and looked through the peephole. Zane's bright blue eyes stared back at her. She opened the door and realized Zane wasn't alone. He'd brought Cass with him.

And Hunter.

"Hunter? What're you doing here?" The words came out more harshly than she'd intended, but she didn't know what was happening right now.

Hunter's eyes widened. "I didn't expect to see you either." He turned to Zane. "Layla's your CIA team member?"

"I didn't know the two of you knew each other," Zane said.

"We went to law school together," Layla said quickly as she exchanged a look with Hunter. She didn't want to get into their past with Zane and Cass. It wasn't relevant to the issues in front of them. "Come in and have a seat." She showed them into the living room and offered them some water and coffee, then tried to steel herself for what was to come. "Will someone please tell me what's going on and why Hunter is here with the two of you?" Her tone was stern, but she wanted answers. Could it be that Hunter wasn't a PI anymore?

Zane and Cass exchanged an uneasy glance. "I'm sorry," Zane said. "Before we talk about Hunter, there's something else. We have news. Bad news."

Like she really needed more bad news.

"There's no easy way to say this." Cass reached out and grabbed Layla's hand. "John is dead."

"What?" Layla's stomach clenched. That was more than bad news. It was devastating.

Zane's eyes met hers. "We found him at his house with his throat slit. The place had been tossed. Just like what happened to Cass's place."

Layla looked at Hunter, who sat with a deep frown on his face. She still didn't know how Hunter was involved in this mess and how he had the security clearance to be having this conversation. And until she knew his role, she couldn't talk about the Mejía cartel. "I can't speak freely in front of Hunter."

Hunter and Zane shared a look. A look that let her know she was in even more trouble than she had thought.

"That's what we need to talk about," Zane said. "Hunter is a contractor for the DEA. He has TS/SCI clearance and has specific permission to be read into our op."

Layla clenched her fists. "I'm sorry, what?" Hunter had

top secret security clearance? She didn't even know where to start her questions.

"Basically, I've been doing freelance work for the DEA for over two years," Hunter said. "Before I started working with them, I had to go through the whole security clearance process."

"How does your work fit into what is going on now?" Layla asked as she tried to put the pieces together as quickly as possible.

"Our team is obviously being targeted," Zane said. "How did the cartel figure out it was us? We've been compromised, and Hunter will be working on figuring out who sold us out. We needed someone from outside our agencies who could step in and be objective."

She frowned. "Does he know all the details of the op?"

"Not yet," Cass responded. "We figured we'd brief him here to make sure we were all on the same page."

Layla nodded but didn't really know what she was agreeing to. How had her world changed so suddenly in just a few moments?

Zane looked at Hunter. "The DEA got intel about a Mejía safe house that was full of drugs and cash. The safe house was going to be the storage area for a large shipment headed north to our border. We had a narrow window to act to secure the safe house, neutralize any cartel activity there, and seize the drugs and money."

Hunter cleared his throat. "This is all about Mejía?"

"Yes," Layla responded.

Hunter turned back to Zane. "You must have had some help in the field. The four of you couldn't have done that alone—no offense."

Zane nodded. "None taken. We had some DEA muscle

with us, but the four of us did all the strategic planning, and we were at the safe house with our guys, watching and monitoring every step of the way."

Hunter leaned forward. "I'll need a list of everyone involved, no matter how tangentially, so I can run deep background on all of them."

Zane started typing on his cell. "Won't be an issue. You'll have it in your inbox within the hour."

"The actual op went off without a hitch," Cass said. "We were patting ourselves on the back, but I guess we celebrated too early."

"So you got the cash and the drugs?" Hunter asked.

"Yes. Everything completely secured," Cass answered.

"Casualties?" Hunter asked.

"None on our side, but the cartel suffered some," Zane said. "But everything was by the book. We didn't take any chances, and our plan was executed to a T."

Layla spoke up. "One of the casualties was Roberto Mejía, the younger brother of Diego."

Hunter let out a low whistle. "If Diego thinks one of you is responsible for his little brother's death, then the threat matrix just went up infinitely." He paused. "There is a possibility that it's not a mole and that you got caught on the cartel's surveillance cameras."

"No, that's not possible. We cut all the feeds," Cass said.

"Maybe you thought you did but there was another system or a backup," Hunter said. "And now the top cartel brass know who you are and are seeking revenge. That would explain the serious nature of the attacks."

Layla had additional worries. "And they're looking for something. Maybe for any of their cash or drugs."

"Why would they think we're dirty?" Zane asked.

"I don't know." It was one of the questions Layla had been debating. She was trying to block out the fact that Hunter was sitting in her living room and instead think about the details in front of her.

"I assume the Agency sanctioned your involvement in this work?" Hunter asked.

"Of course. I would never go rogue. I don't break my word, and they have my unfettered loyalty." She didn't even try to hide her frustration.

Hunter let her accusation go. "The way I see it, you're most likely either dealing with someone on the inside who gave you all up because they cut a deal with the cartel, or you were caught on a surveillance system you didn't know about, and they've tracked you down."

It was as good a time as any to tell them her other unfortunate news, and if Hunter was being read into all of this, then Layla couldn't exclude him. "There's something else I need to tell you all. I have no way of knowing if there's any relation to the situation we find ourselves in, but you need to know that while I was in the hospital, my boss stopped by to tell me that I'm on administrative leave."

"What?" Zane asked loudly. "For what?"

A deep frown pulled at Hunter's lips, but he didn't say anything.

"The IG's office has opened an investigation in which I'm the subject. My boss had zero details, so I'm clueless as to whether it has any connection to this or whether it's just bad timing and one more problem for me to handle."

"Once Mason tells the Agency about the security threat, I bet they'll reinstate you," Cass said.

She doubted that. "Or it will just give them another reason to keep me on the sidelines."

Zane ran his hand through his hair. "I don't like it. What if the cartel is somehow setting you up? Making you take some sort of fall. Or worse."

"Then why bother with the bombing if they cooked up this IG investigation?" Layla asked.

Zane shrugged. "Maybe they're taking this on from multiple angles to cover all their bases."

Layla looked at Hunter, who locked eyes with her. She could tell he wanted to say something but was keeping quiet. "Where do we go from here?" she asked.

Zane stood. "Cass and I are going to stick close to each other. There's strength in numbers. You and Hunter should pair up. We'll work this thing as a team. No solo action. You've already been the target of a bombing, John is dead, and Cass's place was ransacked. We should all be on high alert."

"Wait a minute," Layla blurted before she could help herself. "I don't need to buddy up with Hunter. I can take care of myself. I'm trained for this stuff."

Hunter stood. "Maybe Layla and I should talk about this privately to make sure we're both comfortable with the situation."

Zane arched an eyebrow but didn't argue. "Cass and I will leave you to it, then."

Once it was just Layla and Hunter, he turned to her. "We really need to talk."

Layla didn't know how she was going to handle all these threats—most of all, the one to her heart.

◆

Izzy looked into her boyfriend's warm brown eyes. They'd just finished eating takeout and were now sitting on the couch in her apartment, watching cable news. She'd found out early on that they both shared a love for it, and it was an inside joke that they would do their own running commentary.

But she wasn't in a joking mood tonight.

"Are you finally going to tell me what's been bugging you?" Aiden asked. Aiden was a great guy. He was Jay Graves's son—the Army CID agent she'd become close to while investigating a huge case earlier in the year. "There's absolutely nothing you could've done to stop that bombing. You can't take that on your shoulders."

"It's not that."

"Well, I don't have to use my cop skills to know that something is up."

She'd promised herself she'd never date a cop after what had happened to her. One violent attack by her superior at Arlington PD had changed her forever. But Aiden couldn't be more different from the monster who had hurt her.

"You're right about something bothering me, but it's not the bombing." She took a breath. "You know how much my friendship with the ladies means to me. The three of them have welcomed me and Lexi into their friend group. When Lexi got sent abroad on assignment a few months ago, it became just me and the three of them. I don't know what I'd do without them now that I've experienced friendship like that."

"I'm sensing a *but* is about to come out of your mouth. Whatever it is, I'm here to listen."

Just one of the many things she loved about Aiden. In fact, she felt like she'd fallen in love with Aiden the first time she ever met him. But she needed time—a lot of it—to build a healthy relationship. Thankfully, Aiden was patient and loving. "You're going to think I'm being petty."

He took her hand. "The last thing I'd ever call you is petty. No-judgment zone here. Just tell me what you're feeling."

"I feel like an outsider. I know I have no right to feel that way. These women let me into their lives. They were doing fine without me. But now that I'm in the group, I can't help but feel like there are secrets that I'm not a part of, and that hurts my feelings."

"Oh, Izzy, that's a completely normal reaction. It's hard when you feel like you're the one on the outside looking in."

She nodded. "The weird thing is that I've never felt this way before. They've always gone out of their way to make me feel included. Even though they all went to law school together and have that tight bond, I didn't feel excluded. Then the bombing happened, and everything has gotten weird."

"How do you mean?"

"Layla isn't being forthcoming about something, but I have no idea what it is. The others know it too. I can read it in their expressions. So I'm like the idiot in the dark. And it's clear that they have no intention of bringing me in."

Aiden was quiet for a moment. "Can I ask you something personal?"

"I think we established that a long time ago."

"Do the three of them know what happened to you?"

She sucked in a breath. "No. Only Bailey knows, actually."

"Well, maybe Layla has something in her past that she only wants certain people to know. It's a matter of respecting her feelings. It isn't a reflection on you at all."

"Wow. I guess I hadn't thought about it that way. Now I feel like a jerk for pouting." Izzy hated that self-centered feeling, because it was more out of a lack of confidence than anything else.

"I wouldn't read too much into it. Give her the time and space she needs. She and Viv just went through a crazy traumatic event."

She looked up at him. "You're right, as usual."

He laughed. "Wait a minute. You're the one who usually has a lockdown on that category. Not me."

She smiled. Being with Aiden made her happy, but more than that, she felt completely safe for the first time in a long time. They were building something together, and that meant everything to her. "We can share in being right."

He put his arm around her. "Sounds good to me. How is your work going?"

"I'm still uncertain about whether I should start looking for other jobs."

"NCIS still doesn't feel like your career path?"

She shrugged. "I wish I had more certainty, but I don't. I just can't help but feel like there's something else I should be doing."

"You don't have to decide right away. All the experience you're getting at NCIS will help you wherever you decide to go."

"That's the thing. I'm not sure I want to be in law enforcement. I became a cop because of my dad, and I don't regret that. But I'm wondering if I need to start figuring out my own path."

"Any ideas?"

"You'll laugh at me if I tell you."

"I will not."

She hadn't told anyone this. Not a soul. But Aiden was her safe space. "I haven't made any decisions yet, but I signed up to take the LSAT."

"The LSAT? As in law school?" His dark eyes widened.

"See? You think it's an awful idea."

He shook his head. "No. I don't. I actually think it's a

great idea. But I have to ask—are you sure this isn't just you wanting to have more in common with your friends?"

"No, because only one of them even practices law at this point. This is truly about me."

"What type of law?"

She took another breath, because this is where the rubber would meet the road. "I want to be a prosecutor."

Silence fell between them. Then Aiden spoke. "You want to go after guys like the sergeant."

They'd agreed a long time ago not to speak his name. Not to give him that power over her. "Yeah. I do."

He took her hand. "I'll support you one hundred percent." He paused. "But you realize that nothing you do is ever going to change what happened."

"I do, but I also believe that if I can harness some of my pain and frustration into helping others, in the end, it will also help me."

After another quiet moment, Aiden said, "So, the LSAT, huh? How do you think Marco will handle this?"

Marco was her boss at NCIS, and she had no intention of telling him anything. "Right now he doesn't need to know. I need to make sure I can actually get into a good law school before anything else happens."

"Would you quit NCIS?"

She'd thought long and hard about this. "I think I'd have to. If I'm going to do this, I need to do it right, and that means complete dedication. Let's see how I do on the test and then go from there."

"Whatever you need from me, just say it." He squeezed her hand. "But if you decide for whatever reason not to take that path, you can still do a lot of good at NCIS. Don't forget all the good you've already done in the short time you've been there."

"I know. And I'm not going to make any rash decisions, but I have to explore this option. I've told you before, but your dad really changed my life in the best of ways. He encouraged me to seek counseling, and that has truly helped. And, of course, working with him is how I met you." She smiled, and warmth filled her heart.

"God has perfect timing, Izzy, and seeing that play out in our lives has been pretty amazing."

She had stepped away from her faith for years after her father's murder, but as part of confronting what had happened to her at the hands of the sergeant, she had turned back to God. It hadn't been easy. Largely because she had so much anger, but she was working through it day by day.

"Having you by my side has made all the difference in the world," she said.

"I feel the same way about you."

As she looked into his eyes, she felt like her heart might explode. They were taking things very slowly, but she knew deep inside that Aiden was the man for her. But she wanted to heal as much as she could so she wouldn't be a burden on him. There was no doubt about her feelings, though. She looked up at him. "Aiden, I love you."

He brushed her hair behind her ear and then pulled her closer. "I love you too."

As his lips touched hers, she could feel her heart, which had been so dark and broken, slowly being mended by his love.

CHAPTER
SIX

Hunter sat on the sofa, keeping a healthy distance between him and Layla. When he'd gotten the call from Zane about working on a new assignment, he'd been excited to have another opportunity to work for the DEA. But that had quickly changed once he realized Layla was tied up in this. Her role was still a source of confusion for him, but he'd decided it was best to wait to talk to her when it was just the two of them. He'd gotten the strong impression from Layla that she didn't want to air their dirty laundry in front of Zane and Cass, and he couldn't blame her for that.

Hunter decided to jump right in. "Please tell me everything, because I know you well enough to know that you weren't being totally up-front."

She scowled. "Don't assume you know who I am today, Hunter, and let's start with my questions."

Ouch. He needed to be more diplomatic, or this was going to end badly and fast. "Understood. Sorry, I shouldn't have jumped the gun."

She tucked her foot underneath her on the couch and shifted his direction. "DEA. You work with them a lot?"

At least she was starting with a softball question. "Absolutely. I work with them more than any other agency. I've developed some strong relationships there, especially with Zane, and I enjoy the work. They never have enough manpower, and I thrive on the challenge."

"Why not apply and work full-time with them?"

"I like the flexibility the current arrangement gives me. Being able to take on other work is important to me. It expands my skill set and will ultimately make me a better PI. Plus, the DEA likes that I'm not a full-time employee. It saves them money, but they can use me as they need me. It's a win-win."

Layla arched an eyebrow. "I'm just surprised that you chose to work for them."

"I'm not the only one who has changed." It was true. He'd done a lot of soul-searching to determine which direction to take his career. That he enjoyed the DEA work so much had been a surprise to him.

"So you've been in the field?" she asked.

He nodded. "I've seen some action, but it's never gotten too hot to handle. Since I haven't gone through all the training, they've been careful about how close I get to the danger."

"And that's okay with you?"

She seemed skeptical. He hadn't normally been one to sit on the sidelines, but he understood his value. "For now, yes. I'm still learning a lot, and with time, I'll figure out how best I want to be used by the team. I have a lot of tech skills that others don't have, so I'm more useful behind a computer than with a gun on the front lines, if that makes sense. My real value right now is more on the investigative side than operations."

"It's good to be self-aware," she said flatly.

She wasn't cutting him any slack, and he deserved that response from her, given the past between them. He'd forever damaged their relationship, and he didn't know if there was any coming back from that. "Do you think we can work together on this?"

"What do you mean?"

He didn't want to be too pushy, but they had to address the gigantic elephant in the room. "Can we put our personal issues aside and focus on the assignment?"

"Do we have much of a choice? The DEA hired you. They must think you're the right person for the job. We just need to keep things focused on the work. I want to make it clear that I don't need you as a babysitter."

"I never thought that," he said quickly.

"I'm not the woman you knew in law school."

He couldn't help but smile a little. "So you've mentioned." Which led him to another thought. "Why is a CIA Mideast analyst working DEA ops in South America?"

She stared off for a moment before looking at him again. "Because I'm no longer just an analyst."

"What do you mean?"

"I've started working on the operations side too. Not as a support function from Langley, but actually in the field."

Then it all came together. Layla didn't have a desk job anymore. She was a CIA operative.

❖

"It's not exactly what you're thinking." Layla knew she would have to explain, given what Hunter understood about her work.

He frowned. "I'm confused. You were hired at the Agency

as an analyst, right? Given your degree and your background, you make the perfect Middle East specialist. And now you're somehow tied up with the DEA, running drug ops in South America?"

She sighed. She understood Hunter's confusion. Her father was Lebanese, and she'd gotten her undergrad degree at Georgetown in Arab studies. Given her impeccable Arabic language skills and her subject-matter expertise, she'd been a top recruit for the CIA. "Technically, given the turn of events, I am considered an operations or case officer. Most people outside the Agency call everyone spies or operatives, but we are really CIA officers. It's a complex situation. It was always about me being an analyst. That's the work I love to do—connecting the dots and synthesizing tons of complex information. And, of course, being fluent in Arabic and Farsi is a big advantage when poring over original source materials. But about a year ago, a special assignment came up. It was presented to me as a onetime thing. I can't go into details, but it required fieldwork."

"And I'm guessing this fieldwork took you to the Middle East?"

"Actually, not the initial assignment, no. It was in Europe, but it involved a lot of moving pieces and contacts from many different regions." She took a moment to gather her thoughts and make sure she wasn't revealing too much. "Anyway, I performed well, and even though I told them I didn't want to make the transition from analyst to operations officer, they have subsequently come to me on other special projects. The woman you met in the hospital, Scarlett, works at State and is my interagency mentor. She agrees with the Agency's plan for my career and has pushed me to take any and every field opportunity I can. She believes I'm thinking too small by staying at Langley behind a desk."

"And this cartel op was a month ago? You were actually with them in Honduras, right?"

She nodded. "I was. It was a DEA-driven mission. I was the only non-DEA person on the team."

He ran a hand through his hair. "Layla, if the high-ups in the cartel have put out a hit on you, do you realize the kind of trouble you're in?"

Unfortunately, she did. "I know. And then place on top of that the internal investigation, and things become even more dicey."

"Have you considered that you've formed some enemies at the CIA?"

She'd certainly considered it. "As much as I try to get along with everyone, we all have people we don't see eye to eye with. I've got a couple of people like that. Although I'd hate to think they'd actually try to kill me over our petty squabbles."

"Layla, this is a complete mess."

"Believe me, I know."

"Okay, let's take one thing at a time. You're sure there's nothing your boss said that could tip his hand on what the IG investigation is about?"

She thought for a moment. "No. He was very vague because he wasn't fully read into the details either."

"It's really unjust that they can accuse you, put you on leave, and not even tell you what the accusations are."

It wasn't surprising to her. "Welcome to life at the Agency."

"This is serious."

"I get that."

"You seem almost resigned to the outcome."

"Honestly, the IG investigation is probably the least of my worries. If the cartel is after me, that's my biggest concern, because we all know how they operate. A bureaucratic investigation isn't good for my career, but I have to be alive for that even to be an issue."

"Or the IG investigation could be a ruse to get you out of the protection of the Agency. The cartel could be setting you up."

That seemed less likely, but she wasn't ruling anything out. "I know."

His blue eyes narrowed. "If someone is specifically targeting you, whether it's the cartel or not, once they realize you survived the bombing, they're probably going to make another run at you."

She lifted her chin. "Are you sure you want to work this DEA job, given all this other baggage that comes along with it?"

"Yes," he said with zero hesitation. "I assume you have a firearm?"

"Several, actually."

He moved closer to her. "Good. You should let me check out the security you have here."

She didn't know what she was more afraid of—the threat against her life or spending time with Hunter. "I don't think that's necessary."

"Why the hesitation?" he asked.

"I'm not hesitating."

"C'mon, Layla. I know you better than that."

But did he really know the woman she'd become over the past five years? She was still trying to put her feelings into words when he spoke again.

"If this is about the trust factor, I get it. I really do. You didn't ask to see me, much less work with me in any capacity, and yet here I am." He sighed.

She weighed her options. He said he had security expertise, so while he was at her place, it didn't seem like a bad idea to accept the help. "You know what they say. Desperate times and all."

He gave her a slight smile that showed the dimple in his left cheek. She couldn't afford to let down any walls with this man. Not after what he'd done to her.

"I can tell that smart brain of yours is going into overdrive," he said.

"I just hate being in the dark. There could be something I'm completely missing."

"We'll figure it out. Together."

Together. That was exactly the problem.

◆

On Monday evening, Layla sat in Viv's living room with Bailey. She hated excluding Izzy, but it was for her own good. She refused to put someone else in danger.

"Thanks for gathering, and to Viv for feeding us." Layla smiled warmly at her friend.

"Of course," Viv responded. "Now that dinner's over, you have to tell us what's going on."

Layla looked at Viv and then Bailey. Both women knew something was up. "I trust the two of you with my life. You know that."

"I don't like the sound of this," Bailey said.

"You both already know that my work at the Agency has expanded. Bailey, Viv told me that she filled you in on my last operation."

"Joint op, right?" Bailey asked.

"Yes. With the DEA."

"Go on," Viv said.

"We all know what happened with the bombing, and I've gotten sad news. One of my team members was brutally murdered in his home. His throat was slit."

"Whoa." Bailey stood up and started pacing. "That means someone is trying to take your team out. They're coming after you one by one."

"That's our main working theory, yes. That it's the Mejía cartel as an act of retaliation." Layla explained Roberto's death supercharging any cartel motivation for revenge.

"There's four of you, right?" Bailey asked.

"Yes, and something has happened to three of us." Layla paused. "So far. And to make matters worse, now that I've been put on leave, I have to worry what that's all about."

"Won't the Agency put you in protective custody?" Bailey asked.

"I spoke to my boss late last night. He'd been briefed by the DEA, but because I'm not DEA and was only there in a support function, they're not ready to think that I'm an actual target. He claims the FBI has a suspect connected to a domestic terror group in custody, who has confessed to the restaurant bombing, and that my being there was purely a coincidence."

"Do you trust your boss?" Viv asked.

"No," Layla answered quickly. "Frankly, there are very few people I trust right now, and the two of you are a good chunk of that."

"What do you need us to do?" Viv asked. "Name it."

Layla clenched her fists. "I wanted to let you know what's going on, given I'm not sure I'm going to come out of this alive."

"Don't talk like that," Bailey said. "You helped me when I needed it. I can try to get you into an FBI safe house by calling in some favors."

Layla shook her head. "No. That won't be necessary. I have to face this head on, at least until I know what I'm dealing with. Which brings me to another topic. Hunter."

Viv and Bailey exchanged a look before turning their attention back to her.

"What's going on?" Bailey asked.

Layla took a moment. "Everything is so complicated."

"We can handle it," Bailey said.

"It turns out that Hunter has a preexisting relationship working with the DEA."

Viv let out a low whistle. "That's a far cry from investigating cheating spouses."

"Tell me about it. I knew Hunter would succeed in whatever he did, but I had no idea that he would be doing such high-stakes work. Anyway, one of the DEA bosses approved reading him into our situation and hiring him to work on the investigation. He has top clearances and the whole nine yards. I'm stuck working with him right now, and I'm trying to just push through, but if I'm being completely honest, I don't think I've even begun to process my emotions."

Viv moved closer and touched Layla's shoulder. "It's totally natural for you to have issues with this."

Bailey sat back down. "Did Hunter make an epic mistake? Absolutely yes. But this isn't about love. It's about your life. And as much as I hate to admit it, I think Hunter would lay it all on the line for you."

"But how do I handle this? Having to be so close to him? Having to work with him? I can't trust him." Layla's voice started to shake as she struggled to retain the control she'd barely been holding on to the past few days.

"Bailey may disagree with me," Viv said, "but I think you have to try to compartmentalize as best you can. Think of this as an op you're working. You have far too much emotional baggage to deal with it on the fly."

Bailey looked at her. "I agree. You can't be expected to take on everything at once. Your safety and figuring out who is after you are top priority."

Layla knew her friends were right. "Easier said than done. When I look at him, everything just floods back."

"Including how much you loved him?" Viv asked.

Layla nodded. "Of course."

"You don't want to hear this, but people make mistakes, and they change and grow. That was almost six years ago." Bailey stood again. "He might not be the same man today."

That scared Layla even more, but she wasn't going to verbalize that to her friends. She'd *never* stopped loving Hunter. What a fool she was, and now she had to face him again.

"Where is he now?" Viv asked.

Layla looked at her watch. "Probably on his way to pick me up from here."

"Really?" Bailey said.

"Yeah. Our team lead wants us to work together. He thinks that if the Mejía cartel has put out a hit, then we all have to be on high alert." She opened her jacket, showing her friends that she was carrying.

"I don't like this," Viv said. "You need greater protection."

"My boss isn't budging."

Bailey twisted back her hair. "I'm going to make some discreet inquiries with my FBI contacts and see if they've heard any further details about any cartel retaliation."

Layla's heart sped up. "Please be careful. I don't want your actions to cause you any harm."

Bailey held up a hand. "This coming from the woman who sacrificed everything to help me just months ago. Let me see what I can find out."

"Also, play this out for a moment." Viv leaned forward. "What if your boss is right and the bombing goes out of the equation? You've still felt like someone has been watching you. You can't dismiss that feeling. Going with your gut is the best option."

"Yeah, I'd thought about that, too, but I didn't tell my boss about it, because after he told me I was being put on leave, my antenna went up. He claims it's not his call, but who knows."

"What does Scarlett think?" Viv said.

"That I need to be worried and aggressively defend myself in any Agency probe."

Bailey nodded. "Scarlett's right. Internal investigations can be career killers. You need to think about anyone on the inside who would want you to take a fall. What dirt do you have on them? Maybe you don't even realize you have it, but you might know something that could jeopardize them and they decided to take preemptive action to try to sully your reputation."

Layla groaned as Bailey's words set off a trigger in her mind. Maybe she had been naïve. Because that was something she hadn't thought of yet.

"Why the groan?" Bailey asked.

"My actions got a colleague fired over a year ago. What if this is some type of revenge move on his part?"

"I'd say that's a perfect thing for a PI to look into."

And Layla knew her friend was right.

◆

Hunter sat at his kitchen table across from Layla. They had a lot to tackle, but from the frown on her lips, he figured she had something to get off of her chest.

"What is it?" He hoped it wasn't something he had done. He felt like he was walking on eggshells because he didn't want to upset her. If only she knew just how tangled their past really was, but he'd vowed he wouldn't go there. Nothing good could come from revisiting the past. He'd made a decision, and he had to live with it every single day.

"I realized something tonight that could add another dimension to my problem," she finally said.

As if things weren't already complicated enough. "All right. I'm listening."

"There was a situation at the Agency last year. I reported some inappropriate behavior by one of my colleagues. He was pocketing cash from an asset and misreporting. I went to the IG about his conduct. He got fired. It's possible he's the one who got me investigated."

"But if he's on the outside, how did he make that happen?"

"He still has a lot of friends there who wouldn't think twice about helping him out. Even if it meant planting evidence or even just innuendo about me to stir up trouble."

Hunter jotted down some notes. "I need a name."

"Bryce Wixom."

"I'll check him out."

She looked down at her coffee and didn't make eye contact with him.

"There's more to this story, isn't there?"

"Isn't there always?" she asked.

"Best to just put it all on the table."

68

"Bryce and I were close friends. He took my reporting him as a stinging betrayal, but I never thought he'd actually do anything to hurt me or mess with my career. Maybe I was wrong."

This was starting to make more sense. "When you say close, how close exactly?"

"We were friends. Bryce definitely wanted more, but I tried to keep the lines clear. He could be persistent, to say the least."

Hunter hated this guy already. "So you ratted out this guy who had feelings for you. Sounds like perfect motive to me."

"I don't like the *ratted out* characterization. I was doing what was right. Following protocol. He was the one breaking the rules, and I had a responsibility to report him even if he was my friend."

It was always like Layla to take the high ground and do the right thing. It was one of the many things he admired about her. "You're right. I shouldn't have said it like that, but in Bryce's mind, I'm sure that's how he saw it, and we're looking at this from his point of view right now to determine the risks."

She hung her head. "I'm sorry. I shouldn't bite your head off when you're just trying to help. I'm really on edge right now."

His heart hurt as he watched her try to process everything. "It's going to be okay. Do you have any idea what Bryce is doing now?"

"No. He cut off all communication with me, and I didn't take the time to seek him out. He made his position clear, and we couldn't see eye to eye."

Hunter started typing on his laptop, and within a few seconds he had a hit on Bryce. "Looks like he's gone private sector, working at a DC consulting firm."

"That doesn't surprise me. Bryce was well connected politically and comes from an influential family inside the Beltway." She leaned back in her chair. "I'm just wondering why he would spend the time and energy to concoct claims against me to cause an IG investigation."

"It's possible he didn't, but I'd feel a lot better if we could say one way or the other. We should pay him a visit in the morning."

Layla's dark eyes widened. "*We?* Are you serious?"

"Yeah, it will be better if we're both there. You know him, and I don't. It will help with being able to read his reactions. I also made some progress on the background checks of your DEA support team while you were out."

"And?"

"So far everyone is turning up clean."

"I'm not surprised."

"You always did see the good in people."

"You say that as if it's a bad thing."

He shook his head. "No. It's a good quality, but sometimes it can get you killed."

Layla muttered something under her breath.

"I'm not trying to push your buttons," he said. "I'm really not."

"You always knew how."

"Really? Is that how you remember our relationship?"

"No. What I remember is you cheating on me and breaking my heart."

Talk about the truth hurting. "I can't go back and change the past."

She lifted her hand. "I'm sorry. I shouldn't have said that. There's zero reason to dredge up the past. We're both professionals and have jobs to do."

"You have every right to be upset. If we need to get everything out on the table, you just tell me."

Her dark eyes held so much pain, and it hurt him to think that he was the cause of it. He'd made decisions that had forever changed both of their lives. At the time, he'd acted based on his emotions. But now, years later, he wondered if he had made a terrible mistake.

"No," she said. "There's no point. We've both moved on."

"If you change your mind, let me know." He had a sinking feeling this conversation was far from being over.

CHAPTER
SEVEN

The next morning, Layla found out Hunter's style was to waste no time as they walked up to the swanky DC consulting firm.

"Are you sure this is a good idea?" she asked.

"Better a sneak attack."

"But we might not even get past his assistant."

"Yes, we will."

"Do you know something I don't?" she asked.

"Just watch and follow my lead."

She held back a laugh. Hunter had always been a leader. They'd butted heads over that before, like a million other things. But last night when they'd been talking, so many memories—good and bad—had washed over her.

Hunter knew her, the real her, more than any other man ever had. Since dating him, she'd only let one other person in, and it hadn't ended well. But she didn't want to think about that right now.

She still couldn't fathom what had caused Hunter to cheat on her. He was a man of self-control and discipline. He'd told her that he'd gone out drinking with some law school buddies and things had gotten out of control—hence his ending up in the arms of a girl he'd met at the bar.

But during the three years they'd dated, she'd never once seen Hunter drunk. He was measured in almost all areas of his life. Yeah, he liked danger and adventure—like jumping out of a plane or racing fast cars—but when it came to his social life, his explanation of what had happened always left her feeling like she had never really known him the way he'd known her. And that was one of the things that broke her heart the most.

"Earth to Layla. Let's do this thing."

"Sorry." She put those thoughts out of her mind and got ready to deal with the problem at hand. She thought she'd had a solid friendship with Bryce, but it couldn't withstand her reporting him.

"I'm going to directly confront him," Hunter said. "I'm not expecting him to confess if he is really involved in this, but I want you to be able to see his response. I want your read on him."

"I got it."

They were met by a receptionist in the main floor lobby. "How can I help you?" she asked in a singsong voice.

"We're here to see Bryce Wixom."

"Do you have an appointment?" Her blue eyes locked on to Hunter.

"Just please tell him that Layla Karam is here to see him."

She arched an eyebrow but didn't respond as she picked up the phone and made the call. After a few yeses, she hung up. "You can go up to the tenth floor. Someone there will meet you."

"Thank you." Hunter smiled at the receptionist, and it probably made her day.

They walked toward the elevator.

"See, I told you," Hunter murmured.

"Not so fast, big shot. We haven't actually seen him yet." Bryce wasn't one to underestimate.

"Don't be such a pessimist. We've got this." Hunter pushed the button, and after a few moments, they walked into the lobby of the tenth floor, where they were greeted by another receptionist, this one much younger.

"You're here to see Mr. Wixom. Please follow me."

They trailed behind the petite brunette down a long hallway to an office on the right. She knocked, and Bryce stood up. His eyes lit up when he saw Layla, but then he frowned when he saw she wasn't alone.

"Thanks, Nancy," Bryce said. "Come on in. I'm afraid we haven't met before." He stretched out his hand.

"I'm Hunter McCoy."

"Bryce Wixom. Please have a seat."

They all sat down, and Layla prepared herself for the conversation.

Bryce adjusted his fancy cuff links. "What brings the two of you down here today?"

Before Layla could answer, Hunter spoke. "Do you know anything about the IG investigation launched against Layla?"

Bryce's brown eyes widened. "I have no idea what you're talking about." He turned to Layla. "What is this about, Lay?"

She hated that nickname but didn't correct him. "Please answer the question, Bryce. It's important." She wanted to look him in the eyes and evaluate his response. "I'm in trouble, Bryce. I was at Old Town Grille when the bomb went off."

He frowned, and the mood in the room instantly shifted. "Oh no. I had no idea. I'm glad you're all right."

"Thank you."

Bryce leaned back. "But now I'm even more confused, Lay. Help me out here."

"Someone is giving Layla a really hard time," Hunter explained. "They're coming after her, including the opening of an IG investigation. We have no idea what it's about or who is behind it. Layla is on administrative leave."

"From State?" Bryce arched an eyebrow.

"He knows, Bryce."

With that revelation, Bryce frowned even more deeply. "What's going on here? Why would you have told this guy anything?"

"Hunter knew about my position at the CIA from the very beginning."

Bryce's eyes lit up. "Wait a minute. *You're* the law school guy? The idiot."

"Guilty," Hunter responded. "So yes, I know what Layla does and what you did. We're trying to figure out who wants to harm her, and we would like to strike you off that list."

Bryce shifted his attention back to Layla. "Yeah, we parted on bad terms, but I promise I don't have anything to do with any investigation. I didn't agree with what you did to me, but I know how you operate, so I can't say that I'm surprised. If you're worried about someone gunning for you, it's not me. Look around. I've made a great career for myself here with a lot higher pay."

She studied him closely and wanted to believe him. It did look like he was doing incredibly well for himself.

Hunter cleared his throat. "Do you know of anyone who would want to frame Layla for some type of wrongdoing?"

Bryce looked at her. "You know how things are at the Agency. There's so much backstabbing and maneuvering."

"So you do know something," Hunter suggested.

Bryce shook his head. "Actually, I don't. I was just saying you need to watch your back. Be careful, because there are some real threats out there, and some of them are a lot closer than they may seem." His attention was completely on her now. "Your insistence on playing by the book is antithetical to the way a lot of people operate, but if you're asking me if I ever heard of anyone gunning for you, then the answer is no. Then again, given our friendship, I probably wouldn't have been told. We were friends once, if you remember that."

She probably deserved that jab and decided not to counter him. She wasn't sure if he was telling the truth, but it seemed like he was. Although she had to remind herself that Bryce was a very gifted CIA officer. Lies rolled off his tongue with ease. It was more that she didn't want to believe that he could be trying to hurt her.

"If that's all, I've got other business to deal with." Bryce stood.

They'd been dismissed.

Hunter rose also. "If you think of anything or hear anything, give me a call." He handed Bryce his business card.

"Will do." Bryce turned to her. "It was good to see you, Lay. Please take care of yourself."

Hunter was quiet until they got back down to the main lobby. "Well, what do you think?"

"I actually felt like he was being truthful."

They walked outside and toward the Metro.

"I'm going to do some searching on my end and see what I can turn up on him," Hunter said. "If we find out he has nothing to do with any of this, then we're back at square one on the investigation."

"Unless everything is connected to the cartel. I guess it's naïve to think they couldn't be working things on the inside to get the result they want at all costs, especially given this is about Diego avenging his brother's death."

"Hey." Hunter grabbed her shoulder and pulled her to a stop.

She froze at the touch of his hand.

"None of this is your fault, Layla. We'll get to the bottom of this." They locked eyes for a moment before she turned away. They walked down M Street, headed toward the Farragut North Metro stop.

"I'm glad you're confident about that," she said.

"We have to stay focused, and we can figure this out. I promise you that."

The sound of screeching tires to her left caused her to stop and look over her shoulder. A dark SUV was weaving very quickly down the street. The passenger-side window opened, and she knew they were in trouble.

Her instincts and training kicked in. She tackled Hunter hard to the sidewalk, using all of her body weight and momentum, just as rapid gunshots rang out.

Her breathing was uneven, and she didn't move as the gunshots finally stopped and the SUV screeched away.

"Are you okay?" she asked Hunter.

He looked up at her with wide eyes. "Thanks to you." He took a breath. "But, Layla, you're bleeding."

She touched her left shoulder, and bright red blood stained her hand. She'd been hit.

At the hospital, Hunter paced back and forth outside the room where Layla was being attended to. He couldn't believe she had been the one to protect him and that she'd been hit. She claimed it was just a scratch, but he would feel a lot better once a doctor made that formal determination.

He'd known she had to have skills for the CIA to let her in the field on dangerous missions, but he was experiencing firsthand that she was a trained operative. Thankfully, her quick action had saved them both today. The Layla he'd known in law school had never even held a firearm. The Agency had changed her, but he was glad she was able to defend herself, especially given the danger she now found herself in.

Finally, after what seemed like forever, the door opened and the doctor walked out of the room. "She's asking for you."

"Is she okay?"

"Yes, sir. The bullet just nicked her. She'll be fine." The doctor gave him a pat on the shoulder, and Hunter anxiously walked into the room.

Layla sat on the edge of the hospital bed. Her shoulder had been bandaged.

"How're you feeling?" he asked.

"I told you it wasn't that bad."

"Layla, you were shot!" In what world could she not see that as a big deal?

"I know, but I'll be okay."

"Your quick thinking today saved our lives." He ran a hand through his hair. "You moved a lot faster than I did."

"I've had extensive training, so don't beat yourself up over this. When I started at the Agency, even though I was on the analyst track, they decided to send me to the Farm. I thought it would be good to have those skills and knew I might not get the opportunity again once I was stuck at a desk, so I went along with it. It has definitely paid off, that's for sure."

Those comments only fed into a narrative that was developing in his mind. "Do you think they always wanted you to be a field officer?"

"You know, I've asked myself that question. When they were recruiting me, I made it very clear that I wanted an analyst position. I feel like I'm best suited to a desk job, and they seemed to accept that, but they still wanted me to do the training. They said it would be helpful for me to understand field ops better, since I have a supporting role." She tucked a strand of dark hair behind her ear.

In his mind, she had much more than a supporting role. It appeared Layla had become the star of the entire show. "There aren't that many people with your skill set, Layla. Which makes the Agency investigation even stranger. They need you. It bothers me that they would put such a valuable asset in jeopardy."

"This is probably even worse than we thought and most likely connected to the Mejía cartel. A drive-by on the streets of DC. A team member dead. It has to be linked." She paused. "I called this in to Langley while I was waiting to see the doctor. They're working on getting a security detail posted outside my condo. I figured they would want to do it just to keep an eye on me, if nothing else, but given what happened today, I think it's the right move."

"I agree. I'll feel a lot better knowing you're not alone there. While you were being treated, I did some research on the relationship between the two Mejía brothers."

"And?"

What he had uncovered made him even more fearful for

Layla's life. "They were tight. Really tight. A big age difference between the two meant that Diego was pretty much a father to Roberto."

"That makes a lot of sense. Seeking revenge on behalf of a family member can cause you to act irrationally. The cartel usually wouldn't be so brash, but given the relationship between them, it explains a lot."

"The normal rules aren't applying right now." There was another thing bothering him. "How much money did the DEA seize?" It had to be a big amount.

"In cash, about five million, but the drugs we seized were worth upward of fifteen mil. The response hasn't been the same to each team member. Nothing has happened to Zane. And Cass's place was trashed, but the guy who did it fled. He didn't try to engage."

"Diaz is dead, though, and look at what's happened to you." Thoughts started to come together in his head. "Any reason that they could specifically be out for you and Diaz?"

"If Diego thinks that either of us killed his brother, then maybe. What if they don't even know Zane was on the op?"

"Possible," he said, considering the options.

"What do you think of Zane? You've worked with him before."

He thought the world of Zane and hoped he hadn't misjudged his character. "He's solid. Or at least that's been my experience."

"Mine too." She grimaced as she shifted.

"Can I ask you something a little off topic?"

"Yeah."

"Do you ever wonder what your dad would think of all of this?"

She looked away. "He still believes I work at State."

"You never told him?" He found that hard to believe. Layla and her father were close.

"No. Once I made the decision in the beginning, it just became too difficult to tell him. He's skeptical of the CIA. I understand why he has those reservations."

"But you obviously feel differently, or you never would've taken the job."

She looked up at him. "I do. I'm not completely naïve. I know the Agency does some highly questionable things, but I am a strong believer in the overall mission. And I think deep in my father's gut, he would be too. He hates the violence that has riddled the Middle East. He also recognizes that he has it easier than some others because of our beliefs."

"Isn't that what made you even more attractive to Langley?" It was clear to him that the Agency had sought after Layla even more because of her strong Christian faith. Her religious beliefs were a topic he was grilled about during his initial interview for her background check.

"Yes, and I'm not ashamed of my faith. At the same time, though, I believe in religious freedom. That's what our country was founded on. I want everyone to be treated with respect and dignity. That's what Christ's example was to all of us. Having said that, religion is often used as a weapon—especially in the Middle East. If I can be a part of stopping heinous acts of terrorism, I will do everything I can—and then some—to do so."

"I guess your beliefs haven't changed over the past few years." He hadn't really expected that they would.

She shook her head. "No. If anything, seeing what I see every day has drawn me closer to God. Relying on my faith helps get me through difficult times. What about you?"

He wasn't thrilled to be having this conversation even

though he was the one who started it. But he was not going to lie to her—especially about this topic, knowing how important it was to her. "I've been doing some reevaluating."

She frowned. "Are you having doubts?"

They'd had many talks about their shared faith when they were together in law school, but lately Hunter had started to feel numb about the entire thing. "I don't know how to describe it exactly, but I feel like I've hit the pause button."

"Sometimes you need to take stock and hit reset."

"Just that easy?"

She shook her head. "I didn't say it was easy, but it can be necessary. I find myself in a constant dialogue with God about things. I get frustrated and even angry, but at the end of the day, I know where I place my faith and that He will walk with me through it all."

He wasn't so sure about that. Hunter felt cold. Distant. He couldn't remember the last time he'd actually prayed, but dumping all of that on Layla hardly seemed fair.

Her eyes softened. "What is it?"

"Don't worry about it right now. Take a minute and chill while I call Zane. Then hopefully we can get you out of here soon."

The conversation had taken a turn he wasn't ready for. He was still struggling to answer the major question that lingered in his head: Why had God left him?

CHAPTER
EIGHT

Zane picked up his cell when he saw it was Hunter calling. "What's up?"

"There's been another incident."

Zane looked over at Cass, who sat on the sofa beside him. They had just finished lunch at her apartment and were planning their next move. He put the call on speaker as Hunter recounted a harrowing tale.

"That's brazen, man," Zane said.

"My thoughts too. This is a move right out of the revenge playbook," Hunter said. "Bold, reckless, and with little regard for getting caught."

"Well, cartel hit men don't have a choice. If they're given an order, they have to follow it or be killed on the spot. Where are you now?" Zane asked.

"We're at my place. Layla's upstairs in the guest room, resting per doctor's orders. I'm trying to figure out the best way to help. I'm worried about her safety, but the CIA is stationing a security detail at her condo that will be ready by tonight. I'm not letting her leave here until that's in place."

Zane looked at Cass, who was frowning. "That's good news. I'm glad she let Langley know. Given the threat level, I wouldn't say no to any offer of security."

"She isn't exactly trusting them right now, and I can't blame her, but she felt she had no choice in the matter."

"I'm going to let the DEA know. This was our op. I want Mason to be fully in the loop on this."

"All right. I'll stay in touch."

"Roger that." Zane ended the call. "What's up, Cass? I can see those wheels turning."

She rubbed her bloodshot eyes. "Why not try to kill us all?"

"What, do you have some sort of death wish?"

Cass shook her head. "Of course not, but the guy at my place didn't even make an attempt on my life. You haven't been targeted at all. Why?"

He bristled. "You can't possibly be insinuating that I'm somehow involved in this."

She laughed. "I know better than that."

"All right." He didn't really think it was a laughing matter, but she didn't appear to be accusing him of anything.

Cass shifted on the couch to face him. "Think this through. Why focus on Diaz and Layla? Maybe if we figure that out, we're closer to breaking this thing open."

He could only hope. "Could the cartel believe that the two of them are responsible for Roberto's death? Maybe holding them specifically accountable. It could be that they don't know I was there but determined that you three were. And maybe they had some reason to believe you or Diaz had some of the cash or drugs at your place. That's my best working theory."

"But why me?" Cass asked.

"Not that much of a stretch to think one of us could be dirty."

She sighed. "Yeah. I guess there's no reason to feign surprise at that. But why target *me*?"

He couldn't hold back his smile. "Maybe they think you're the most likely candidate of the group."

She punched his arm. "It would definitely be you before me."

He'd worked with Cass for years and trusted her completely. "But it's a good question. Why *did* they think it was you? Rack your brain. Is there anything that could give the cartel even the smallest indication that you might be a dirty agent?"

Cass sat quietly for a minute. "No secrets, right?"

"I sure hope not." He wondered what bomb she was about to drop.

"I haven't been intentionally hiding this from you. There just hasn't been a reason to bring it up."

"Go on."

"My little brother has a gambling problem. So much so that he got on the wrong side of some really bad guys."

"Uh-oh." He hated to think about the implications.

Her dark eyes softened. "I had to protect him."

His gut clenched. "What did you do?"

"I emptied my savings and took out some loans to pay off his debts. If someone were to do a profile on my financials, they'd see all of that, and it wouldn't be a stretch to assume I could be vulnerable."

"Cass, your brother is lucky to have you." Zane paused, considering his words carefully. "I'm guessing Mason doesn't know about this."

She shook her head. "And you can understand why."

DEA agents were supposed to immediately report to their boss anything that could be used as leverage against them. "I do. But now, what are we going to do about it?"

She rubbed her temples. "You want to go to Mason."

"Not necessarily," he shot back. "We should think this through. We don't want to have you sidelined."

She put her hand on his arm. "Thank you for having my back, Zane."

He placed his hand on top of hers. "We're a team, Cass. Partners don't cut and run, and neither do Marines."

She smiled. "Once a Marine, always a Marine."

"Oorah!"

"All right. So we keep this information to ourselves for now." Her phone started beeping, and she picked it up. "Looks like we're being summoned to a meeting with Mason."

Zane stood. "Maybe he's finally got some intel to help us."

"I hope so, but I'm not holding my breath."

He started walking to the door, but she caught his arm. "We're good, right?"

"Yes. Don't worry about it. We need to focus on the immediate threat." He just hoped there weren't more surprises yet to come.

◆

Izzy knew Aiden was slowing his jogging pace so she could keep up on their evening run, but he wouldn't admit it. That was just the type of guy he was. She shouldn't put him on a pedestal, but he hadn't given her any reason to do otherwise.

When her phone started vibrating in her shorts pocket, she pulled it out and stopped. "Your dad's calling."

Aiden frowned. "That's strange."

She placed the call on speaker. "Hi, Jay, I'm out jogging with Aiden."

"I'm sorry to interrupt, but there's something you need to know right away."

Fear struck her as she started to imagine worst-case scenarios. Had something happened to one of her friends? "What?"

"He's been murdered," Jay said flatly.

"Who?" She had no idea what he was talking about.

Jay sighed loudly. "*Him.*"

Izzy dropped the phone, and it bounced into the grass.

Aiden picked it up. "Dad, we're still here. I'm lost. Is this a case you're working?"

Izzy felt flushed as a swirl of emotions bubbled up inside her. She was certain Jay was talking about the man they'd agreed never to name again, but she had to be one-hundred-percent sure. "The sergeant?" she whispered.

"Yes," Jay responded.

"But how? When?" Her mind raced.

"Two days ago. And, Izzy, I'm not going to tell you any more than that."

"Why?" A moment ticked by. A moment too long. "What aren't you telling me?"

"The less you think about him, the better. I just wanted you to know that he can never hurt you again."

Deep inside her, she felt a mix of relief and fear, because there was more to the story. As her feelings swirled, she wasn't sure whether she wanted to cry or celebrate. But that was something she would keep to herself for now.

"Dad, we'll talk to you later. I'm going to get Izzy home."

"Thanks, son."

The call ended, and Izzy stood as still as a statue.

Aiden pulled her into a tight hug. She took a minute just to try to steady her breathing.

"I've got you," he whispered into her ear.

Those words were all it took to break her. The tears started flowing down her face, and her whole body shook as sobs threatened to overtake her. The man who had done so much to damage to her—both physically and emotionally—could never hurt her or anyone else again.

After what seemed like an eternity, she willed herself to let go of Aiden.

"Do you want me to go back and get the car to pick you up?" he asked.

"No. I'd rather run. I just need a second." She needed a lot more than that, but for now that was all she'd take.

She'd thought about putting a bullet through the sergeant's brain on countless occasions, but she also realized that doing so wouldn't take her pain away. But someone had killed him, and she couldn't help but wonder who.

They ran in silence, and she pushed herself as hard as she could, flying faster than she ever had before. The pure adrenaline burst from the unexpected news propelled her all the way back to her apartment complex.

When they walked up to her building, her stomach dropped. The doors of a dark sedan parked out front opened, and two Arlington PD detectives stepped out to greet her.

◆

Layla had been called to an offsite DEA meeting at Mason's condo. With each passing minute, she was becoming more convinced that they were caught up in something bigger than the one op they'd performed in Honduras.

Hunter was even more on edge than usual as they walked

up to Mason's front door. "I know you probably don't want to hear this, but I'm wondering if there's a possibility that the Honduras op was unsanctioned. Why not meet at HQ in Pentagon City?"

"An off-book op?" That thought hadn't even occurred to her.

"Yeah, as in someone wanted it to happen, but it didn't go through the proper chain of command."

"I guess that's one thing to put on the table."

She rang the doorbell, and Mason opened the door. The tall, brown-haired supervisory agent greeted her warmly. "Come on in, both of you. The whole gang is here. We need to talk."

"Why meet here?" she asked, unable to help herself.

"I'll explain." He turned to her. "And I'm glad you're okay."

"Thanks."

They were led into Mason's large living room, where Zane and Cass sat in two navy blue chairs.

"All right." Mason remained standing as Layla and Hunter took seats on the couch. "It's time to read everyone into the bigger picture here."

"There's a bigger picture? I don't like the sound of that," Zane said.

Mason nodded. "I have kept you all in the dark, but I had my reasons. The Honduras op was only one small piece of a larger DEA covert operation to try to take down the Mejía cartel."

"And why didn't we know about the rest of the plan?" Cass asked. "We all risked our lives down there."

Mason lifted his hands. "If I need to leave for a minute and let all of you trash-talk me so we can get down to business, let me know."

There wasn't an ounce of humor in Mason's suggestion. Layla kept her mouth shut, but Zane didn't.

"We have a right to be angry, but we also need to get to the information, since we are the targets here. So please continue."

Mason crossed his arms. "The plan against Mejía is totally need-to-know. We have multiple operations running, and no one on those assignments knows about the bigger picture. Leadership made that decision to decrease the chances of leaks and to give ourselves the best chance of disrupting and ultimately destroying the network."

Layla still felt unclear. "How does this fit together with the current threat assessment?"

"We've believed for some time that someone at the DEA is working with Mejía, but because of the larger plan, we have to be extremely careful about how we handle the insider. If we can continue to keep things compartmentalized, then we can feed information to each team and determine who might be the traitor. Also, a new development I want everyone to be aware of is that we haven't determined for certain but believe one surveillance camera got missed in the chaos at the Mejía safe house, and that's how you all got identified."

Layla was quickly processing everything he was saying. "And maybe Zane wasn't caught on that footage?"

"That's our current theory," Mason said. "We also don't know why Cass's situation was a break-in instead of a hit job, but we have to assume all of you are in danger." He looked away and then made direct eye contact with Layla. "And, unfortunately, there's more bad news."

"What?" she asked.

"The Agency is being cagey about you, Layla. I couldn't get a word out of them on this supposed investigation they're conducting, and I'm going to be totally frank here. I got the sense that they're trying to disassociate themselves from you."

She'd had the same feeling. "I know, but I have no idea why. I guess the cartel could be linked to that, too, but then again, if they're trying to kill me, why go through the trouble of cooking up something with the IG's office?"

Hunter cleared his throat. "Regardless, Layla is a prime target here. I hope the DEA isn't going to throw her to the curb like CIA has."

"No. At least not if I have anything to do with it," Mason answered. "Layla was a key part of this entire operation and the success we had. I don't know what kind of games Langley is playing, but we want no part in it. However we can help, we will, and that includes you, Hunter, providing her with personal protection."

Hunter laughed.

"What's so funny?" Mason asked.

Hunter looked at her. "Layla's the one who saved me from getting shot, but yes, I'm here to do whatever I can."

Layla was thankful again that her training had kicked in yesterday, and as a result, they both got away relatively unscathed. "You know that the Agency stripped me of my passport and wants me to stay in town."

"You could defy them," Cass suggested. "Go off the grid. We could help you."

"To what end? I can't hide forever." Frustration was building up inside her. "And I've got Agency security detail posted at my condo, watching my coming and going. Feels more like surveillance than security, but at least it's something."

Mason finally took a seat. "I get that this situation is far from ideal, but all we can do is take it one step at a time.

We're investigating Diaz's death as hard as we can. We're putting resources behind this thing. If anyone wants a DEA safe house, just say the word. All options are on the table. But I do ask that you not reveal to anyone the larger plan for Mejía, because that investigation is critical to being able to determine who is dirty on the inside."

That statement got some affirmative murmurs from the group.

"And, Layla, I can't tell you what to do about the Agency, but it wouldn't surprise me if they have you under surveillance that goes beyond the security detail at your condo, so just keep that in mind."

As Mason said those words, she wondered immediately if the tail she'd suspected from the past few weeks was CIA and had absolutely nothing to do with the cartel. She wasn't going to verbalize that concern to the whole group, but a sick feeling formed in the pit of her stomach. If she was being watched as a result of this IG investigation, then the subject matter was even more serious than she had previously considered. Someone was really out to get her.

❖

Mason had requested a one-on-one meeting with Hunter after the group meeting, so Layla was waiting for him in the living room. He wasn't sure what Mason wanted, but he was open-minded as he followed Mason into the kitchen.

Mason took a quick drink of coffee. "I need you to add another project to your plate."

"What is it?" Hunter asked.

"For now, I'm going to ask you to keep this aspect of your work to yourself. No one else, understood?"

He didn't like the direction this conversation was going.

"What is it?" he repeated. He needed more information before he made any decisions.

Mason ran his hand through his hair. "More bad news. We've discovered that we're missing five hundred thousand dollars from the money seized on the op."

Hunter felt his mouth drop open. He hadn't been expecting that. "Are you sure?"

"Positive."

"And you want me to investigate the team to see if any of them took it?" Hunter assumed that would be the task.

Mason nodded. "Yes. Everyone on the op has to be investigated. That means a deep dive on financials and the money trails. Hopefully you'll be able to exonerate the core team, and we can move on to everyone else who made the trip, but I have a bad feeling about this."

Hunter did too. One thing he knew in his gut was that Layla was no thief. He doubted any of the team was, but his emotional reactions wouldn't satisfy the DEA. They wanted cold, hard facts. The problem was that he was concerned this could end badly once Layla realized he was trying to dig up dirt on her—and the others. But he didn't really have a choice in the matter. This was his job and his reputation. "I'm on it."

"Good. We'll have to talk to everyone about this, but first I wanted you to dig in and see what you can find. Then, after you get some investigating done, we'll start questioning everyone."

"That sounds like a plan."

"Any updates on the mole investigation?" Mason asked.

"Everyone is a suspect until they're not." Well, almost everyone.

"Even me?" Mason quirked an eyebrow.

"Yes, sir. Even you."

Mason nodded. "I can handle that."

"What about Layla's involvement in this?"

"She's not the insider. One, she doesn't fit the profile, and even more importantly, she has only worked one op with us. There's no way she has the connections and background to be useful to the cartel. It has to be someone who has experience working this stuff."

Hunter wanted to make sure this was crystal clear. "So you're okay if she provides me with input on the investigation?"

Mason nodded. "As long as you don't bring up the money, yes. And I know she has her hands full right now with all the op fallout and the IG investigation."

That was an understatement. "Tell me about it."

"Anything you can share?"

"I think she's being set up. I guess there's a possibility the cartel is behind it, but that doesn't sit well with me. I believe it's something else, but we haven't figured out what it could be yet. But I plan to keep pushing."

"The cartel's style is more direct. Unfortunately, we don't have to look further than Diaz's death to show us that. And that's on top of all the other threats and attacks."

"Yeah."

"I hope you're considering the possibility that Layla has crossed someone at the CIA—and they are seeking revenge. Agency types can be pretty brutal once you pull back the spy exterior."

Hunter knew that fact all too well. "Yeah. We're looking at all angles, but it's slow going."

"Seems like you'll have time to work on this, and since there is a tie to Layla, I know you'll want to get to the bottom of things." Mason paused. "I may be overstepping my bounds here, but were the two of you a thing?"

Hunter sighed. "We used to be together years ago. It ended badly. Very badly."

"And now?" Mason raised an eyebrow.

"We're just trying to get through this mess, but we're on good terms. At least I feel like we are. Who knows where things could go after all this is over. Assuming it's ever over."

Mason patted him on the shoulder. "It's going to be. We're going to take down the Mejía cartel. I can feel it. We've been close before, but they're getting sloppy because Diego is acting emotionally, not as a shrewd leader. That will be their downfall."

"I hope so. I'll do my part."

Mason slid a USB drive across the table. "This has everything that has been accumulated so far on both investigations, including bank records and a possible suspects list within the DEA. You're not bound by anything on here, but use it as you see fit."

"Thanks. I'll start reviewing this right away and then let you know what else I might need access to." Hunter could only hope that he wouldn't find a traitor in their midst.

CHAPTER
NINE

The next morning at Hunter's office, Layla sat at the large oak table, staring at the piles of paper in front of them. "I'm telling you right now, I don't think anyone on the team is the mole." She'd been giving it a lot of thought and couldn't bring herself to suspect any of them.

"I tend to believe that, too, but the heat is on everyone except you."

"That's because I haven't done enough DEA-related work to cultivate the types of relationships needed to pull this off." She thought for a moment. "But the rest of the team has."

"That's where we need to begin. If we can clear people, then we can move on to the next person and at least narrow down the pool of possibilities. I've printed out everything from the file that Mason gave me."

"You've worked with Zane and Mason before. You don't think it could be them, do you?"

Hunter shook his head. "No, but I told Mason I wouldn't cut any corners. So I still need to review their files and look for any red flags. But before all of that, I wanted to see if you'd be interested in helping out with interviews of other DEA personnel."

"Of course. Who are we targeting first?" She might as well stay busy and help Hunter, because she couldn't do any work for the Agency right now, and sitting around twiddling her thumbs wasn't an option.

"There are two people who have worked with Cass and Zane. Mason pretty much told them they needed to cooperate. The first one should be here any minute."

"Name?"

"Darnell Lopez. Forty-five, been with the DEA for fifteen years. Before that, he was a cop. Solid record."

"I don't think I've met him, but honestly, everything was so fast and furious with preparing for our Honduras op that I know I don't remember everyone I met at the DEA."

Layla took a few minutes to study Darnell's file so she could be helpful in the interview, although she planned to defer to Hunter, since this was his gig. She'd only pipe in if she thought she could be useful.

It occurred to her that she was completely focused on the investigation—and not letting her thoughts be preoccupied with the past or even the present with Hunter. She thought that was a big step forward for her and an important piece of being able to leave the past in the past. Maybe Viv had been right all along and this was exactly what she needed to get some real closure once and for all.

When Darnell entered Hunter's office, she rose from her seat and introduced herself, but she kept her State Department cover firmly intact. It wasn't unusual for State and the

DEA to work closely together. Darnell had jet-black wavy hair and big brown eyes, but she definitely didn't remember meeting him before.

"Thanks for coming in on such short notice." Hunter offered him coffee, and they all sat around the table.

"Mason said it was important, so here I am," Darnell said. "Although I will tell you that I've already talked to the internal investigators at length. Twice, actually."

Hunter nodded. "I'm sorry if this will be redundant, but we're just trying to get to the truth."

"If the DEA decided to hire a PI, it has to be serious." Darnell's dark eyes shifted from Hunter to Layla. "I'm an open book. Ask away."

Hunter opened the folder in front of him. "Let's talk about your experience with a few people, starting with Zane Carter."

"Zane is the real deal. We had an instant connection because we were both Marines. If you're looking for someone dirty, Zane is not your man."

"You say that with a lot of confidence," Layla said.

Darnell focused on her. "You're right, but I have no hesitation in doing so. Zane is the type of guy you want to have your back in a fight. He's fiercely loyal. And he's not driven by power or money or anything like that. He's got a good head on his shoulders and truly wants to help people, and that's a rare find, in my opinion."

She looked over at Hunter, who was jotting down notes.

"Zane never expressed any frustrations to you about promotions or anything like that?" Hunter asked.

Darnell shook his head. "No. We've never even talked about promotions, period."

It was clear that Darnell wasn't going to speak one ill

word against Zane, but she let Hunter finish up his line of questioning.

"All right," Hunter said, shifting topics a few minutes later. "What about Cass Ruiz?"

Darnell laughed.

"What's so funny?" Layla asked.

"The fact that anyone could think Cass is a double agent is laughable. She's a firecracker. One of the toughest agents I know—man or woman. Strongly committed to the DEA's mission. You're barking up the wrong tree."

"Money can convince a lot of people to do things they would not otherwise do," Hunter said. "Even good people can be corrupted."

Darnell nodded. "But nothing Cass has ever done would make me question her."

"But you didn't have an absolute reaction like you did to Zane," Layla had to point out.

"True. I can't be as certain about Cass because I don't know her as well as I do Zane, but I still think she's clean. You asked my opinion, and I'm giving it to you."

Hunter shifted in his seat. "What about this—is there anyone you've ever worked with at the DEA who you *do* believe could have divided loyalty?"

Darnell didn't immediately respond. Layla wondered what he was keeping to himself.

"The answer I could give you is one you won't like," Darnell said.

"I don't have an agenda here except getting to the truth," Hunter said. "Don't give us a sanitized version. The truth is the truth."

"I appreciate hearing you say that." Darnell took a breath.

"Here's the thing. I don't think anyone inside the DEA is working with the Mejía cartel."

Well, that wasn't what she'd thought Darnell was going to say. "What do you mean?"

He cleared his throat. "It's more likely that someone outside the DEA is the problem. Most likely CIA."

Layla sucked in a breath, but thankfully neither man saw her reaction. Could it be possible that someone at the Agency was behind this?

"Do you have anything concrete that you're basing this on?" Hunter asked.

"Hard evidence? No. But there are rumors among some of my contacts in the field. My informants have heard rumblings about an insider working for the cartel. I pushed them to try to get more facts, and I couldn't get a name, but all of them said it wasn't a DEA person."

Layla looked at Hunter. If this was true, then that could have big implications. "But wouldn't it have to be someone, even if it was CIA, who had connections to the cartel?"

Darnell nodded. "Absolutely. But unfortunately, there are a lot of CIA officers in South America. It's a long list, and I don't have anything specific to go on."

"This is very helpful," Hunter said. "If you hear anything else from your sources, can you contact me right away?"

"Will do. I hope this thing can be wrapped up quickly."

After Darnell left, Layla turned to Hunter. "That was a curve ball."

"But one that you're uniquely situated to handle. You need to see what you can dig up from your Agency contacts, but you need to be discreet."

"For a million different reasons." She sighed. "Darnell

seemed to have solid intel, but I still think you have to push through vetting the DEA people in case he's wrong."

Hunter gave her an affirming nod. "Yeah, I was thinking the same thing."

"I'll get right on the Agency angle." She wondered if all roads would end up leading back to the CIA.

◈

Izzy had been frantically trying to get ahold of her friends all morning, and she finally ended up at Viv's door.

"Izzy, what's wrong?" Viv asked. "You sounded distressed on the phone."

Izzy let out a sigh of relief when Viv opened the door. "Thank you for seeing me. I'm so glad you're not at work."

"I'm working the late shift tonight. What's going on?"

Izzy knew her red eyes showed she'd been crying. Ever since the visit yesterday from Arlington PD, things had become a whirlwind. But she'd told them that if they wanted to talk to her, she'd need an attorney present. Given that she used to be one of them, they seemed cooperative, but they had insisted that she be ready for the interview Thursday morning. Which meant she needed an attorney ASAP, because she had yet another secret hanging over her head.

Viv hadn't been her first choice. Not that Izzy didn't love and trust her, but Bailey was the only one of them who knew the history. Given Bailey was out of town today on assignment, Izzy had come to Viv because Layla had so much on her plate.

"We're going to need to sit." Izzy looked into her friend's hazel eyes and decided that she had no other choice but to cross this bridge right now.

"Go into the living room. I'm going to bring in some water."

Izzy took a few steadying breaths—something she'd been forcing herself to do since Jay had called yesterday. She sat down, and a minute later Viv walked into the room with a bottled water.

"Whatever it is, just tell me, and we'll figure out a plan."

Izzy smiled. "Thank you." Viv was probably the quietest of the group of friends, but she had a huge heart. "This is a very difficult conversation to have."

"Take it slow. I'm in no rush."

Izzy closed her eyes for a second, asking God to help her. "Back when I was an officer for Arlington PD, I was assaulted by a sergeant."

Viv's eyes widened, but she didn't say a word.

"I was able to fight him off and escape, but it was the scariest and most horrific time of my life. It happened late at night in his office. My clothes were ripped, my body was bruised. But more than that, I was severely traumatized by it."

"I'm sure you were," Viv said softly. "Izzy, I had no idea about any of this."

"I've only ever told a few people about it, but it's definitely shaped my life and continues to impact me personally and my relationships."

Viv took her hand. "Whatever I can do, just name it."

Izzy decided it was best to just spit it out. "The sergeant who assaulted me was murdered three days ago, and Arlington PD wants to talk to me."

Viv's mouth dropped open, and she didn't immediately respond.

"Yeah, that's how I felt too." She wasn't surprised by Viv's reaction. Izzy had kept this secret so closed off that there was no way anyone would have had any suspicion.

"Do they think you could have something to do with this?" Viv's voice cracked.

"I haven't talked to them yet because I need to get a lawyer. You know Aiden's dad, Jay, the one I worked with before? He's the one who told me. He's also the one who urged me to get help initially when I was struggling." She took a breath. "But he's not the reason I need a lawyer."

"Then why?"

"I think I know why the police want to question me."

"All right. Before you say anything else, I need you to request me to represent you."

"What?" Izzy didn't understand what was happening.

"It won't be a long-term representation, but given the legal implications of what I think you're going to say, I want this conversation to be protected by attorney-client privilege."

Izzy wasn't sure how this all worked, but she trusted Viv. "Okay. I'd like you to represent me."

"I accept. Please continue."

"About a month ago, I ran into the sergeant at a coffee shop in town. He invaded my personal space. Tried to touch me." A chill went down her back as she recounted the story.

"Oh no," Viv said.

"Yeah. It shook me. Unfortunately, that wasn't the end of it. About two weeks ago, he showed up on my jog. There's no way it was a coincidence. Then he started texting me."

"Uh-oh."

"Yeah. I sent some texts back that could be misconstrued, especially if taken out of context."

Viv sighed. "Did you threaten him directly?"

There was no doubt. "Oh yeah. I was pretty clear on that point. I was livid and afraid, but I didn't want him to see my fear. I wanted to face him down and wanted him to know that I wasn't going to let him touch me ever again."

Silence hung in the room. Izzy knew her admissions could make her look like a suspect.

"You need a top-notch defense attorney," Viv said.

"I can't really pay top-notch rates." She had a little savings put away, but given lawyer rates, she wasn't sure that would do the trick.

Viv's eyes lit up. "I have someone in mind who might take on your case pro bono. Of course I'd defend you in a heartbeat with everything I had, but that would be doing a huge disservice to you, since I don't practice criminal law. We have to do much better than what I could provide in terms of representation, but one thing I can do is find you an attorney."

Izzy felt her eyes fill yet again with tears. "I didn't do it, Viv."

Viv squeezed her hand. "I know that, Izzy. I know you and your heart. No matter what was done to you, you believe in the justice system to right wrongs, not in vigilantism."

Izzy shook her head. "But that's the thing you don't understand."

"Tell me. Help me understand."

She needed Viv to see where she was coming from. "I *have* wanted to kill him. To make him pay for what he did to me. For the torment and pain he put me through every day of my life since the attack. I've felt unsafe around men ever since this happened to me. I've lived through so many sleepless nights, ongoing nightmares, fears, and insecurities. All because he attacked me. So when I sent those texts, there were moments when I felt like I could've acted on them. If he had tried to hurt me again."

Viv's eyes met hers. "It's completely natural for you to feel that way, and if he had tried to hurt you, then you would have been acting in self-defense. But you didn't do it. Yes, you may have wanted to act on those feelings, but you exercised self-control. That's the truth, and once everything is investigated, the police will see that."

Izzy wasn't so sure it would be that easy. "Someone did kill him, though, and I have no idea who."

"How long was he on the force?"

"A few decades."

Viv leaned in. "Hmm. Cops make a lot of enemies. I'm sure they'll be focusing on a variety of options."

"They must have found those text messages, though." A chill shot down Izzy's back at the thought of reliving this entire nightmare.

"I'm going to call my friend. Maybe we'll get lucky with her availability. Give me a few minutes."

Viv left Izzy alone in the living room because she probably wanted the privacy to talk to the lawyer first before Izzy got involved. She closed her eyes. *Lord, I'm not strong enough on my own to handle this. Please help me.*

It was a prayer she'd found herself praying ever since she reconnected with her faith months ago. She'd tried fighting her battles alone and had failed miserably. With God, she still felt weak, but there was a sense that she could face her struggles, knowing she wasn't alone anymore.

There were days when she was still angry at God for what had happened to her. For her father's death. For so many things. But she'd also felt His mighty hand guiding her through the dark nights. His gentle voice coaxing her to open her heart to Him and to others. He'd brought amazing people into her life just when she needed them most. Seeing

Him work in her life in real time had a tremendous impact on her.

So yes, she still had her doubts, but God's love was more powerful than anything. It had pulled her out of a dark abyss when she hadn't even wanted to live anymore.

Viv rushed back into the room, her face flushed. "I got her. She's coming over."

Izzy blew out a breath in relief. "Thank you. Words aren't even enough."

Viv insisted that Izzy eat something while they waited, because she hadn't had anything but coffee and water all day. When the doorbell rang, Izzy prepared herself to meet the attorney.

The door opened, revealing an auburn-haired woman with brown eyes.

"Piper Alexander, meet Isabella Cole."

Izzy offered her hand to Piper. "Please call me Izzy."

"Nice to meet you." Piper then gave Viv a big hug.

"Okay, Izzy. Now that you have an experienced criminal defense lawyer, I'm going to turn over the representation to her and let you two talk alone in here." Viv led them into the kitchen. "I'll be upstairs in my bedroom if you need anything."

"Thank you again for everything." Izzy squeezed Viv's hand before Viv left her alone with Piper.

As she sat across the table from this woman she'd just met, Izzy realized she was putting her trust in Viv. If Viv vouched for Piper, then that would have to be enough for her.

Piper pulled a legal pad from her bag and set it on the table. "Izzy, you should know that I am a criminal defense attorney, but that I also have experience doing pro bono work representing victims of domestic violence."

"I'm not a lawyer, but isn't it odd to work both sides?"

"It is a bit unorthodox, yes, but I'm never adverse to any of my clients on the criminal side, and lawyers are encouraged to do pro bono work. Criminal defense is my specialty, but I wanted to bring up my other experience because, from the little Viv told me, I thought it would be helpful for you to know."

Izzy nodded, not sure what to say.

"We'll take this nice and easy. Instead of starting with the difficult experiences of your past, why don't you tell me exactly what you know about the case." Piper's pen was at the ready.

"Not much. The person who was killed is Sergeant Henry Tybee." Saying his name made her want to vomit.

"All right. How would you like us to refer to him?"

"You can tell that I don't like saying his name?" Was she that transparent?

Piper leaned in. "It's actually very common in these circumstances. So whatever you tell me is what we'll go with, but I should warn you, the police will most likely refer to him as a victim."

Izzy had thought about that, because she knew police procedures like the back of her hand. Having to deal with it in her own life was another experience entirely, though. "I'm pretty good at compartmentalizing. I'm just going to have to use those skills here. Between us, let's just call him the sergeant. I can't control what anyone else is going to call him."

Piper made a note. "What can you tell me about the sergeant's death?"

Izzy took a moment to explain who Jay and Aiden were and then described the phone call from Jay.

A deep frown pulled down on Piper's lips.

"What is it?" Izzy sensed something was really wrong.

"I'm just trying to figure out the lay of the land here. I know you don't want to hear this, but I have to think about all the possibilities. Is it possible that either of them could be under the microscope too?"

Izzy's stomach clenched. "Why would you say that?" She didn't see what the two of them could have to do with this.

"Given what you've told me, it's possible that Jay and Aiden are also going to be questioned. My top priority as your attorney is *you*, but my years of experience tell me that *your* top priority may not be you. It might be Aiden or Jay or both of them. So we need to get all that out on the table right now."

Izzy's pulse quickened at the implications. "There's zero chance that either of them murdered the sergeant. I can promise you that."

"They love you, right? You basically said that Jay is a father figure in your life. He's the one who convinced you to seek help. You also said that you think Jay previously confronted the sergeant, then the next thing you know, the guy takes early retirement. You have to admit that looks suspicious at the very least."

Izzy lifted her hand. "You don't know Jay. He's a man of honor. A Green Beret. An Army CID agent."

Piper shook her head. "Actually, with each word out of your mouth, he sounds more and more interesting to the police. It's possible that Arlington PD wants to question you because they think Jay's the guilty party."

The thought of them going after Jay almost felt worse than having them come after her. He'd had such a positive impact in her life and had helped her so much. There was no way she would do anything to put him in jeopardy. And that was why she had to fess up to Piper. "I don't want you to talk like that. I appreciate what you're doing here, especially taking this on pro bono, but I am loyal to these guys, and I will have their backs no matter what."

Piper arched an eyebrow. "You wouldn't testify against them?"

"Absolutely not." There was zero chance that would ever happen.

"You believe they're innocent?"

"With every fiber of my being, and that's why I also need to share some things with you that might explain why the police want to question me." Izzy steadied herself and continued to recount to Piper what she had told Viv about the text messages and the encounters she'd had with the sergeant.

Piper ran her hand through her hair. "I'm not going to lie to you. This does make things more complicated."

"How do I handle the questioning? Do I tell them about this up front, assuming that they already know or will soon find out?"

Piper tapped her pen on the table. "We need to be careful with how we play this. I want you to be honest if asked. But I'm not sure I'm at the point where my legal advice is for you to just spill your guts."

She had to put her trust in Piper right now. Izzy wasn't an attorney, but she realized that these facts didn't look good for her.

Piper took a sip of water. "Let's get back to the details. You know he was killed, but nothing else?"

"Nothing. Jay wouldn't tell me."

"Okay, don't go investigating. Let's get through the interview in the morning. I have a feeling you're not going to know the answers to most of their questions anyway, but it's time for some ground rules."

"I'm listening."

"Don't answer any question immediately. Give me a second to make a determination about whether you should answer it. There's a tendency to want to get your story out there. Don't do it. Answer just the question asked. I think our discussion on the text messages shows you how important this can be."

"Should I be taking notes?"

"I'd prefer you just listen. Any notes you take could potentially be discoverable in any litigation."

"Okay." She hoped she could keep this all straight. She'd never been on this side of questioning before. "How much detail am I going to have to go into about the attack?" That was one of the biggest things bothering her.

"The attack is your motive. I'd prefer to minimalize the discussion as much as possible, but I have to be forthright with you and say that's probably not going to happen. They're going to ask for details. The worse the attack was for you, the stronger the motive you would've had to kill him. They know that. It won't be any type of secret strategy."

Izzy bit the inside of her cheek. "I don't know how I'm going to handle that."

"Just do the best you can. And while we're on the topic, you'll need to walk me through it. That way I can know best when to cut off the questioning."

For the next half hour, Izzy powered through and told her story in painstaking detail—going to the sergeant's office, what started out as a friendly career discussion, and then when he first touched her. She'd immediately backed off and tried to pass it off as a misunderstanding, but he would have none of that. The violence that ensued was as vivid today as it was when it happened. She didn't sanitize anything. She told every detail exactly as she remembered it, including how violent he had become and how much he had hurt her. As she finished up, she realized fresh tears were flowing down her cheeks.

But what surprised her was seeing the tears in Piper's eyes. Then Piper took hold of her hands. "When Viv told me the basics of your story, I knew you had been through a lot, but hearing it in your own words is compelling. And the events that have transpired with him coming after you recently and harassing you adds to the situation." Piper looked away.

Something even more was bothering Piper. "What are you really thinking?"

"You have the perfect motive for murder."

CHAPTER
TEN

On Wednesday afternoon, Layla waited for Scarlett's arrival at her condo. They were going to have coffee before Layla met Viv and Izzy for dinner. They'd been texting each day, with Scarlett checking in to make sure Layla was safe.

After getting her college degree, Scarlett had gone straight to the DEA and quickly risen through the ranks by proving herself in the field on dangerous ops time and again. She'd worked with the Agency multiple times, and Scarlett had confided in Layla that the Agency had recruited her hard. But Scarlett had other ideas. She loved the thrill of fieldwork, but she also had diplomatic ambitions. Being at State opened different doors.

While Scarlett had never come out and said it, Layla thought that she might even have political ambitions down the road. And working in high-level diplomatic jobs at State was a great résumé builder. Layla had even considered whether State might be a good fit for herself initially, but the Agency needed her skills a lot more than State did, and Layla desperately wanted to serve her country in the best way possible.

When the doorbell rang, Layla went to tell the Agency guard that it was okay to let Scarlett in.

"Thanks for breaking away from work for coffee."

Scarlett greeted her with a warm hug. "Of course. I had a few errands I had to run, so it worked out perfectly to swing by here. How're you holding up?"

They walked into the kitchen. "Considering all that's happened, I'm doing okay. Each new day, things seem to get more complicated." Layla picked up the coffeepot and poured them each a big cup. "And you see my security detail is in full force."

Scarlett sat down at the table. "Well, that's actually a great idea. I'm sleeping better at night knowing you're not here all alone. Those guys are highly trained and ready for anything."

Layla scoffed. "Including monitoring my every move."

Scarlett didn't seem fazed by Layla's sarcasm. "On that point, have you heard from the IG's office yet?"

Layla shook her head. "No. It seems they're operating on their own timetable, and that only adds to my already high stress level."

Scarlett picked up her yellow coffee cup. "I know I sound very suspicious about this, but I can't help it. What I haven't told you yet is that I've lived through this process."

"Really?" That came as a surprise.

"Yes. I was a young DEA field agent. An investigation was opened on my entire field team. They put us through the wringer, but I never, not once, showed weakness. In the end, they folded, we were all completely cleared, but that put a bad taste in my mouth forever when dealing with internal investigations. So if it seems like I'm coming in hot on this, I am."

It was just like Scarlett to lay it all out there. It was one of the things that made their friendship work so well. Layla didn't like passive-aggressive types. "Thanks for sharing that. At least I'm in good company."

Scarlett smiled. "I did make some informal requests from my side to Langley."

"And?"

"They're being tight-lipped. Usually I can call in a favor and get what I need, but not on this one." Scarlett sighed. "And that's what really concerns me. Everything about this screams to me that they think they have something big on you, but they don't have quite enough evidence yet to act on it."

Layla groaned. "But I'm telling you, there's nothing." She had spent countless hours thinking about this, and absolutely nothing came to mind. She was a rule follower through and through. She had memorized Agency protocol from day one and had never broken it.

Scarlett patted her arm. "I believe you, but that's all the more cause for concern, because it means someone set you up."

"We talked to Bryce."

Scarlett's eyes narrowed. "That guy is a piece of work, but I don't know that I can see him taking things this far. Anyone else you can think of on your enemies list?"

"My what?"

Scarlett lifted her hands. "C'mon. We all have one."

Layla didn't think she did, but now, staring at Scarlett, she wasn't so sure. "I don't try to make enemies."

"Of course not, but our intentions don't always matter. I'm sure there are other people at the Agency who would like to get rid of you. Think of your competition."

"What do you mean?"

"Your contemporaries who want promotions and see you as a threat. It's no secret that you're a rising star with unlimited potential. You've already been rapidly promoted, leaving others in the dust. They can't compete with the substance you bring to the table, so maybe someone has decided to play dirty to get what they want."

Maybe Layla was living in too insulated of a bubble, because these things hadn't crossed her mind.

"I can see I've unloaded a lot on you. I don't want to stress you out, but I wouldn't be a very good mentor or friend if I didn't help you navigate these troubled waters, and to do so, you need to have your eyes wide open. You must fight for this the same way you'd fight on a mission or in your analytical work. I've seen how tenacious you are when you're working. Take that same passion and focus and use them here. Don't let them railroad you, Layla. You've worked too hard for that to happen."

"And the Agency wonders why I want a desk job."

Scarlett laughed. "You're more talented than you even realize, you just don't have the confidence yet to see it. But enough of all this. If I do hear anything, I'll contact you immediately, and my earlier advice stands. Lawyer up before you submit to any questioning. Even if they claim it will be informal. There's no such thing. Okay?"

"Understood." Layla would just have to be patient, because the IG was clearly running at their own speed.

"Anything new on Mejía from your side?" Scarlett took another sip of coffee.

"Our best guess is that either the team was caught on a surveillance camera we missed or that someone on the inside sold us out. The same person they suspect has been feeding intel to the cartel for quite a while to help them stay one step ahead of DEA."

"How careful were you with the electronic surveillance?" Scarlett asked.

"I thought we were completely buttoned up, but Mason thinks we missed one of the cameras. DEA is actively investigating the mole. Hunter has also been hired to conduct a separate independent investigation."

"Really?" Scarlett smiled. "How are things going with him?"

She'd told Scarlett about the Hunter saga years ago. "It's not easy, but our personal baggage has to wait. There's no time to get distracted by all of that right now."

"I know you may think that, but baggage has a way of always being there. That's why they call it baggage." Scarlett sighed. "But I am a complete and utter failure in the romance department, so don't take advice from me on that front."

That wasn't true, as far as Layla was concerned. "You're single by choice, Scarlett. You've had plenty of guys interested in you."

Scarlett grinned. "Thanks for helping support my narrative."

Both of them laughed, but Layla had one more serious topic to get to. "There's something else I wanted to run by you."

"Shoot."

"There's new information that the DEA mole could actually be CIA."

Scarlett's eyebrows went up. "Really? Now, isn't that interesting. How reliable is the intel?"

"Seems like it could be legit, but I wanted to pick your

brain. You know a lot of the Agency officers who work in the region. I've done some digging, and one name keeps coming up as a potentially promising lead."

"Who is it?" Scarlett asked.

"The last thing I want to do is wrongly throw someone under the bus, because I'm living through that situation now, but I trust you, and I know you'll be discreet about this."

"Absolutely. My lips are sealed."

She knew Scarlett wouldn't act on anything she was saying. "The name is Keith Hammond."

Scarlett's eyes lit up. "Yes, I'm familiar with Keith. He's been in Honduras off and on for the past couple of years. He's known as a tough operator who isn't afraid to make waves. I can't say that he has anything to do with this, but he would be a good possible fit for the profile."

Layla grabbed Scarlett's hand. Maybe this would be a much-needed break. "That's valuable insight. We'll run it down, and I promise we won't do anything that will compromise him without real evidence."

Scarlett squeezed her hand. "I'll do anything I can to help you, but I'm worried about your safety."

"But you just commented on my great security detail."

"They're only here with you at your condo. When you leave, you're out there on your own."

"Not exactly. Hunter is my shadow right now."

"That's a good thing. Keep it up. I can't say I'm a big fan of him, given how he treated you, but it seems like he still cares about you and is willing to go to the mat. You need people like that surrounding you."

"Yeah. I can't live under a rock forever, but the way I understand it, if Diego wants you killed, then you don't make it out alive."

Scarlett patted her shoulder. "Drug lords may have a lot of power, but you still have the resources of the US government behind you and a great head on your shoulders. You're going to make it through this."

Layla looked down. "I can't say the same about John Diaz."

Scarlett hung her head. "John was a great agent and a good man. Really a decent guy, and there aren't many men like that anymore."

"You know how these cartels work a lot better than I do. Why haven't they touched Zane? He was on the op."

"Maybe they don't know he was there. That would be my best guess. Or they have a bigger plan for him down the road. Or . . . I hate to even say this."

Layla shook her head. "No. Zane isn't working with them."

"You have one of the kindest hearts of anyone I've ever met, but that's also your blind spot. I'm not accusing Zane. I'm just pointing out once again that you need to keep your eyes open, okay?"

Layla knew in her gut that Scarlett spoke the truth. The question now was what she was going to do about it.

◆

Hunter sat in his office, staring at his computer in frustration. He'd been tasked by Mason to find out who had stolen the cartel cash, but unfortunately, even after all the work he'd been putting in, he was no closer to finding the culprit.

He'd received a load of documents from the DEA that had been secured through warrants to a variety of banks and financial institutions. He'd been sworn to secrecy, so he hadn't been able to talk to Layla about any of this, and he felt the weight of guilt at poring over her finances—which he'd done because he wanted to satisfy himself and Mason that Layla was clean. Layla's finances were exactly what he'd expected. She lived a reasonable lifestyle, putting a good part of her modest government salary into her savings account. He didn't find any suspicious accounts or activities. No questionable transfers. Her biggest splurges seemed to be at her favorite clothing store, a boutique in Georgetown, and those purchases only happened a couple of times a year.

Now he was deep into the other core team members' information. He noticed that Cass's savings account was depleted. He would be on the lookout for any other indicators of financial stress. Making some notes for follow-up, he decided to review Zane's documents.

He was surprised to see the size of Zane's accounts. This guy had money. Lots of money. But would he be so brazen as to steal cash from the cartel and then put it all in his domestic accounts? Hunter's best working theory was that the stolen money had ultimately ended up offshore somewhere. But Zane's financial situation meant he needed to do more digging. He knew Zane was former military, which also didn't explain that amount of cash. The number of zeros was enough to make Hunter's head spin. This man was beyond rich.

After putting in a number of hours, Hunter headed over to Elijah's place. Hunter had decided to hang out with him while Layla saw her friends for dinner. He hated to leave her, but she'd shown him just how capable she could be. And he knew she wouldn't be alone, because she was going to Viv's house.

"Talk to me, man." Elijah handed him a soda and took a seat in one of the huge chairs in front of the flat-screen TV. A game was playing, but he'd put it on mute.

"Layla is in danger. I can't go into the details, but I'm worried about her."

"Worried as a friend or something more?"

"You know the answer to that already."

"So that's what's got you so wound up?"

Hunter let out a frustrated groan. "Layla's still upset about the past. She's focused on the present, which is a good thing as far as her security goes, but when she looks at me, I can't help but feel like she's staring right through me."

"What did you expect? That she'd just fall willingly back into your arms?" Elijah shook his head. "No way."

"I get that. It's just all business between us. Like we're partners working an investigation."

"Isn't that *exactly* what this is?" Elijah pulled the ottoman forward and propped up his feet.

"Yes, but you know that's not what I want."

"Do I? And more importantly, does Layla?"

"Obviously I haven't broached that topic."

"You need to be patient. If the two of you are ultimately meant to be together, then it will happen."

"You're not going to start preaching at me, are you?"

"Do I ever preach at you?"

"Sometimes." Hunter laughed. "Seriously, though, you've respected my feelings on that front. For the most part," he added quickly. Elijah was as rock-solid as they came in his faith, and Hunter was on shaky ground at best.

"I know I've given you some room to work through your faith struggles, but ultimately God is still there waiting on you. You just have to look in the mirror and ask yourself what it really is that has you so wound up. You have to be truthful with yourself, because I feel like you're in denial."

"What's that supposed to mean?" Just because he was

having doubts didn't mean he was in denial. "I'm facing this thing head on. It's just that I don't like what I see. What I feel."

"You were never that good at the feelings thing."

Hunter leaned back in the armchair and sighed. "You wear yours on your sleeve, and I keep mine wrapped up tightly in a box."

"That, my friend, is the problem. Look at me right now and honestly tell me what has you so angry."

"Decisions I've made."

"Be specific."

"What happened with Layla."

Elijah raised an eyebrow. "Don't you mean what you did *to* Layla? How you cheated on her and broke her heart? No need to sugarcoat it."

"Right." It was much more of a tangled web than that, but now wasn't the time or place for that discussion.

"It seemed to me before like you had taken personal responsibility, but now, hearing you talk, I wonder if that's not completely the case."

"It's more complicated than you know."

Elijah shifted in his seat. "Is it, though? You made a mistake. A very bad mistake. You say you've moved on, but there's something still holding you back."

"You're right."

"Whatever that is, no matter how small or big, that's what you need to take to God. Get His help."

Hunter admired his friend's faith, but he just wasn't feeling it. "Why would He help me now? He didn't before."

"God works in His own time. We can't expect to understand all of His ways."

"Easy for you to say."

121

"Now, wait a minute. We've been through too much together for you to act like I've had an easy path in life."

Hunter was kicking himself. "You're completely right. I'm an idiot, as usual, saying stupid things. I can be a bit self-absorbed."

"You think?" Elijah laughed. "But don't be too hard on yourself. I give you tough love because I'd want the same thing from you. When I went off the rails sophomore year, you were there to help get me back in line."

Hunter remembered that all too well, but he'd do it again in a heartbeat. "At least neither of us has had a meltdown at the same time."

"And let's keep it that way." Elijah took a sip of his drink. "Is there anything I can do to help out?"

"Not at the moment, but that could change."

"I'll be on standby. Just call if you need me."

"Thanks, Elijah. For everything." Just talking had actually helped him feel a little better.

"No problem."

Hunter picked up the remote. "So how's the game so far?"

CHAPTER
ELEVEN

Layla looked at Viv and Izzy as they finished up dinner. Bailey was still out of town for work. They'd kept the dinner conversation light on purpose and were avoiding the serious topics until after they'd eaten. But the story Layla had just heard from Izzy was anything but light. It was gripping and scary, and Layla was glad that the man who had hurt Izzy was dead. She couldn't help those feelings.

"So you got a lawyer?" Layla asked.

"Yes." Izzy looked at Viv. "Thanks to Viv."

Viv tucked a stray hair behind her ear. "She's an old friend who practices criminal defense. Her name is Piper. She'll go with Izzy to her interview with Arlington PD in the morning."

Suddenly Layla wasn't so sure that her problems were as bad as she'd thought. "I'm so sorry, Izzy. Is there anything else we can do?"

Izzy shook her head. "I'm just ready for this nightmare to be over once and for all, but it appears we may still be a ways from that."

"What is Aiden saying?"

Izzy gripped her coffee cup. "He's worried about me."

Layla had to ask. "Did he know about what happened to you?"

Izzy looked away. "Yes, but he's one of the few people who did. That's all about to change in this interview, and I'm really dreading it."

"It's like you're having to relive the trauma all over again. It's so unfair," Layla said. She turned to Viv. "Isn't there something Piper can do?"

Viv picked up her mug. "She'll try to cut it off if they start to badger her too much, but she can't stop it entirely."

"You're stronger than you think, Izzy." Layla wanted to encourage her. "You're a fighter, and as long as you tell the truth, then you should be fine."

Izzy raised an eyebrow. "That's sweet of you to say, but I don't believe you really think that."

Viv shifted in her seat. "Let's try to stay positive here, ladies. Izzy's got top-notch counsel, and more importantly, she has the truth on her side. We will be here for you each step of the way."

Izzy smiled at Viv. "You've done so much already."

"You'd do the same for us."

Izzy lifted her hand. "Enough about me. Layla, how are things going with you?"

Layla had embraced the few moments of respite from having to face her situation. But since Izzy was there, she could only say so much. "Things are about the same."

"And Hunter?" Viv asked.

Layla knew Viv was asking about Hunter not just because it was a favorite topic of hers, but to divert the conversation. "It's been hard working with him."

Izzy leaned forward. "I still don't get why he cheated on you in the first place."

"Believe me, I've asked myself that question a million times." Layla took a sip of water. "The answers he gave were never satisfying, but sometimes people just make mistakes. I know I've made my share."

"There's mistakes, and then there's *mistakes*," Izzy responded. "If I were you, I'd confront him about it. I realize I'm coming into this really late in the game, but an outsider's perspective is sometimes useful. I don't think you've really moved on. You need more closure. Once you have that, maybe you'll be able to take the next step in your life free from that lingering burden."

Maybe Izzy was right, but that would mean fully opening up an old wound as opposed to the current situation of just picking at it. "I'm not sure how I'll end up handling it."

"Hunter's still single, isn't he?" Viv asked.

"Yeah. It appears that way." Layla paused. "Hey now, don't go getting any crazy ideas. I don't know how I'd ever get past the betrayal. Even if I could be on better terms with him for my own sanity, starting a relationship is a completely different question."

"People can change," Viv said.

"But loyalty is everything," Izzy added.

"Isn't love everything?" Viv asked.

Layla laughed. "Well, aren't you the romantic?"

Viv sighed. "Maybe I'm projecting. My love life is nonexistent."

Izzy smiled. "I can see if Aiden has anyone he could set you up with."

Viv threw her head back. "Please don't make me sound desperate. Even if I am."

That comment got a much-needed laugh from all of them, which Layla knew was Viv's intention. Viv wasn't desperate, she was just picky—and Layla appreciated that. It wasn't that easy to find a guy who could appreciate all they did in their careers and still be a loving and faithful man.

Her phone rang, and she saw it was Hunter. "My chariot has arrived." She turned to Izzy and grabbed her hand. "You'll be fine tomorrow." She saw the worry in Izzy's blue eyes, and it broke her heart. "Come here." Layla gave Izzy a bear hug and prayed that this investigation wouldn't victimize her young friend a second time.

◆

Zane walked Cass up to her house. They'd gone back and forth about a DEA safe house, but for tonight, Cass had stood her ground and wanted to go home. That meant Zane needed to check it out and satisfy himself that it was secure. There was no way he'd be able to sleep tonight without making sure his partner was safe.

"I'll be fine, Zane. I appreciate your concern, but it appears Layla is target number one."

He grabbed her arm before she opened the door. "Wasn't Diaz target number one?"

She frowned. "Yes, and I didn't mean to diminish his murder. My only point is that they don't seem intent on killing me and you. At least not yet."

"Let's keep it that way, okay?" The words came out harsher than he'd intended, but she didn't say anything else as she unlocked the front door.

Cass walked over to the alarm keypad. "That's strange. The alarm isn't on."

"Are you sure you set it?" he asked.

"I thought so, but maybe with everything on my mind, I forgot."

He pulled her back toward him. "We can't take any chances. We'll clear the house room by room."

"Split up?" She pulled her gun.

"No. Stay together."

Her eyes locked on to his. "I was hoping you'd say that."

His heartbeat sped up as his senses screamed to him that there was something wrong. "Does anything look out of place?"

She shook her head. "Not yet."

They moved into the living room and then into the kitchen and office.

"Clear," she said.

"Up the stairs. You have multiple bedrooms up here, right?"

"Yeah. Mine is the one on the left."

He'd been to Cass's place many times, but he usually stayed on the first floor. They reached the top of the stairs. He was intently focused on what was in front of him, expecting danger at any moment. He readied himself to go into the first bedroom on the right.

But when he heard Cass scream, he spun around. Someone must have been lying in wait in the bedroom on the left.

The man had his beefy arm wrapped around Cass's neck. She was thrashing about, but it wasn't doing much good.

Zane rushed toward the attacker, feeling confident that he could take him in hand-to-hand combat.

But then the man pulled out a gun and pushed it into Cass's ribs, causing her to scream in pain. "Put down your gun or she's dead."

Zane wasn't playing this game. Not with his partner and friend's life. There would be no bartering. Yes, it would be nice to take this guy alive and interrogate him, but Cass's life was the most important thing to him.

"You're going to kill me anyway." Cass's eyes widened in fear. She was trying to send him a message.

"No. I need you alive. Diego wants to talk to you," the assailant said.

"Talk about what?" Cass asked with a strained voice.

"Diego isn't going to rest until he finds the person who killed his brother."

With that admission, Zane knew he had no other choice. If he laid down his gun, he would most likely be killed, and Cass would be taken and tortured. Something he couldn't allow under any circumstance. He had to take the shot.

Zane squeezed the trigger twice and hit the assailant in the head.

Cass let out a shriek as the man flopped to the floor. "Zane!"

"I wasn't going to negotiate with him. I couldn't let him take you."

She threw her arms around him, and he pulled her in close. Her body shook in his arms.

"It's okay. He can't hurt you now."

After a moment, she stepped back. "He came out of nowhere."

Zane squatted down and checked the body for ID, but there was nothing. "Let's call this in."

"Zane," she whispered.

He looked up. "Yes?"

"I think I'm ready for that safe house now."

❖

Layla and Hunter had just gotten a disturbing call from Zane about an attack at Cass's place, letting them know she was being moved to a DEA safe house. According to Zane, the man specifically said that Diego wanted to question Cass.

Layla couldn't dwell on it too much right now. Since Cass was safe, they had other immediate business to attend to.

"We should be there soon," Hunter said.

Layla had told Hunter about Keith Hammond, and she'd reached out to Keith to set up a meeting. Keith had been friendly enough on the phone, but Layla hadn't revealed why she wanted to talk to him. He'd probably acted out of professional courtesy, since they were both employed by the Agency.

They'd decided to meet at a coffeehouse in Arlington at nine that evening. Given there was a possibility that Keith was working for the cartel, Layla was glad Hunter was with her. There were no good reasons to play the lone wolf right now. Although it would be nice to get a break in the case, she hoped Keith was clean—it would help restore some of her fragile faith in the Agency and its operatives.

"Let's talk Keith Hammond," she said to Hunter, ready to tackle the mission at hand. They'd gotten his file from Mason. She didn't have full access to CIA files right now, but Mason had been able to go through one of his contacts to get it.

Hunter glanced at her. "He's been with the Agency for fifteen years. He was recruited right out of college."

She'd committed Keith's background to memory. "Fluent in Spanish and Portuguese, he was placed in South America from the get-go and has spent his entire career working in the region—including a long stint in Honduras."

"Service record is impeccable. He's received several commendations. No disciplinary actions," Hunter added.

"Were you able to check his finances?" she asked, always thinking about monetary motive.

"Yes. From what I could find, it all looked good, but someone with his experience and connections could probably do a good job of hiding money if that was the goal."

"How did your questioning of the other DEA employees go?" Layla asked. He'd conducted several interviews without her.

"Nothing as illuminating as our talk with Darnell. Most people claim to know nothing, and they also have very high opinions of their colleagues."

"I get that. No one wants to believe that the people they trust and work with every day are playing on the bad guy's team."

"I'm sensing a *but* here," Hunter said.

"This entire experience has led me to question a lot of my basic assumptions about my work."

"Pretty soon you'll be just as cynical as me."

She smiled. "I sure hope not."

The tension between them seemed to be easing as the importance of the case was elevated above her feelings about the past—and the present. Although she hated the fact that when she looked at Hunter, she still felt butterflies. Major ones.

It reminded her of when she had first met him at law school orientation. They'd locked eyes, and she just knew she had to meet him. When he'd introduced himself and they found out they were in the same section of classes, it was like her world was falling into place. Even after everything they'd gone through and the pain he had caused her, he still affected her like no other man ever had.

"Here we are." Hunter pulled up and found a metered parking spot on the street.

She pointed. "I see Hammond waiting outside." She recognized him from his file.

They got out of Hunter's SUV and started walking toward the coffee shop. As they waited for the light to change so they could cross the street, a car whizzed by them.

Layla had taken one step into the crosswalk when gunshots pierced the night.

She started running toward the coffee shop with Hunter by her side, and together they reached the horrific scene.

Keith Hammond lay on the sidewalk—his lifeless body riddled with bullets.

CHAPTER
TWELVE

The next morning, Hunter still couldn't believe the turn of events. He and Layla were at his office, waiting for Mason to arrive. She'd been visibly shaken after witnessing the shooting, but he had been as well. One minute Keith Hammond had been standing in front of the coffee shop—unassuming, waiting for what he believed was just a routine meeting with an Agency colleague—and the next, he was violently gunned down in cold blood.

"Do you think the cartel killed him so he couldn't speak to us?" Layla asked.

"That seems like a plausible explanation, but how could the cartel have found out about it?" Hunter asked.

Layla bit her bottom lip. "Maybe he was under surveillance, and they heard our phone conversation. I identified myself to him. That would've been enough for the cartel, even if I didn't bring up the reason I wanted to meet with him."

Hunter hadn't slept much last night as he replayed the events in his head. "If he was dirty, why would the cartel have wanted to kill him? Wouldn't they have wanted to keep him in play?"

"That's a good point. Unless they thought he was about to turn on them, and they decided to take him out."

Mason walked in a few minutes later. "How are you two doing?"

"All things considered, okay," she answered. "Unfortunately, we can't say the same for Keith Hammond."

"FBI is taking the lead on the murder, but we're being read in because of the suspicions raised about Hammond's allegiance."

"Any updates?" Hunter asked.

"Good thing you got the license plate, Hunter. We were able to run that, and it was a stolen vehicle. Given the tactics used, we are operating under the assumption that this was a cartel hit, but we can't say at this juncture whether Keith was working for them and what the motivation was for the hit. FBI is going through all his electronics now, and if they find anything, we'll be notified."

"If he was the mole, that would mean the cartel has lost their inside man," Layla said.

"That would be a good thing," Mason responded. "But I'm not ready to call this open and shut. For one, we're not sure he was the mole, and on top of that, we can't guarantee that he was working alone if he was. That's why I wanted to talk this through. Hunter, keep doing your work. If Keith wasn't involved and just got caught in the crossfire, then we still have someone out there working against our interests. There's too much riding on this one to be wrong."

"No cutting corners," Hunter said.

Layla cleared her throat. "If Keith wasn't dirty, given his extensive time in the region, he still had to be a known player to the cartel. When I reached out to him, maybe they got spooked."

Hunter hated to think about that, because he knew Layla would obsess over her role in his murder even though it clearly wasn't her fault.

Mason frowned. "That's one of the many questions the FBI will be looking to answer. We can't do anything about their investigation. The process has to unfold, but we can make sure that we're doing everything we can to identify the true traitor."

"Understood," Hunter said. "There is still a list of people I'm working through on the DEA side."

Mason nodded. "Keep up that work, and I'll let you know if I hear anything from the FBI. And be extra vigilant. Layla, you still have Agency security at your condo, right?"

She nodded. "Believe me, they aren't going anywhere. They're watching me like a hawk."

"Good. I'll be in touch." Mason exited the room as abruptly as he'd appeared.

"I guess we have our marching orders," Layla said.

◆

Izzy was trying her best to hold it together. It helped that Piper had a death grip on her arm as they walked toward the main precinct for Arlington PD late Thursday morning. She'd known she would have to deal with the assault forever, but now that the sergeant had been killed, it put a whole new spin on things. She was just trying to take it one step at a time, but her footing was uneasy.

At least she'd never have to face that brute again. He was

dead. He couldn't hurt her, but his memory still threatened her entire well-being.

"Keep doing the deep breaths," Piper reminded her.

They walked through the front doors that she'd been through many a time. But as her foot crossed the threshold, she flashed back to the last time she'd been here. The sergeant winking at her. Touching her shoulder. She had recoiled in disgust . . . and wished him dead.

"Izzy, did you hear me?" Piper asked.

She hadn't heard a thing. "No. I'm sorry."

"I asked if you wanted to go to the restroom before we head into the meeting."

"No. Let's just get it over with."

They were greeted by two detectives in the main lobby. "I'm Detective Stewart," the tall, older woman said. "And this is Detective Bryant." A shorter, younger man with a shaved head offered his hand.

It didn't surprise Izzy that they had a female detective involved in the questioning. That had to be by design. To Izzy, though, it didn't matter whether the detective was male or female—the pain was still the same for her to have to relive. She understood more than ever why victims of sexual assault didn't come forward. Being questioned and prodded about the most personal and intimate details of your life came at a huge price. But given that this was a murder investigation, she didn't really have any say in the matter.

"Thank you for coming in," Detective Stewart said.

Before Izzy could answer, Piper jumped in. "My client is here purely as a courtesy. I hope you'll keep that in mind."

"Of course," Detective Stewart said.

They didn't take Izzy to an interrogation room but instead led them into one of the conference rooms. Izzy had wondered how they were going to play it, and so far they were following the good-cop routine. How long that would last was the big, open question.

Everyone took their seats around the large conference room table. Piper sat next to Izzy, as she had expected. Piper was her lifeline and had made it clear that she was going to be her protector today. Izzy couldn't imagine for one second doing this alone.

Detective Stewart's beady brown eyes homed in on her. "You understand, Agent Cole, that you're here regarding the murder investigation of Sergeant Henry Tybee. We've got some questions that we're hoping you can help us with. Okay?"

"All right." At hearing his name, apprehension filled Izzy's body. She kept trying to take deep breaths like Piper had instructed. She worried that soon all her preparation was going to fly out the window.

"Let's start at the beginning. Do you have any idea why you're here today?"

Izzy remembered Piper's instructions. She wasn't supposed to speculate. "It would be helpful for you to tell me."

"What do you know about Sergeant Tybee's murder?"

She paused as she'd been taught, but when Piper didn't interject, she answered. "All I know is that he was killed. That's where it stops and starts."

Detective Stewart shot Detective Bryant a look before she turned her attention back to Izzy. "Sergeant Tybee was shot. It appears a struggle ensued, based on wounds on the sergeant's body, and he was killed with his own weapon. We think maybe he was killed in self-defense."

Ah, and they were looking into women who might fit the bill—Izzy included.

Detective Stewart looked at her notepad. "How did you know the sergeant?"

"I worked with him." Short, simple statements. Just like she'd practiced with Piper.

"Did you leave Arlington PD because of him?"

Talk about not much of a windup. But Piper had also instructed Izzy that she had to be truthful at all costs—even on the difficult topics—because if they caught her in a lie, they would use it against her. "Yes."

"Why?"

She sat silently, not sure how to answer.

Piper touched her arm. "Detective Stewart, let's not dance around the issues here. If you have a direct question to ask my client, then please do so."

Detective Stewart nodded. "Very well. What I'm about to tell you is disturbing, but it's not my intent to upset you. Do you understand?"

A wave of unease rushed through her in anticipation. "Yes."

"When we searched the sergeant's home, we found these." Detective Stewart opened a manila folder and slid it across the table.

Izzy leaned in and scanned the pictures spread out in front of her in bright vivid color. Pictures of her. Candid shots—her at the grocery store, coffee shop, jogging. Her breath caught as she started to see dancing stars in front of her eyes. She might be sick.

Piper noticed her reaction. "Take a deep breath, Izzy. Here's some water. I think she's going to need a minute."

Detective Stewart nodded. "Of course."

They sat in silence that hung in the air like a heavy weight as Izzy tried to think through what she was seeing. How long had the sergeant been watching her? When he'd confronted her, she'd had no idea that he'd been lurking in the shadows. Finally, she spoke up. "Obviously I didn't know about these."

Detective Stewart leaned in. "I know this is difficult. Just please bear with us for a few more minutes, okay?"

Izzy nodded.

"We're still combing through a lot of evidence, including electronics, but there's something I have to ask you about."

She knew it. This was about the text messages.

"Agent Cole, were you violently assaulted by the sergeant?"

Izzy sucked in a breath. "Yes."

"Sexually assaulted?"

"Yes." It was like she wasn't even sitting there answering the questions. Her whole body turned numb as she tried to fixate her gaze on the clock behind the detective's head. Anything to avoid eye contact during this topic.

The detective jotted down a note. "So that's why you left Arlington PD, right?"

"Yes." She shifted in her seat, waiting for the next question. They still hadn't brought up the text messages. Was it possible they hadn't found them yet?

"Who did you tell about the alleged assault?"

This time she didn't wait for Piper, and she looked right at Detective Stewart. "It wasn't an alleged assault, Detective. It was an assault." Her nails dug into her hands under the table.

Detective Stewart cocked her head. "Regardless of the terminology, who did you tell about it?"

"And that's relevant how?" All of a sudden, any desire she'd had to cooperate had left. Those photos had rocked her to the core.

Piper leaned toward her ear. "Izzy," she whispered. "You

can answer this. They already know the answer, most likely. Remember everything we talked about."

"I assume you're asking for those people who knew before the murder?" Izzy asked.

"Yes," Detective Stewart said.

"My Navy counselor, plus Jay and Aiden Graves and Bailey Ryan."

"Anyone else?"

She shook her head. "Not before the murder. No."

"Were you aware that Jay Graves confronted the sergeant?" Detective Bryant finally spoke up.

"I didn't know specifically, but I had my suspicions when I found out the sergeant took early retirement. Jay and I never spoke about it."

"You and Jay are close, right? You're dating his son?" Detective Stewart jumped right back in.

"We formed a bond while working a case earlier this year. That's how I met Aiden."

"In fact, Jay is like a father to you?"

"If you're asking that, then you already know that my father was killed. Shot dead in the line of duty, and yes, Jay is like a father to me. But I'd prefer to cut to your ultimate question. Do I think Jay killed him? No way."

"Why?" Detective Bryant asked.

"Because Jay is a man of honor and integrity. He's not a murderer, even if someone deserves it." As those words came out, Izzy realized her mistake.

"And you believed the sergeant deserved to die, didn't you?" Detective Stewart asked.

Piper grabbed Izzy's elbow. "Don't answer that. Detective, as I said, we are here as a courtesy. Do you have any evidence tying my client to this murder?"

"Not at the present time, no," Detective Stewart said. "And I apologize. We're just trying to gather all the facts, and the sergeant appears to have had a fixation on Agent Cole. An obsession. When was the last time you saw him?"

Izzy looked at Piper, who nodded. She couldn't lie about this, because if she did and they found out, it would make her look guilty. "A couple of weeks ago, the sergeant showed up while I was jogging."

Detective Stewart frowned. "What happened?"

"I told him to leave me alone," she whispered.

"Had you seen him recently before that?"

She nodded. "Yes, at a coffee shop in town. I thought that might have been an awful coincidence, but when he turned up on my jogging route, I realized that it had to be intentional."

"And I assume that frightened you?"

"I didn't want to have anything to do with that man," Izzy shot back.

"Have you ever been to his house?"

She shook her head. "No."

"Are you certain of that?" Detective Stewart asked.

"Yes. That isn't something I'd forget." The thought of being at his house sent another round of chills down her back.

Piper stood. "I think we've done enough for today."

"Are we done?" Izzy asked, unsure what to do.

Detective Stewart's expression softened. "Yes. I know this is extremely hard for you."

She was about to say something, but Piper jumped in. "We're not trying to be obstructionist here, but my client has already been through enough."

"Just one more quick thing. I need to ask where you were four nights ago."

"At home," Izzy answered softly.

"Alone?" Detective Bryant asked.

"Yes."

"And did you stay at home all night?"

"Yes. I left the next morning for a jog around five thirty."

"All right," Detective Stewart said. "Agent Cole, we're not the bad guys here. As much disdain as you may hold toward Sergeant Tybee, his murderer still deserves to be brought to justice."

"That's easy for you to say," Izzy blurted.

Detective Stewart quirked a brow but didn't say anything. Piper took Izzy by the arm and led her out of the room.

"Sorry." Izzy turned to Piper once they were down the hallway. "I couldn't hold my tongue any longer."

Piper patted her on the shoulder. "You did as well as could be expected under the circumstances."

"What do you think?"

"Let's get outside."

A minute later, they were walking to the car. "So?" Izzy wanted Piper's perspective.

"They clearly don't have any actual evidence against you at this point, but the fact that the sergeant was so obsessed with you isn't great."

"Tell me about it." Izzy considered what had just happened back in the conference room. "Do you think they have anything on Jay?"

"You sound concerned. If you're convinced he didn't do it, then everything should be okay."

"I know he didn't do it, but I've seen enough to know that sometimes the facts and the law get all twisted up." It was yet another reason she was tossing around the idea of law school and ultimately being a prosecutor. "Can I ask you a totally unrelated question?"

"Sure." Piper started up her car, and they pulled out of the precinct parking lot.

"Why criminal defense? You seem like the search-for-justice type."

Piper laughed. "I am, and that's exactly why I do criminal defense. As you just said, not everything is always so clear-cut. Of course, not every client I have is innocent, but they all deserve their opportunity to be heard—or not heard, as the case may be. The right to take the Fifth, to have qualified counsel. Those things are important to me, because I believe in the integrity of the justice system as a whole."

"I guess I never thought of it like that."

"Then maybe something good can come out of this bad experience."

"Maybe so." Izzy had a lot to think about. "Do you think we did the right thing by not volunteering the information about the text messages?"

Piper frowned. "I wanted to see how it went in there before offering up additional information. Let's sleep on it, and depending on how things proceed, we can make a decision about the texts."

Izzy had to trust Piper on this. She was the expert. "I'm just relieved she didn't make me relive the attack blow by blow." She'd stayed up all night worrying about that.

"I am too, but this was just the first interview. I don't want you to think you're in the clear, as far as that is concerned. It could quite possibly come up again, and she might be much more aggressive with you."

Izzy groaned.

"Are you going in to work?" Piper asked.

"Yeah. I can't just sit around and mope all day. I also have to talk to Marco and let him know what's going on."

"Your boss?"

"Yes. I've been dreading having this conversation, but now I have no choice. For all I know, they're going to want to question him, too, and I need to be the one to tell him about all of this."

"The less you tell him about the history, the better. Got it?" Piper asked.

"Understood." Although right now, she didn't feel like she understood anything.

CHAPTER
THIRTEEN

Layla walked into the living room of her condo. "They want me at Langley tomorrow." She sat down beside Hunter on the couch. She'd just gotten off the call.

He frowned. "For what?"

"The IG's office said they had questions for me. I guess they're finally ready for my interrogation."

He turned toward her. "What if you get there and they decide to take you to a black site, and we never hear from you again?"

She blew out a breath. "Don't you think you're being a bit melodramatic?"

He placed a hand on his chest. "Me? C'mon, Layla. These aren't games you want to play. I know you believe in the Agency and all the good they do, but do you really have any doubt in your mind that they would turn on you if they thought you were dirty? I think you've been set up, and we have to assume they will do everything in their power to get answers from you that match their expectations."

As much as she hated to admit it, Hunter had a point. If none of the other stuff had happened and this investigation was in isolation, that would be one thing. But she couldn't close her eyes and pretend like everything was going to be okay. "All right. What do you suggest?"

"Bring your lawyer."

"But I don't have a lawyer."

He stood up. "You do now."

She couldn't hold back her laughter. "You're *not* a lawyer, Hunter."

"Hey, I am an active member of the Virginia and DC bar. Just because I don't have a law practice doesn't mean I'm not legit. And if they deny you legal counsel, then we just say *thanks, but no thanks* and hightail it out of there."

She considered his offer. As much as she hated to admit it, he was right. She'd been at Langley long enough to know that if she had been set up, there could be disastrous consequences. Scarlett's words of advice echoed through her brain. This was far from a routine legal inquiry. "Scarlett told me I absolutely couldn't go in there without an attorney and that it would be foolish to represent myself."

"Sounds like great advice to me. I hope you'll take it."

"You realize that if you're right and there's danger involved, then you could be put right in the middle of it."

He nodded. "I'm not going to let you down this time."

And there it was. The opening for the conversation that the girls had encouraged her to have. Was it now or never? Would there ever be the exact right time? "About that."

"Yeah." He sat back down.

"Can we talk?" she asked.

Hunter looked away for a moment before making eye contact. "I wondered how long it would be before we had this conversation."

"You look like you're dreading it." Probably not as much as she was, but this seemed like a necessary evil if she was ever going to move on with her life. And that was something she desperately needed to do. Living in the past with his memory always floating around was not healthy.

"I knew this day might eventually come, but honestly, I never thought it would be under circumstances remotely like this." He paused. "I've been having internal debates about whether I should reach out to you for a long time, but I didn't want to invade your life. I felt like the last thing you deserved was any more heartache from me, so I decided it was best to try to keep the past in the past."

"Why did you think reaching out would cause me more heartache? What could possibly be worse than what you did?" She couldn't stop talking now, as her emotions simmered dangerously close to the surface. "We had plans to build a life together. To get married, have a family, the whole nine yards, and you just threw it all away on a one-night drunken hookup? That wasn't the man I fell in love with, and I've questioned over and over in my mind how we could've ended up there. What did I do to push you away? I thought we had promised each other that we would build our relationship on trust, love, and our common faith." Finally, she took a second to regroup and see how he would respond to her allegations.

"I deserve all of that and more. And I think you finally deserve the truth." He took her hand and squeezed it.

Her pulse quickened. "What do you mean? I know the

truth. I may not know every sordid detail, but you can spare me that."

He hung his head.

"Hunter, is there something else you're not telling me?"

His blue eyes met hers. "I lied to you, Layla."

She pulled her hand back. "Was it more than just a one-time thing? Is that it?" She tried to move farther away from him, but he grabbed both her hands and held on tightly. "What?" It came out as a whisper, because the look in his eyes told her that something was really wrong.

"Layla, there was no blond undergrad. No drunken night at the bar."

Her voice shook. "I don't understand what you're saying."

He looked away again, and she feared that what he was going to tell her would be even worse than the lie she had believed all these years.

"Hunter?" This time she tightened her grip on him.

"That entire story was fabricated."

"But why?" Her thoughts were jumbled, because none of what Hunter was saying made any sense at all.

"Do you remember what was going on in your life during all of that?"

How could she forget? It was one of the most defining moments of her life. "Of course. I was in the final stages of my interviews with the Agency." She looked him in the eyes, and then a sick feeling formed deep within the pit of her stomach.

"I was interviewed about you for the background check, and that was all standard operating procedure."

"I remember you telling me everything went fine." That conversation about the background check visit was vivid in her mind.

Hunter took a breath. "And it was, but then I got a visit from a completely different man."

She felt her heart cracking into tiny pieces all over again, because deep in her gut, she knew where this might end. "What did this man say to you?"

"A lot of things, but the bottom line was that if I really loved you, I would break it off. That the country needed you more than I did, and that ultimately our relationship would be a liability not only to your career but to the Agency."

She felt her mouth drop open. Had the CIA really tanked her relationship? "But why? Most recruits have relationships of some sort. I admit the success rates of CIA marriages aren't the best, but still, it's completely normal for CIA employees to get married."

"You were what he described to me as an HVR."

"HVR?"

"A high-value recruit. Only one percent of recruits fall into that category. You speak Arabic fluently, you know the Middle East like the back of your hand, and you have a first-rate academic pedigree. They literally saw you as a once-in-a-lifetime hire and were willing to do whatever it took to make sure you could succeed there unencumbered."

"Why didn't you tell me?" Her voice cracked.

"He told me if I spoke a word of any of it to you, they'd cancel your conditional offer of employment, and he didn't seem like the kind of guy to make idle threats."

She sat in silence, holding tightly to his hands, because she didn't know what else to do. Her entire world had been turned upside down. But the feeling that hit her the hardest was anger. Not at Hunter. No—it was at the CIA.

"They took everything from me." Fresh tears started to flow down her cheeks.

Hunter pulled her close and wrapped his arms around her while she cried. She knew she'd never be the same.

◆

Layla had stopped crying, but that didn't make Hunter feel any better. He had wanted to hold her since the moment they'd parted years ago, but this wasn't how he'd wanted it to unfold. Although he had to admit that it felt like five thousand pounds had been lifted from his shoulders. He'd never told a soul about any of this. Not even Elijah, who heard about everything else in Hunter's life. This had been his dark secret to bear alone.

"You let everyone believe you were a cheater to try to protect me?" Layla looked up into his eyes.

"I loved you. I felt like it was my only option. You were so high on the Agency gig. That's *all* you talked about. How you wanted to become a top-rated analyst and save lives. Thwart the next 9/11. Be the one who could see things that others couldn't see. Connect all the dots. There was no way I was going to take that away from you. It meant far too much."

"I don't even know how to begin to process all of this," she whispered.

"Do you want a few minutes alone?" He was willing to give her all the time she needed.

"No," she responded quickly. "I have questions."

"Whatever I can answer, I will." That was the least he could do.

"This man who came to you. What was his name?"

"Riley Brown."

Her eyes widened. "Are you sure?"

"Well, I can't be sure he was telling the truth, but that's what he said his name was."

"What did he look like? Do you remember?"

How could he forget? "Yeah. White guy, I'd say in his late fifties, with dark hair graying at the temples. Probably about five ten, light eyes. Do you know him?"

She nodded. "He's high up at Langley, but not in the DA."

"DA?"

"Directorate of Analysis—my division. Riley's from the Directorate of Operations, aka the clandestine service." She shook her head. "If the DO's involved, they had this planned all along."

"What planned?"

"That I'd come in as an analyst, and they'd make me a field officer even though I told them I wanted a desk job. If Riley Brown came to you, they were working me from day one, and I never saw it coming. I've played right into their little web of tricks."

He put the pieces together quickly. "But why not just re-cruit you for the clandestine service from the beginning?"

"Because I made it clear from my first interview that I wanted to be an analyst."

"And they didn't want to take no for an answer." He had to ask. "Do you think any of that history and their plan for you has anything to do with the IG investigation?"

"I doubt it, but at this point, everything is on the table. Honestly, Hunter, my mind is blown right now."

He knew he might be pushing his luck, but he took her hand again. "I'm so sorry about all of this."

"Me too," she said softly. "This is all the more reason to take you up on your offer to go with me tomorrow as my attorney."

"Layla, I know we can't turn back the clock, but I vow to

you right now that I'm going to stick by your side through this."

"I believe you."

As he looked into Layla's dark eyes, he wondered if there was any chance of starting over with her.

CHAPTER *FOURTEEN*

"I'm dreading this." Izzy walked into Arlington PD with Piper by her side.

Piper nodded. "I know, but after giving it some thought, I think we need to get out in front of this. Even if the sergeant deleted those texts, there's a chance they could get them from your phone through a subpoena, and I don't want to be put in that position—I don't want to put *you* in that position—given we can explain this. It will be better if we set the stage as opposed to the other way around."

Izzy reluctantly agreed, but those texts were damaging. Once she realized the sergeant had been following her, a flood of emotions had gone through her. It started with fear, but then it quickly turned to red-hot anger. And when he had tried to touch her, the rage inside her was just too much to contain. She'd lashed out in the texts. But she had not killed him, even if she had wanted to.

Detective Stewart met them in the lobby. "Agent Cole, Ms. Alexander, what can I do for you?"

Piper didn't hesitate. "We have some information we'd like to provide."

"Let's go to the conference room and talk." Detective Stewart led them down the hallway.

Izzy started feeling sick again but tried to keep her emotions in check. She took a seat beside Piper and let her take the lead.

Piper looked directly at the detective. "When we were here last, you laid a lot of information on Agent Cole. She was clearly disturbed by the information you provided about the sergeant's home."

"Yes, and again, I'm sorry for that," Detective Stewart said.

"In the interest of full transparency and cooperation, we wanted to provide you with some additional information regarding recent interactions between the sergeant and Agent Cole."

Detective Stewart raised an eyebrow. "I'm listening."

"Izzy, you can explain," Piper said.

Izzy swallowed. It seemed she had no other alternative. "After the sergeant showed up on my jogging trail, he started texting me."

"Really?" Detective Stewart said.

It appeared the detective hadn't known that tidbit. "Yes, and I responded. I told him to leave me alone, and in those texts, I did threaten him."

"Are you willing to turn over those texts voluntarily?"

Izzy shot a glance at Piper. "That's up to my lawyer."

Detective Stewart gave her a slight smile. "Ms. Alexander, what do you think?"

153

"I'm inclined to advise my client to cooperate because she has nothing to hide. Yes, she was incredibly angry at the sergeant, but there is a big difference between making a threat in a text and acting on it—especially when you're talking about someone who has a sterling record in law enforcement."

"I feel a catch coming on here," the detective said.

"No catch. Just a cautionary statement that you take my client's cooperation into account. Agent Cole did not harm the sergeant, regardless of the text message exchange. That's the bottom line."

"But you would've liked to?" Detective Stewart asked Izzy.

"At the time I was angry, but I didn't see him again after those texts, so there was no issue. I tried to focus on my work and not think about him."

Detective Stewart leaned forward. "You did the right thing by bringing this fact forward. It seems the sergeant was an avid texter, but we have no way of knowing if we have a complete set of his messages. We're going through them now."

Izzy wondered if he was harassing other women via text as well. She also wondered if he had other shrines at his home. Why was he so focused on her? The thought gave her another chill. "Detective, I didn't kill him."

"I'm just gathering the evidence," Detective Stewart said.

It wasn't lost on Izzy that the detective hadn't agreed with her statement but instead deflected.

"Do you need anything from us right now?" Piper asked.

"Besides access to those texts, no."

"We'll get those to you." Piper stood.

Izzy was ready to get out of there. Once the two of them were outside, she turned to Piper. "I sure hope we did the right thing."

"I know you're nervous, but we couldn't risk it coming out and making you look guilty for hiding it from the police."

Izzy knew Piper was right, but she felt like she had just dug her hole even deeper with Detective Stewart.

❖

At Langley, Layla braced herself for a big pushback from CIA security over Hunter's presence, but surprisingly, they hadn't given her any grief.

The man who sat beside her now wasn't the Hunter she was familiar with. He wore a dark navy suit and tie. He'd even brought a legal briefcase. They were at a small conference room table, waiting for the IG team to arrive.

She'd had a hard time sleeping last night after Hunter had told her the truth about their past. Everything she thought she knew about how their relationship ended had been a lie. But not one driven by Hunter—it had been the CIA's doing, and she was having a hard time coming to grips with that. She wasn't naïve. She knew the personal sacrifices that people made every single day to serve their country at the Agency, but she'd never expected it to become so personal to her. What bothered her most was that they had taken her choices away. The powers that be at Langley had unilaterally determined that they knew best how she should live her life.

The door opened, and two men walked into the room, along with her boss, Brett. She wondered if he was going to be involved in this.

"Layla, thanks for coming in." Brett gave her a forced smile.

Like she had much of a choice. "Of course."

She turned her attention to the two men she didn't know. One was quite a bit older than the other.

"I'm Frank Gibson," the older man said. "And this is Monty Hicks. We're both with the IG's office."

Hunter rose and stretched out his hand. "I'm Hunter McCoy, Ms. Karam's attorney."

Brett eyed Hunter but didn't respond directly to him. "Layla, I just popped in to make sure everyone was situated here, but I won't be sticking around for the questions. The IG's office prefers it that way."

She did too. She wasn't sure Brett was really on her side. "Okay, thank you."

Brett gave a nod to the guys from the IG's office and walked out of the room.

"Let's have a seat," Frank said. They each passed over their business cards. "Ms. Karam, we usually don't allow attorneys in our investigations, but given the circumstances, we have no objection, since Mr. McCoy has the proper clearances."

"And what are the circumstances exactly?" Layla asked. She appreciated that Hunter was there, but she was going to speak up to protect her interests as well.

Frank cleared his throat. "Ms. Karam, you're familiar with the known terrorist group called Al-Nidal, correct?"

She hadn't been expecting that to be where the questioning would start. "Yes, of course, they're part of my portfolio."

"Meaning?" Monty asked.

"You'll have to excuse Monty. He's new to this job, so he'll have more questions," Frank said.

Layla was skeptical about that claim, but she focused on answering the question, assuming that the sooner she did, the sooner she'd find out what this was all about. "That means that I study the group in hopes of becoming an expert so I can aid operations and any other analytical efforts we have."

Frank nodded. "Have you ever met any members of Al-Nidal?"

Before she could answer, Hunter grabbed her arm to stop her from responding, but she waved him off. "No. I haven't."

"Are you sure about that?" Monty asked.

"I'm one hundred percent sure. I think I'd know if I'd met a known terrorist." Layla's frustration level was building.

Monty opened one of the many folders in front of him and slid a picture across the table. "Do you know who this is?"

Layla sighed. This was quickly going nowhere, in her opinion. "Of course. It's Omar Assad."

"And who is that?" Monty asked.

Layla wasn't sure why they were playing dumb. "He's the number two in Al-Nidal. Basically, he's Abu Rihal's deputy, and Rihal runs the organization from some unknown location in Syria."

Frank leaned forward. "Do you know Assad?"

She tried not to get too impatient with this line of questioning, but she failed to understand what they were driving at. "No. I've studied him intensively, but I don't know him personally."

"So on the record today, you've never met?" Monty asked.

"No. Don't you think if I'd met Assad, I would've immediately filed a report? That kind of thing isn't exactly a run-of-the-mill occurrence."

"We actually agree with you. Let me show you something else." Frank nodded to Monty, who pulled out another photo.

As she looked at it, her stomach clenched. The photo appeared to be of her and Assad sitting at a coffee shop in Paris. A coffee shop she'd been to last year on her first field assignment. She remembered it very clearly, and she also remembered that she had never encountered Assad there.

"Does that refresh your recollection?" Frank asked.

"Don't answer that," Hunter said. "I need a moment to confer with my client."

A sly smile spread across Frank's lips. "By all means."

Layla and Hunter stood and walked over to the corner of the room.

Hunter leaned down. "Talk to me, Layla," he said in her ear.

She looked up at him. His face was so close to hers, but she didn't want the IG men to hear their private conversation. "I've never met Assad, and I certainly didn't have coffee with him."

"Are you sure? Not even as an asset?" he whispered.

"No," she shot back.

"Then someone has gone through a lot of trouble to make it look like you did. If I had to guess, there's going to be more evidence tying you and him together."

"This is crazy. What do you think I should do?" A million thoughts zapped through her brain, but she was having trouble formulating the best course of action.

"We could stop the interview now, but it might make more sense to keep going and see if they'll show any more of their cards. You just keep telling the truth, and let's try to get all we can out of them. It's best to know what we're up against."

A wave of nausea threatened her. "This is bad."

He took her hand and gave it a quick, reassuring squeeze. "We'll get through it."

His multiple references to *we* were the only thing keeping her steady at this point. She really did feel like Hunter was going to stand beside her no matter what happened. Given his act of sacrifice years ago, she had no doubts that he'd go to every length to protect her.

She took a deep breath and walked back over to the table. "I don't know Assad."

"But that is you in this picture, right?" Monty asked.

"It looks like me, yes, but I never had coffee with Assad. I was at that coffee shop by myself, conducting surveillance. It was my first field op, so I remember it very well."

"Okay." Monty pulled out another picture. This one appeared to be taken from outside of a hotel room window, and she could be seen through the glass, standing with Assad's arms wrapped around her. She thought she might be ill.

Frank crossed his arms. "Ms. Karam, do you deny having a romantic relationship with Assad that started in Paris of last year?"

Her heart felt like it was going to beat out of her chest. These allegations were almost too much for her to handle. Not only that she was knowingly working with a terrorist but also doing a lot more than that in a hotel room. "I unequivocally deny that."

Monty leaned forward. "So you didn't spend the night together in Paris?"

Now she was moving from frustration to outright anger. "Absolutely not. This is insane."

"Maybe you thought you were working him? Turning him into an asset?" Frank asked. "That would be smart. Is that what happened here? Just tell us if it was. That would help us put together all of your actions. The Agency doesn't frown upon using whatever it takes to bring in high-value assets. Just tell us what you did. Did you try to turn him?"

"I can't tell you something that didn't happen. I never met him, and I most certainly didn't try to turn him through whatever tactics you're insinuating."

"Then how do you explain these pictures?" Frank asked.

She lifted up her hand. "Let's back up a moment. Who took these photos?"

Frank frowned. "I'm not at liberty to provide information on how we acquired the pictures."

"They must be fabricated," she replied quickly.

"Our initial analysis tells us otherwise," Monty said.

"With the advances in AI technology, these things can be faked, and it's almost impossible to detect. Yes, it would take someone with access to high-end technology, but I believe this is a setup, and you guys are falling for it."

"You know we will polygraph you," Frank said.

"I welcome that." She paused, thinking about how far she should go. "You two need to consider that if I'm telling the truth, someone went through a whole lot of trouble to frame me. Should I also remind you that I was a target in the restaurant bombing?"

Frank shook his head. "Our best and current intel doesn't support you being a target. We have a homegrown terrorist taking complete responsibility."

Isn't that convenient?

"I think you gentlemen have gotten your questions answered." Hunter rose from his seat.

Frank stood as well. "Yes, we have what we need for now." He turned to her. "You'll be contacted about coming in for that polygraph. And given the totality of the circumstances, we have decided that it is best for you to stay at a CIA safe house."

She hadn't been expecting that. "Will I still have the security detail?"

"We don't think that's necessary at an Agency safe house. Of course, we'll keep close tabs on you, and if the situation changes, we'll adjust quickly."

She studied him, unable to hide her skepticism. "I just want to understand the terms of engagement here. Am I free to move about as I want?"

Monty nodded. "Yes. The safe house is something the DEA was pushing for as well, and as we said, I believe it makes sense, given everything that has happened. However, we reiterate our request that you stay in the greater DC area. You'll be sent the details on the safe house and can move in tonight."

Layla wanted to hold her tongue but couldn't. "When you find out that I was right about this, I want a full exoneration statement placed in my file. Are we clear on that?"

Frank leaned against the table. "If you're telling the truth, then that shouldn't be an issue. If, however, the evidence shows otherwise, then the Agency intends to pursue all legal remedies at its disposal."

She wanted to throttle him, but she fought to keep her cool. Sensing that she was about to blow, Hunter took her arm and guided her out of the room.

They didn't say much until they had driven off Langley's campus, but she was about to erupt. "Can you believe that?"

She turned toward him, but he kept his eyes on the road as he responded. "Someone wants you out of the Agency and is willing to go to great lengths to make that happen."

"How does this tie in to the DEA angle? We need to think about timing. Could this case against me have been created and put in motion after we were outed during the DEA op?"

"I find it difficult to see how they could've pulled that off, unless whoever is responsible knew about your DEA activity before your team was actually attacked. For me, the even bigger question is why the Agency is handling it this way."

"What do you mean?" she asked.

"Think about it, Layla. If those investigators *really* thought you were cavorting with a well-known terrorist, don't you think they would've locked you up somewhere?"

She rubbed her temples as her head pounded. "You're wondering why they let me go? I know the answer. They're watching me now. They want to see if they can catch me in the act. That whole bit about my security detail being released since I'm at a safe house? That was just them trying to make me think I have some freedom of movement, when really, I bet they're going to be watching me closely."

"That's a good point. And I know we've been down this road before, but we have to revisit it. Do you think Bryce could have anything to do with this?"

"He seemed sincere when we met, but he's also a trained liar."

"How're his tech skills?"

"Good. I doubt he personally would've been able to doctor the photos, but he knows people who could. He has extensive contacts."

"I'm going to talk to him solo," Hunter said.

"Do you really think that's a good idea?"

"Yeah. I'll get more answers without you there."

She flopped back into her seat. "Whatever you want to do on that front is fine with me."

"How're you holding up?"

She sighed. "I'm all right, I guess. You didn't actually think for a minute that I could've done those things, did you?"

He shook his head. "Of course not. I know you better than that. And even if you were trying to turn an asset, you wouldn't have gone to his hotel room."

"I could've changed a lot since we were together," she suggested.

He glanced over at her. "You're solid to the core, Layla. You can't be shaken. Especially when it comes to your beliefs."

If only he knew how much she had gone through since they'd been together. "Thank you for saying that, but there have been a lot of times when I've wondered how I was going to make it through. I've made some mistakes and gone through some really dark spots. The doubts have piled up."

He raised an eyebrow. "You? Have doubts? No way. That's not the Layla I remember."

"I hurt so badly after what happened with us that I truly wondered if God was there. I asked why He'd chosen to abandon me. What had happened to us? We were both people of faith. I never understood, and now I see I was wrong about all of it."

He sighed loudly. "The whole God-working-all-things-together-for-good thing doesn't always pan out, does it?"

"Do you really believe that?" she asked softly.

"Honestly, Layla, I'm not sure what I believe anymore."

She couldn't help herself as she placed her hand on his forearm. "God hasn't left you, Hunter. I promise."

He shot her a glance. "Can you really make that promise?"

"With every ounce of myself, I believe that. God's there even when we think we can't feel Him or hear Him. Sometimes it may just be a whisper in the wind or a beautiful sunrise, and that's all it takes to remind me that the Lord is so much bigger than us. Than this earth. Than our lives. He is everything and everywhere, while at the same time He cares about each of us."

He looked over at her before focusing back on the road in front of him. "I do not doubt your conviction for a moment."

"What do you doubt, then?" she asked.

"God's ability to care about a man like me."

"Hunter, you're a good man," she responded quickly.

He laughed. "You wouldn't have said that a few weeks ago, would you?"

She sat silently for a minute. "Actually, I would have. I thought you did something awful and that it never made sense, but that's different. If you had done it, then it would've been a bad mistake, to say the least, but that doesn't change who you are—and that's a good man."

"Then, once again, Layla, you're a better person than I'll ever be. And maybe in that is where I find my answer."

She shook her head. "No, Hunter. God's grace doesn't work like that. It's not a game board where He's keeping score."

"I hope you're right, because I'd be losing big-time right now."

"We *all* would be." She struggled to find the right words to say to him and didn't push the topic any further, but she couldn't help but believe that this conversation was far from over.

CHAPTER
FIFTEEN

Izzy sat next to Aiden on the couch while Jay sat across from them in one of the large chairs. She wanted to talk to both of them even though Piper told her she probably shouldn't. But Izzy wasn't focused on just the legal case. She wanted to make sure she was doing everything she could to protect the two men who meant so much to her.

Jay had changed her life in immeasurable ways, and she'd never loved anyone like she loved Aiden. She didn't know if it would be possible to love anyone else like that again.

She had to get them up to speed. "Thanks for getting together tonight. Both of you know I had my second interview this morning with Arlington PD."

Aiden took her hand. "I'm sorry I couldn't be there with you."

"It wouldn't have worked, given the circumstances, but I know you always have my back. Both of you." She breathed in deeply, considering her next words very carefully.

"You know we do," Jay added.

"And that's why we're here. The line of questioning they went through made me think that either one or both of you could also be questioned by the police."

Neither man seemed surprised.

"You expected that?" she asked.

Jay nodded. "I did. Given my interaction with the sergeant, I figured they would check me out, and now, with your relationship with Aiden, he's also in the mix. They wouldn't be very good cops if they let all of that slide."

That wasn't the way she was looking at it. Everyone was talking about how the sergeant deserved justice, but she still hadn't accepted that and probably never would. She couldn't have them wrongfully caught up in her mess. "Jay, I dragged you into this to begin with. Let me help you."

Jay smiled. "Izzy, you didn't drag me anywhere, and I wouldn't change a single thing about how I acted."

"Maybe we're all just being paranoid," Aiden said. "I haven't been contacted by anyone yet."

Izzy looked at him. "It's just a matter of time. There's something else too." She took a moment to gather her thoughts. She knew they were not going to like what she'd learned. "I found out that the sergeant had been following me. He had pictures of me at his house."

Aiden's eyes flashed with anger. "No way."

"Unfortunately, yes," she said softly.

"Izzy, I hate to say this, but that only makes your situation more difficult," Jay said.

"You sound like my lawyer."

"The bigger question here is who did kill him," Jay said. "We know it wasn't one of us."

"He was an officer for many years. Probably made his fair

share of enemies," Izzy said. "But would that be enough for murder?"

Aiden took her hand. "Let's have a little more faith in Arlington PD here. Give them a chance to do their jobs. This is all very personal for us, but I want to believe that they will get this right, and the culprit will be brought to justice."

She didn't share his sunny viewpoint on the topic. "You're more optimistic about that than I am. Something about the way the detective scrutinized me gave me pause. Which brings me to my next point."

"Yes?" Aiden squeezed her hand.

"I'm going to do some investigating of my own."

"Whoa. That can't be a good idea." Aiden turned toward his dad. "Talk some sense into her."

Jay let out a big sigh. "I agree with Aiden on this one, but I don't think you're going to listen to us, so if you do decide to start snooping around, you don't need to do it alone. We don't know exactly what's going on here, and there's no way to know whether it's bigger than the sergeant's death. I'm going to head home and leave you two to talk," he said. "Izzy, you know you can call me at any time."

"I do know. Thank you, Jay. For everything." He'd been a source of strength and stability, and she thanked God for bringing him into her life. She stood and gave him a hug. A piece of her wondered if she'd be able to call him Dad one day, but she couldn't get ahead of herself where Aiden was concerned.

Once Jay had left, she focused on Aiden.

"You know I just don't want any more harm and pain to come to you, Izzy, but if you're dead set on conducting your own operation, then you can count me in. Where do you want to start?" Aiden asked her.

"I don't think there's a blueprint for this, but as much as I'd like not to, we start with the sergeant. We do a deep dive on social media, background, anything we can find." The prospect of coming face-to-face with more of the sergeant's secrets was disturbing but unavoidable. She needed to do this.

"Which means we have to start asking questions," Aiden said. "That could raise eyebrows. Are you really sure you want to do this?"

She was, because there was no other choice in her mind. "If word hasn't already gotten out that the detectives talked to me, believe me, it will. I can handle the heat. I came clean with Marco, and he was very supportive, including offering me any time off I needed to deal with this, which I accepted. My head isn't in the work game at the moment. The truth is the most important thing to me right now, and making sure we're all in the clear."

"Sounds like a good plan to me, but are you ready for what you might find?"

"What do you mean?"

"What if the answers out there are difficult to handle?"

"I don't think we're going to find evidence of the sergeant's sterling reputation. In fact, I think it's going to be just the opposite. He had an obsession with me, but I doubt I'm the first or only woman he fixated on. I bet there's a long list of women out there."

And that fact scared her.

"We'll get through this," Aiden said. "We're a team, remember? We made that pact from day one. It's one of the things that has made our relationship so solid."

She smiled. "Since you came into my life, I see things differently. I was in such a dark place before. The lack of trust, the pain and fear. But being with you has shown me another way."

He pulled her close to him. "I worry that this ordeal threatens to take you back to that very dark place, and I don't want you to go there."

She sighed. "I don't either, but if I'm forced to go, I know that you'll be by my side this time."

"Always. If you'll let me."

She closed her eyes and rested her head on his shoulder. She didn't think he was making a real *forever* statement, but she did have hope that one day they would get there. As long as her past didn't overtake her.

◆

After the ordeal at her house, Cass had welcomed the DEA safe house. Zane was pacing around the kitchen, trying to figure out their next move. The target still didn't seem to be on his back, and his top priority was keeping Cass safe.

He'd never seen real, true fear in her eyes until she was in the arms of her attacker. He hated that he'd had to kill the guy—one, because he never liked to take a life, and two, because that meant they had no leads. Zane felt pretty confident that he could've gotten some actionable intel out of the hit man, but if he had to go back and do it again, he would make the same decision. Cass's life was paramount.

His phone rang, and he saw it was Mason. "Hey."

"All secure on your end?" Mason asked.

"Yeah. Cass is resting right now."

"Let me guess—you're stewing."

"Wouldn't you be?"

"I always am. We're alike in that way." Mason chuckled. "But I have an update for you."

"Good."

"We got a hit on the perp who attacked Cass. His name

is Rod Gaynor, and he's a known mercenary. Works for the highest bidder and has cartel contacts."

"And you think the cartel hired him for this job?" Zane asked.

"I can do you one better. We were able to trace a couple of his offshore bank accounts, and he was wired money from one of the Cayman banks that is a favorite of the cartel. It's not conclusive evidence, but it points that way."

"That makes sense. All the more reason why it's good Cass is in the safe house. They'll just send someone else. We have to figure out how to get the kill order removed."

"If you have any ideas, I'm all ears," Mason said.

"Not yet, but as long as that order is out there, Cass is in danger. Layla too. Although there seems to be a lot of other stuff going on with Layla, and I'm not sure it's all related to our op."

"I can't be either, but I'm still willing to help her in any way I can. She's been a real team player, and I appreciate that. We can't always say that about Agency types."

"I want to help her too. I have no idea why Langley is giving her a hard time," Zane said.

"If we get to a point where you think you can't trust her, for whatever reason, I need you to let me know."

"I doubt that's going to happen, but I get the request."

"I'll be in touch."

Mason ended the call, and Zane turned around as Cass walked into the kitchen. Her hair was pulled back in a low ponytail, and she wasn't wearing a stitch of makeup, but she still looked pretty.

As that thought crossed his mind, he had to check himself. Since when did he look at Cass like that? All of this danger they were facing was messing with his head.

"What is it?" Cass asked. "What's wrong?"

He quickly shook off those thoughts and tried to get his head back in the game. "Nothing. We got an ID on your attacker. Standard merc with financial ties to known cartel accounts."

She pulled her hair out of the ponytail, letting it loose on her shoulders. "It's like whack-a-mole at this point."

He moved toward her. "Hey now. You can't have a defeatist attitude. We'll beat this thing. There will be a way."

"We've talked about this before. Once the cartel orders the hit, the only way you get off that hit list is if you're dead. And before you even suggest it, no, there's no way I'm going into WITSEC. That would require me to give up everything. The only real solution is to take down the Mejía cartel. Did Mason say anything about the traitor on the inside?"

He shook his head. "No. I don't think he's at liberty to talk about any of that."

"If they can figure out who that is, maybe we have a fighting chance at beating them."

"We'll push Mason if we need to. There's got to be a way out of this, and we'll find it together."

Her expression softened, and she moved closer and took his hand in hers. "I can't thank you enough, Zane. I knew as my partner that you would be there for me, but you've stepped up in ways that go far beyond the call of duty."

He squeezed her hand. "You would do the same for me, and I want you to keep your head up. This could be a long battle."

She looked up at him with her big brown eyes, and he felt a punch of desire.

"I can fight as long as you're with me," she said softly. Then she put her arms around his neck and rested her head on his chest. Her hair smelled like flowers. She felt so small pressed against him, and his need to protect her only grew stronger.

What was he supposed to do now? He figured this was likely just her wanting to be comforted. He was a jerk for thinking of anything romantic, but his brain didn't appear to be winning that battle.

She pulled back a little but still held on to him. "Sorry if I'm being needy. It's totally not my style."

He smiled. "I know that."

Cass looked away, and he could've sworn that her cheeks reddened. He wasn't sure what was going on here, but he needed to put a little distance between them. He let her go, reluctantly, and went to the refrigerator, pulled out two bottled waters, and gave her one.

"Were you able to sleep at all?" he asked.

"Only a few minutes, but maybe that means I'll actually get some rest tonight." She took a sip of water. "I want to go in to work tomorrow. I can't just sit here all day. I'll feel better if I can focus on something else."

"We'll just have to be extremely careful getting back here to make sure we're not tailed."

She grinned. "We're pros. I think we can handle it."

"All right. We'll go to the office in the morning." He was glad she was joking around. It was better than the alternative. He could handle the lighthearted banter much better than those big brown eyes that seemed so fearful.

"I'm starving. They said they stocked this place with groceries. I'm going to whip something up. You want in?" she asked.

"You know I never turn down food."

"Isn't that the truth? If you stay in here with me, though, I'm going to put you to work."

"Whatever you need, but you know I'm pretty incompetent in the kitchen."

Cass laughed. "Lucky for you, I'm not. C'mon. Wash up, and let's get to work."

◆

First thing Monday morning, Hunter showed up unannounced at Bryce's office, but this time he'd come alone. He'd expected Layla to put up more of a fight, but she'd readily accepted him rolling solo.

There was no doubt a shift had occurred between them once he'd told her the truth, but he still didn't know if the damage was irreparable. He hoped it wasn't. He even found himself praying it wasn't, but he wasn't sure that God was paying attention to his prayer attempts. Although he knew deep inside that he hadn't made a true effort at reconnecting and most of his reaction was based purely on fear for Layla. If going back to God meant He would keep Layla safe, then Hunter would consider it.

He'd opened up to Layla about his faith struggles, and true to form, she had pressed him to examine why he felt this way. He wasn't an examine-his-feelings type of guy. He was more of the lock-it-away-and-try-not-to-think-about-it type.

And that was exactly what he did as he was led back to Bryce's office.

Bryce stood. "I figured I'd hear from you again."

"Do you know why I'm here?"

"I assume it's still about the IG investigation into Layla."

Hunter's instinct to come at Bryce a second time had been right. "So you do have more information."

Bryce motioned for him to sit before he did the same. "I

hate to say this, but there are some nasty rumors that Layla is playing both sides of the fence."

"Rumors from who?"

Bryce's jaw twitched. "They're coming from Agency sources, but I'm not going to name names. You should know this is very serious, though."

"Do you have any further insight into what, specifically, they are claiming she did?"

Bryce ran his hand through his hair. "Not many specifics, but it had to do with her work regarding Al-Nidal."

This whole thing stank more and more by the minute. "Do you believe any of it?"

Bryce laughed. "C'mon. Layla is great at many things, including being one of the best subject-matter experts that Langley has. She's able to see the big picture *and* understand all the details. She speaks the language, she understands the culture. But a super spy? No way. She's too honest. She doesn't have the edge to work assets in the field—at least not yet. And to tell you the truth, I don't think she wants to have those skills. She wouldn't hurt a fly. Her heart is too big for subterfuge."

"Then why the push for her to be in the field?" That was a nagging question Hunter couldn't answer.

"Because the higher-ups believe they can take raw talent in any form and mold it into what they want, even with reluctant recruits. The problem is that Layla doesn't want that kind of life and is set in her ways, and that's where the tension lies."

"Shouldn't the Agency be satisfied that she's so good at her analyst job and leave her be?" They were already demanding so much from her. Had taken so much from her.

Bryce cocked his head. "You'd think. If you want my

opinion—and I assume you do, or you wouldn't be here—Layla crossed someone and doesn't even realize it. And now they're out to get her."

"Quite an elaborate scheme for revenge, don't you think?"

Bryce leaned forward. "You might not understand just how cutthroat the intel community is. I still sleep with one eye open."

Hunter needed to push him again. "But you wouldn't hold such a grudge?"

"Of course I would, but it's hard to dislike Layla. I was seething after she ratted me out, but I eventually got over it. She has principles, which isn't something we see very often these days. I care about her and would never want something to happen to her. That's how friendship works. You might blow a gasket, but at the end of the day, you move on because they're your friend."

"But the two of you haven't remained friends."

"Look, it has taken me a good long while to get over it. But I am now, and if she reached out, I think we could be friends again."

A shot of jealousy went through Hunter.

"I'll tell you this," Bryce continued. "If you really want to get at the person who could've done this to her, you need to check out Nick. He had a lot of reasons to set her up."

"Why didn't you tell me about him before?" Hunter felt his temper starting to flare.

"I've already said too much. You need to talk to Layla about Nick. It's complicated. Very complicated. And the last thing I want to do is get in the middle of it."

Hunter realized Bryce wasn't going to give him anything else, so he thanked him for his time and hightailed it out of the building. He wasn't sure who this Nick character was, but he intended to find out.

But first he had to get back to his work on who had stolen the cartel money.

He made his way back to his office and booted up his computer. One thing he had discovered rather easily was that Zane Carter came from serious family money. It appeared that he might be estranged from his wealthy father, but that hadn't changed the amount of money Zane received from the family empire. The interesting thing from the cash flow that Hunter examined was that it didn't seem like Zane ever touched the money. It was spread out among multiple accounts with various banks, but the amounts only increased in time with interest—there were no withdrawals. He figured there was a deeper story there, but it wasn't one he needed to jump into, because he'd found out what he needed: Zane was clean. He had more money than he seemed to know what to do with and no cash influxes from any other source. Hunter couldn't be certain that Zane wasn't the mole, but his gut told him no on that score.

He'd finished rummaging around in Mason's and Cass's finances as well, and so far there was nothing tying anyone on the team to the missing money. Cass did have money troubles, it appeared, but he hadn't yet found any evidence connecting her to the cartel money.

He'd learned early on in his career as a PI that paper trails could be hidden, especially when dealing with offshore accounts. He intended to focus on the dark web and other means to ferret out the real thief. It wouldn't be easy, but they needed answers.

CHAPTER
SIXTEEN

That evening Layla sat in Hunter's SUV in the driveway of the CIA safe house in Arlington. The two-story light blue colonial didn't give any sign that it was an Agency property.

"We have to assume there's audio surveillance inside," she said. "So we need to be careful what we say."

Hunter nodded. "I'm going to bring in my detection equipment to sweep for bugs so we can speak more freely inside."

"That's a great idea. We can sweep daily to be on the safe side. How did it go with Bryce?"

"He's pointing the finger at some guy named Nick—and he said to talk to you about it because it's complicated."

She rolled her eyes.

"Who is Nick?"

"Nick Foster's one of the deputy chiefs in the DO. He's about ten years older than me, but he's on the fast track to be at the top. He reports directly to Riley Brown."

"You can't be serious. How does Nick play into all of this?"

"Nick has been the loudest advocate for getting me into the field. He's been taught by Riley that the real top people at the Agency need to be in the field, not behind a desk."

"Okay. Well, at least this sounds like it may be a promising lead."

She looked away, dreading the conversation that was about to ensue. "It's not so simple."

"What?"

"It's not good."

"Just tell me, and we'll work through it. None of this is any good."

She prepared herself for a negative reaction from Hunter. "Nick and I were romantically involved."

Hunter's jaw twitched, but he didn't say a word. His face said it all.

"Yeah. I told you it was bad. Let's get out of here and take a walk, and I'll explain." They got out of the car and started down the neighborhood sidewalk.

"It was an actual relationship?" Hunter asked.

"Yeah, but we had to keep it under wraps, given the optics. We weren't in the same chain of command, but still, I didn't want anyone to know. That was part of the appeal, I guess. And he was so interested in me and my career, I kinda got wrapped up in all of that. When things got a bit too intense for me, I bailed, and it didn't go well."

"Why didn't you say anything earlier? He could be the one targeting you."

"Because I knew you'd think less of me."

He put his hand on her back. "Layla, that's not possible. We're human. So you dated this guy. It's not the end of the world, but it could have a big impact on this investigation. Did others know?"

"Bryce figured it out. That was another reason I was so hesitant to ever get involved with him. I'd been down that road once with someone at Langley, and I wasn't doing it again. Beyond Bryce, I don't know if Nick told anyone. If I had to guess, I'd say no. He liked to play things close to the vest in all aspects of life. It made him feel more powerful. I was naïve. He was so smooth, and I fell quickly."

"How long ago were you with Nick?"

"About a year. I ended it. In total, we lasted about four months."

"Bryce thinks Nick could be out for revenge. Would Nick be aware of the IG investigation?"

"Before I saw the content of it, I would've said no, but if they're saying I'm working with Al-Nidal, I'd have to think that someone has briefed him or will brief him very soon on that, given his seniority level."

"I think you have to talk to him."

She groaned. "I can't get into Langley."

"I assume you know of other ways to contact him?"

"Yes." Although that wasn't what she wanted to do. Dealing with Nick was never a simple task. His complex nature was one of the many things that had drawn her to him, but that felt like a lifetime ago now.

Hunter put his hand on her shoulder and turned her toward him. "Look, this isn't easy, but if you want to keep your career at the Agency, I think this is the best path. You need to confront him."

Except, at this point, she wasn't sure what she wanted anymore. Everything she'd thought she understood about her world had been turned upside down. But because of that, this wasn't the time to make rash decisions. She needed to think logically.

"You're right." She would have to buck up and figure out what, if anything, Nick had to do with this.

"When's the last time you talked to him?"

"It was before the Honduras op. He had to give the ultimate sign-off for me to go, but it was a purely business conversation. No-nonsense. In fact, it's been like that since the initial explosion of anger after I broke it off."

"Then the sooner you can connect with him, the better."

"I know where he likes to hang out after work."

"Then we'll check it out."

She shook her head. "I need to talk to him alone."

"That's fine, but wherever you're going, I'm going with you."

"All right." She knew he had a point, but having him involved in the conversation would be a nonstarter.

"Are we going to talk any more about the elephant in the room?" he asked.

She'd wondered how long it would be before he brought that up. She looked at him. "I'm still in the processing phase."

"I don't blame you. I know I can never say I'm sorry enough."

She'd tossed and turned last night, going over every bit of their conversation. Questions still loomed large in her mind. "Was the cheating thing really the only way you thought you could break up with me?"

He rubbed a hand down his face. "I needed a deal breaker, and that's the only thing I could come up with. I was a little worried you still might forgive me because that's the type of loving person you are. That's why I tried to make the story egregious and act like I wasn't sorry. If I had shown true remorse, I thought that there might be a possibility you would want us to push through it."

She wondered if he was right. Would she have taken him back? "That confused me so much." She'd cried herself to sleep so many nights because of his callous attitude. Knowing now that it was all a farce to try to give her what she had thought she wanted more than anything—the job at the Agency—tore her up.

He took her hand and held it tightly. "The last thing I ever wanted was to hurt you—just the opposite. But I did hurt you, and it impacted you even more than I thought it would, and for that, again, I'm sorry."

There were some important things she needed to get off her chest. "I accept your apology, and from here on out, you don't need to keep apologizing to me. I understand why you made the choice you did. I remember clearly that at that time all I did was talk about how excited I was to start my CIA career. And since I could only tell a select number of people, that meant you heard it even more. I don't place blame on you, but I do place it on the Agency. They shouldn't have thought so little of me that they had to play such ridiculous games. Games that ended up irreparably impacting my entire life." She paused. "God has a larger plan at work in this, and that's what I'm trying to focus on."

Hunter squeezed her hand. "I'm not so sure about God's plan, but I am glad you were brought back into my life." He took her other hand in his and held them both. "Layla, the timing of this isn't ideal, but if we're going to have total honesty between us, then I should tell you that I have never stopped loving you."

Her breath caught at his bold admission. She couldn't find words. Her eyes started to fill with tears. There was so much emotion bubbling up inside her. After all these years, the dam was about to burst.

Hunter pulled her into his arms. It was like he understood what she needed. And as he held her, so many memories came flooding back like a raging sea. How much she had loved him. Their plan for a life together. How the two of them just made sense. But now, over five years later, here they were again. A different time and place, and she'd gone through so much in life and lived to see many things that she'd never thought possible. She'd grown up in so many ways and was much more mature now than she had been back then. There had also been a number of mistakes and ups and downs that all led her to where they were standing.

Her life now in danger, God had somehow worked His almighty plan to bring Hunter back to her, and she felt like maybe this was more than just Hunter walking with her through this trial. Maybe, just maybe, this could be more.

He lifted her chin, and they looked into each other's eyes. She wanted to tell him how she felt, but she couldn't. Not just yet. But he knew her well enough to know that she still had feelings for him. There was no doubt. The chemistry between them still burned brighter than the summer sun.

She held her breath, waiting to see if he was going to lean in and kiss her, but he didn't. Instead, he pulled her closer and tightened his grip around her.

In that moment, she felt content for the first time in years. Even though there was so much havoc surrounding her, she was ready for a new chapter in her life. And she prayed that Hunter might be a part of it.

CHAPTER
SEVENTEEN

On Tuesday, Zane and Cass spent a long day at the DEA office, trying to get some work done. They still had other active files and investigations that needed their attention, and Zane was glad for a distraction from the looming threats to the team.

But the bottom line was that they were still targets—or at least everyone else was.

"You look deep in thought," Cass said.

"Yeah." There were too many things clouding his mind. She nodded. "I can guess what about."

Before he could confirm what she already knew, the door to the conference room opened, and Mason walked in.

"Zane, I need to talk to you alone for a minute," Mason said flatly.

Cass stood. "I'll head to the break room so you guys can talk."

Zane wasn't sure why Mason was kicking Cass out, but

once it was the two of them, he watched as Mason frowned. "I recognize that face. What's the problem now? Because I can't deal with many more of them."

Mason stuffed his hands in his pockets. "The team working on the investigation into the mole thinks they have intercepts between you and a member of the cartel."

"What?" Zane felt his jaw go slack. "Are you serious?"

"Yes. Combine that with the fact that you're the only member of a four-person team who has not been targeted directly, and those running the investigation believe you need to be questioned."

Zane muttered some words that he probably shouldn't say. "This is insane."

"I know. I don't think for one minute you're dirty."

"Then help me get out of this mess." His voice got louder with every word.

Mason crossed his arms. "That's my plan, but you have to talk to the team leading the charge. My hands are tied on that, but I already planted the seed with them that you're not the problem here. If they look deep enough, they'll figure that out."

Thoughts started to race through Zane's mind. "Maybe this was the plan the entire time."

"How so?" Mason leaned against the table.

"They frame me to take the fall by purposely not attacking me. I'm painted as the traitor, and the real culprit keeps working for the cartel on the inside."

Mason drummed his fingers on the table. "Sounds plausible to me. We have to figure out what those intercepts are they claim they have on you, though."

"There's nothing legit there. I can promise you that." Zane hoped Mason would see the truth here.

"Okay. Defend yourself vigorously, and we'll get through this. I don't think the team really thinks you're the mole, either, but they wouldn't be doing their jobs if they didn't run this thing down."

"The mole isn't me, but it is someone who has skills and is dangerous. We all need to watch our backs."

Mason nodded before pausing. "How is Cass holding up?"

Zane wasn't going to reveal just how vulnerable he thought Cass had become, because as much as he trusted Mason, it just wasn't something he thought he should say. Cass needed time to get her head on straight, and she had earned that time without his color commentary on her mental state. "She's solid. It's been a lot to take in, but she'll be fine."

"Cass is a great agent, but she hasn't seen combat like you and me. I just want to make sure she's emotionally okay. Do you think she'd be open to counseling?"

Zane hesitated. "I don't know."

"Your face says it all. I didn't think she'd want to do it either, because she'd be afraid it would make her seem weak, when that's completely not the case. Do me a favor and ask her about it. I'd prefer she agree to it as opposed to it being an order coming from me."

"Understood." Zane would see what he could do.

Mason left him alone, and in a few minutes Cass returned with two cups in her hands.

"Coffee for you."

"Thanks."

She sat down, and he did the same. "What was that all about?" she asked. "Mason seemed even more serious than his normal self."

Best to just lay it out on the table. "He was giving me a heads-up that I'm going to be looked at."

Her eyebrows went up. "Looked at for what?"

"As being the inside man."

She let out a loud laugh. "Wow. This really is amateur hour around here if that's what's happening. Is this just because no one has directly come after you?"

He shook his head. "No. That's just an add-on. They claim they have evidence on me. If there is any supposed evidence, then someone wants me to take the fall for this."

She grabbed his arm. "We can't let that happen. Just let me know how I can help."

He was acutely aware of her hand lingering on his arm. "Will do. Right now, I just wait until I talk face-to-face to the investigation team." He placed his hand over hers and turned toward her. "There is one more thing."

"Uh-oh. I don't like the sound of this."

"Mason wants you to go to some counseling sessions."

She broke the contact between them and pulled away. "I hope you told him that would be completely unnecessary and a waste of time."

"I told him I thought you were doing well and that I felt you'd resist this."

"And you were right!"

"But he asked me to try to sweet-talk you into it because, Cass, he's going to make it mandatory if you don't go willingly."

She threw her head back and groaned. "If I were a guy, we would not even be having this conversation."

He didn't fully agree with that. "I believe it has less to do with gender and more to do with your experience."

"You're a Marine, so you can handle it."

"Do I sense some sarcasm there? I'm just being honest with you. I saw all manner of things when I was on my two combat tours. Mason is well aware of that, because he was there too. You didn't go through that, and he just wants to make sure you're handling everything okay. It has been a lot, and even though we see things on our DEA ops, what has transpired over the past couple weeks has been on a different level."

"You're obviously right about our experiences being different, and up until the last attack, I think I was pretty composed. Unfortunately, you've seen some of my weaker moments."

"I would never hold that against you, and I promise I didn't give Mason any indication that you were weak—just the opposite. You're strong, Cass, and a great agent."

She sighed. "Okay. I'll do it, but only because I don't want a mandatory order in my files."

He smiled. "Good. Let's get out of here and call it a night."

Layla looked at Hunter as they walked toward the door of the trendy Georgetown hotspot. "Nick will be hanging out at the bar. Please keep your distance. I need to do this alone. If he thinks I've brought someone with me, it will be a completely different conversation, and I'm not sure I'm going to get a second shot at this."

"Absolutely. But if there's any problem, I'll be there in a second."

"There won't be. I can handle Nick." Or at least that was the message she wanted to convey to Hunter. She didn't want him to think Nick was in control.

"If he's not here, we can wait and see if he shows."

She looked down at her watch. "Let's hope he hasn't changed his routine too much. Let me go in first. Give me a minute before you follow."

"Roger that." He looked around, surveying their surroundings.

Taking a deep breath, she opened the door and walked into the restaurant. This Georgetown hangout was known for its power-player lunches and after-work happy hours with the movers and shakers in town. Nick always got the best tables for dinner, and he basically had his own seat at the bar.

When she'd dated Nick, they'd come here often. She still hated a lot of the decisions she'd made where he was concerned, but she'd tried her best to give those regrets to God and move forward.

When she spotted him at the corner of the bar in his usual seat, a wave of memories started to overtake her—some good and some bad. But right now she was on a mission. There was no time for regrets and recriminations.

As Nick's eyes met hers, they widened.

"Anyone sitting here?" she asked.

He motioned for her to sit down.

"Thanks."

"You tracked me down outside of work, so something must be on your mind. Wanna have a drink?"

The bartender stood in front of her. "Club soda with lime, please." She turned her attention back to Nick.

"I'm guessing this isn't a social visit." He lifted his glass to his lips.

"It's not." She moved in closer to keep her voice down. "Are you read into the IG's investigation of me?"

He arched an eyebrow. "You realize it's probably inappropriate for us to even be *having* this conversation."

"Now you're going to worry about what's appropriate or not?" The words were out of her mouth before she could stop herself.

He set down his drink. "Fair enough. Yes, I actually just got briefed today."

"It's all lies, and I need your help." The words gushed out quicker than she had intended.

Nick sighed. "I know things didn't end great between us. I was a big jerk, but I care about you, Layla."

"You wouldn't have done this to me." She truly felt that in her gut and had decided to take this approach and see how he responded instead of accusing him outright.

"Never. I'm not the enemy here. I want to see you succeed." He touched her arm gently before moving back. "And I think you know that, or you wouldn't have come to me."

"Actually, Bryce suggested you might be behind the whole thing."

Nick rolled his eyes. "We both know that's crazy. You fully understand what my job is like and what my aspirations are. I opened up more to you than I have to anyone. I couldn't handle a scandal like that. Can you imagine? 'Top-ranking CIA official sets up his ex'? Talk about a career killer."

She knew Nick wanted to be the CIA director one day.

He looked directly into her eyes. "Have I ever lied to you?"

She thought carefully. "No. Actually, you haven't." He'd said a lot of things to her—some not very nice during the breakup—but he had always been open with her.

"In our line of work, there are a lot of lies and deceptions, but I've always been honest with you."

She had to ask him something else. "Were you the one behind the plan to get me into the field? Riley going to Hunter back during my recruitment—was that all you?"

He shook his head. "No. That was all Riley. He was instantly fascinated with you and your background and was going to stop at nothing to make sure you got into the Agency and ultimately into the field. I agreed with his assessment and was on board with everything, but he was the driving force."

She wasn't sure if that made her feel better or worse.

"Did Hunter tell you?" Nick asked.

"Yes, but only recently. I believed a lie for all those years. And you knew it too and didn't say anything to me about it when I confided in you." That stung. It really did.

"It wasn't my place. Riley had sworn me to secrecy years ago, and I keep my word. But Riley isn't your enemy either. If you're looking that way, you're barking up the wrong tree. Riley would put it on the line for you, and if he wasn't out of the country right now on assignment, he'd probably be in the IG's office, trying to help you even though he shouldn't be."

She decided to take another path. "Then, who do you think my enemy could be?"

He inched closer to her. "Have you considered that someone on the outside is pulling the strings here, maybe using internal contacts to make it happen but driving the process externally?"

She had considered that. "It's an option on the table. I'm sure they briefed you on those crazy pictures of me. You know I would never do that."

Nick nodded. "I do. But, Layla, given my position, I'm not supposed to interfere with an independent IG investigation."

"Even if you know they're wrong? Even if you risk losing your supposed rising star?" She couldn't help herself at this point.

"If I vouched for you in a more personal sense, don't you think that would raise a lot more questions? We don't want people talking about our relationship. That is in the past, and frankly, it's none of the IG's business, and I wasn't about to make it a part of this. That could've put even more heat on you."

"And you."

He grinned.

"Why are you smiling?" Frustration built within her.

"Because it's good seeing you fight for yourself. Facing tests like this will make you better, sharper. Especially in the field."

"But I don't want to be in the field." Why did they refuse to accept her wishes on that?

"You're far too gifted to be stuck behind a desk. I read the reports from the Honduras op. You were a vital part of the team."

"I think you're exaggerating." She'd just been following the lead of much more seasoned field agents.

He shook his head. "Not at all." He took her hand. "Listen, Layla, I need to stay on the sidelines on this one. You'll come out stronger for it. I have the utmost confidence in you, and the IG's office will get to the truth. I know that's not the answer you were looking for, but it's the best I can do."

"Just promise me one thing."

"Okay."

"If I wind up dead, you'll help clear my good name."

CHAPTER
EIGHTEEN

Watching that Nick guy fawn all over Layla had been sickening. And when Nick had taken her hand, it was all Hunter could do not to react. But he'd sat quietly at his table, brooding and trying to read lips the best he could without staring. It was the longest twenty minutes of his life.

Now they were in his car so they could speak freely without the prying ears of the Agency. He'd taken extra precautions to make sure there weren't any surveillance devices in his home or car for that very reason. They already had enough eyes on them.

"You're keeping me in suspense," he said. He didn't want to push her, but he also really wanted to know what had happened.

"Sorry. I'm just replaying the conversation in my head."

"No need to apologize. I can try to be patient." *Try* being the operative word. He glanced over and smiled at her.

She gave him a weak smile in return. "Nick says he wasn't involved in this, and I believe him."

"Isn't that good news?" He knew there was more to the story.

She shifted in her seat. "Yes, but he also said that he can't interfere in the investigation and then gave me this big pep talk about how this was just going to make me a better agent and I'd be stronger for it."

"I saw him touching you." It came out more accusatory than he had intended.

Layla sighed. "Yeah, but it wasn't a romantic gesture. That is over, and he knows it."

Hunter had been shocked that Layla had carried on this secret relationship with a top-ranking CIA official, but he certainly didn't judge her for it, although it seemed like she was judging herself pretty harshly. "I wasn't trying to insinuate anything except for my dislike for the guy."

They drove in silence for a few minutes before she spoke again. "Nick also suggested that someone outside the Agency could be behind all of this."

Hunter nodded. "The cartel has eyes and ears everywhere."

"I guess it's possible, but it seems like an elaborate ruse for the cartel to orchestrate. Why not just kill me?"

"True." He looked in his rearview mirror. "Hey, let's put that on pause for a second. I think we may have a tail."

She turned and looked. "I see them. Black Chevy SUV. The question is whether it's the Agency keeping tabs or someone else."

"Let's see. Hold on." He slammed on the brakes and took a sharp left. Then he floored it before taking a hard right.

"Where did you learn to drive like that?" she asked.

"You're not the only one who has had training. Mine has just been a bit more informal. Call it on-the-job training." He gritted his teeth as he watched the rearview mirror.

"I think you lost them." She let out a sigh.

He wasn't taking any chances. He accelerated down the road and then headed toward the highway.

"The Agency is probably trying to keep track of my whereabouts. As if the safe house isn't enough."

He actually hoped it was the CIA following them. If it was someone from the cartel, they were in grave danger. "The Agency we can handle. What we don't want is more cartel hit men on our trail. I feel like a sitting duck out here."

"Yeah. I agree with you."

There was only a moment for him to regroup before, out of the corner of his eye, he saw another black SUV barreling toward them. It was a different vehicle than before. Without even thinking, he spun the wheel at full speed, and they did a one-eighty. He peeled out the other direction.

"Nice move," she said. "I don't think that was the Agency. We shouldn't go to your place or the safe house. Let's just keep driving for a while and make sure we're in the clear."

"I'm on it." He glanced at her and saw that she'd pulled her Glock out of her jacket and had it sitting in her lap.

They rode in silence for a few tense minutes as he replayed the sequence of events in his head.

She looked over at him. "That wasn't a coincidence. It could've been a two-man team trying to box us in."

"Which is why your idea about continuing to evade and escape is a good one."

She smirked. "They teach us a few things about evasive maneuvers at the CIA."

"I bet they do." He paused, wondering if he should broach this topic. "Can I ask you something?"

"Sure," she said.

"Why are you so against fieldwork? You're obviously talented at it."

"It's hard enough to live the double life I do with my State Department cover as an analyst. Being able to shift personas and work people is not my strongest point. Yes, I'm good tactically, but I don't think I have what it takes to be cutthroat in the field. And you have to be. People's lives are literally on the line. The top guys are caught up with how I look on paper—my language skills, my academics— but in the field, executing on all of those things with real people is not easy."

That made sense to him. "You're too transparent. You don't want to work an asset and tell lies and weave up a story, do you?"

She shook her head. "No, and that's what's required. I keep telling everyone that, but they just keep pushing it. The Honduras op was a bit different because I wasn't working any assets. I was just executing a mission and providing intel and analysis."

"You didn't even mention the danger element."

She gave him a smile. "There's danger in every part of life. I have to rely on God's protection whether I'm running a field op or driving to the grocery store. It's all in His hands."

She'd come back to the faith topic again. He was still struggling with how to verbalize his issues with her.

"I take it from your silence that you disagree with me. What changed, Hunter? I know what strong faith you used to have. I lived it with you for three years."

"I wish I could make you understand why I feel the way

I do. There's just a big gulf between God and me. I don't know how to explain it, but I feel cold, unwanted. Numb."

"Did you stop going to church?"

It went much deeper than just church attendance. "Yeah, a while ago. I wasn't connecting anymore, and it felt a bit hypocritical to keep going, given my feelings."

"Maybe it's just time for a change. Try out a different church."

"That requires effort."

"Are you saying you don't want to put forth effort anymore when it comes to God?"

Ouch. "Well, when you put it that way, it sounds awful, but I'm trying to be brutally honest with you. No sugarcoating, just telling you exactly how I feel. What I've been struggling with."

She touched his arm. "I'm not judging you, Hunter. I'm just trying to understand what the root cause of the issue is."

"I don't know the answer to that either."

"You're not alone. God is still here. Here with us right now, and I'm not going anywhere either." She paused. "Maybe you don't think He's in your life because you don't want Him there."

She had just hit the nail on the head. "You might be right," he said softly. "But I'm tapped out, Layla. I just don't have it in me right now to have some big come-to-Jesus moment. I just don't."

"It doesn't have to be like that. Hunter, you came to Jesus years ago. You told me about it, remember? We shared those stories together. Once you make that commitment, He's all in forever."

He checked his side mirrors, and everything was still clear. "You're on a roll tonight, preacher."

"I'm being serious. Don't believe the lies you hear in your head. You are not too far gone." She sighed. "I talked to you about the rough time I had after we broke up, but I also had a really rocky road after I split up with Nick."

"Questioning your faith?" He had a hard time believing that, given what he knew about her.

"I'd say it was more anger than questioning. I didn't like the person I'd allowed myself to become with Nick, and for a while I blamed God, thinking I could shift the blame from my own personal decisions and actions to Him. I went into a bit of a tailspin. But after I stopped feeling sorry for myself, I realized that yes, I had made mistakes, but God understood I was flawed. I didn't have to wallow forever. I could pick myself up and move on, knowing that God's love was enough. Definitely more important than the love and affection of any man."

"Nick really did a number on you, huh?"

She shook her head. "No, it's not fair to lay blame on him. I just allowed myself to be seduced by his power and influence. That isn't the type of person I am at my core, but at that point in my life, I wasn't seeing clearly. Nick was just being Nick. He treated me well, and I believe he did care for me a lot. Probably even loved me. But it wasn't a healthy relationship. Our values didn't line up, and instead of being strong, I allowed myself to be manipulated and fell into what he wanted instead of sticking to my guns." She sighed again. "But I learned a lot of important lessons, including what it's like to fall really far and be able to get up again. It wasn't on my own strength, though. I thought I could make it on my own, but all of that showed me how much I need the Lord in my life."

"You're stronger than you think."

"Maybe, but it's also dangerous to think that we're invincible. That we are in control of everything in our lives."

"I rarely feel in control of anything." He swallowed. That was an unexpected admission.

"But you shouldn't feel uneasy about that. God's got it. He's got you."

Her impassioned words struck a chord with him. Maybe he had been too boneheaded about his relationship with God. Thinking that he could just muddle through. Hearing what she'd been through and seeing how she handled herself made him rethink things.

Movement behind them caught his eye. A car was quickly gaining on them. "They're back. Another vehicle."

"This makes no sense. How could that be possible?" she asked.

A thought occurred to him. "I checked the inside of my vehicle for surveillance equipment, but I didn't check externally for a GPS tracker."

"That has to be it. Which means we're like a homing beacon. We've got to get to a Metro station, dump the car, and move."

Once again her quick thinking was coming in handy. He'd have come up with something, but her plan was better. "If they get too close, fire a warning shot. If they're just surveillance, they'll back off."

"Roger that."

"We're in between Clarendon and the Virginia Square-GMU Station. We either circle back to Clarendon or go forward to GMU. Any preference?"

"Clarendon gives us more options. Circle back." She rolled down her window, readying for anything. "ETA is probably ten minutes." She looked behind them. "They're gaining."

"Take the shot if you need to, but wait until the last minute. We need to preserve ammunition."

"I've got an extra clip."

Of course she did.

"And, Hunter, my gut is that these guys are not from Langley. This has to be the cartel."

"Got it." Deep down he'd felt the same way, but hearing her say it was chilling. The Agency would only go so far at this point, given the early stage of the investigation against Layla. But the cartel was a completely different story. The men they hired didn't care about human life. They had zero moral compass and thought nothing about killing in cold blood. And right now they were barreling down on them.

"They're getting closer. Can you go any faster?"

"Yes." He pushed his foot down on the accelerator. "Once we get off the highway, though, it's going to be tough to keep up this speed. We need to shake them."

"I'm a really good shot. I can probably take out a tire."

"Okay, you just tell me when. I'll slow down when you're ready to get you closer."

"Let's go a little farther." She turned to face the rear of the car, getting ready to lean out the window.

His pulse thumped loudly as adrenaline soared through him. He had to focus. Their lives depended on it. He still couldn't believe that Layla had turned into an expert markswoman, but it was just one of the many changes about her. As he looked over at her, she closed her eyes for a second. This had to be even worse than he thought.

When her eyes opened, she looked at him. "I'm ready when you are."

"Okay, get ready, because I'm going to slam on the brakes."

"Understood." She braced her knee against the seat.

He took a deep breath and then punched down hard on the brake pedal. The car trailing them was now right up on them. He heard gunshots, but they weren't just from Layla. The car behind them had opened fire, and Layla was exposed.

"Get back in the car!"

"One more shot." She was true to her word. She took the shot and slid back inside.

He punched the gas and watched in the rearview mirror as the pursuing car skidded to a stop.

"You got them. Front right tire."

"I told you." She sighed loudly. "Now, let's get to the Metro before anyone else pays us a visit. We need to get out of this alive."

CHAPTER
NINETEEN

Layla was putting on a tough exterior for Hunter, but deep down she was afraid. The coordinated attack on them tonight screamed professionals, and that pointed to the cartel still being intent on taking her out. But she had wanted Hunter to remain in control, since he was driving, and she knew that if she showed her anxiety and fear, it would have negatively impacted him. So she'd put on a brave face and relied on her training to get her through it.

They still weren't in the clear, but at least they were out of Hunter's car and on the Metro. "I don't spot anything," she said.

"Me neither."

"We should get off in two stops and change lines, just to be on the safe side." There was another alternative, but she hated to bring it up.

"Sounds like a plan."

Hunter had become very quiet, and she thought he was

probably freaked out by all of this. Especially her hanging out the window of his SUV to take shots at the enemy. It surprised her, too, but she had been trained, and thank God, because it was coming in handy right now. When she'd been on the Honduras op, Zane had shown her some additional tips and tricks that he learned in the Marines. Growing up, she'd never been around guns of any kind. Her dad had seen and heard about enough violence as a child in Lebanon that he insisted they take a different path.

But here she was, many years later, literally fighting for her life.

"This isn't my first choice, but I could call this in to the Agency," she said. "They'll probably wonder why I don't return to the safe house anyway."

His crystal-blue eyes locked on to hers as the Metro doors opened and they got off. "I understand your hesitation, and I'm right there with you, but I think they need to know. It also bolsters your version of the story."

"It bolsters the truth," she said flatly.

"Who would you call?"

"Two options. My boss or one of the IG guys."

"You should call Frank Gibson. He's the senior investigator, and it was clear to me that he was running the show. Tell him what's happened. I can be your witness."

She held back a laugh. "Hunter, I don't think they'd take either of our words for anything right now. They have me in compromising photos with a known terrorist, and you're acting as my attorney—and I'm sure those men know exactly who you are my from personnel file. Hopefully they'll be able to provide some additional protection. If they bug out, we'll call Mason to see if he can do anything."

Hunter nodded. "Regardless, we need to let Mason know

what happened. For all we know, the others could be impacted as well."

Good point. The last thing she wanted was for something to happen to Cass and Zane. Diaz had already lost his life. Her heart hurt, thinking about his untimely death. She'd connected with him instantly on their trip to Honduras. To think that the cartel had killed him still shook her to the core.

Sensing her pain, Hunter took her hand as they walked down the Metro platform. Feeling his strong grip on her hand gave her some reassurance. At least she wasn't alone.

She pulled out her phone and the business card from Frank Gibson to dial his cell.

"This is Gibson," he answered.

"Frank, it's Layla Karam."

"I just got a report from our team that you haven't been to the safe house since early this morning."

"Yeah, that's right. Things got heated."

"How so?" Frank asked.

"We had three different cars come at us in a planned tactical assault. Finally we dumped Hunter's SUV and got on the Metro. We believe his vehicle has a GPS tracking device on it, because there's no way they could have located us so quickly each time we shook one of their vehicles."

"And who, exactly, do you think is after you?"

She had to bite her tongue not to lash out. "Well, honestly, my first thought was that there was some Agency surveillance on me, but as the aggressive nature of the pursuit continued, it became clear that it probably wasn't from Langley."

"It's still your contention that this is all related to the cartel?"

"Yes, sir, it is. They fired at us. I returned fire, taking out one of their tires, but we could use some help at least getting coverage back to the safe house."

"Where are you now?"

She rattled off their exact location and prayed that he would act.

"We'll send someone. Standard extraction protocol. Stay alert."

She sighed. "Thank you."

"Just for the record, I don't think this means you're innocent. In my mind, there could be a threat against you from the cartel, *and* you could be in with Al-Nidal. But if I'm wrong, the consequences for an operative of your caliber are far too high, and I'm not the reckless type."

She wanted to correct him and say that she wasn't technically an operative, but she let that one go. If he was going to help, then that was the biggest thing she needed, and there was no point in picking a stupid fight. "We'll be standing by."

The call ended, and she turned to Hunter, who was continually looking around.

"It's going to be okay," she said.

He raised an eyebrow. "Shouldn't I be the one telling you that?"

She smiled. Even in the midst of this danger, they complemented each other. "We're a team, remember?"

"You've been the team leader today, Layla. MVP all the way."

It was nice to hear that he had confidence in her, because sometimes she didn't in herself. Everything today had been about training and pure instinct and, most importantly, God's strong hand guiding her when she wasn't sure what to do.

Hunter squeezed her hand. "How long do you think it'll take them to get here?"

"If he puts in a priority call, we can have a team here in ten to fifteen minutes. There are a lot of internal Agency assets in this area. That plays in our favor. Stay alert, though."

"Understood. How did Frank seem?"

"He doesn't believe this means I'm innocent. He thinks I could be guilty and still have the cartel threat. I can't really blame him. If I were in his shoes, evaluating the file, I'd probably think I was guilty too—or at least I'd have a strong suspicion that I'd want to run down completely before any exoneration could occur. Those pictures are unsettling."

For the next fifteen minutes, they walked briskly but not so fast as to call attention to themselves.

Hunter nodded his head forward. "Those two guys at twelve o'clock. Do you think they're yours?"

She looked to where he had indicated and saw two men dressed casually but walking with purpose. When one of them made eye contact with her, she knew it was their way out. "Yeah. That's them. Let's cross the street."

"But why? Shouldn't they come to us?"

"No. Now that we've made contact, we'll meet up about two blocks from here. Just follow me."

Hunter did as she instructed, and they walked in silence until they reached the rendezvous point, where a gray SUV with tinted windows was waiting.

"Get in," one of the men told her.

She must have gotten through to Frank for him to send a three-man team to extract them. She jumped in the back seat and slid over for Hunter to get in. The last man, the one who had spoken to her, got in and hopped over their seats into the third row of the Durango.

"I'm Sawyer," he said. "And that's Ace and Dax up front. Do you think you were followed here?"

She shook her head. "No. I think we were able to shake them on the Metro."

The tall blond nodded and then turned to Hunter. "You dumped your car?"

"Yeah, near the Clarendon stop. I think it has a GPS device on it somewhere."

Sawyer looked over his shoulder and then back at them. "We'll have it picked up and cleaned and taken to the new safe house. We can't take a chance that the cartel knows the original location, since Hunter's vehicle was there."

"I don't know when they put on the device," Hunter said.

"Another reason we have to be cautious." Sawyer's light brown eyes focused on her. "I read your file—or at least what they were willing to give me."

She could only imagine what that contained. "Did they tell you about the investigation?"

"Yeah," Sawyer said. "Seems like you've gotten yourself into a bit of trouble." He smiled.

His reaction let her know that he didn't really think she was guilty, and she wanted to reiterate that. "I haven't done anything wrong. Someone is trying to set me up."

Sawyer chuckled. "For an analyst, you sure do have a lot of problems."

"Tell me about it," she muttered.

Sawyer leaned forward. "But that's the thing, right? Your personnel file has you working in the DA, but that doesn't line up."

"I am an analyst. I *want* to be an analyst." Maybe if she said it enough, someone would finally listen.

"But the Agency has other thoughts on her career," Hunter piped up.

"They have a way of finding people's talents and putting them in the right place," Sawyer said. "Maybe you should just go with it and see what happens."

She threw up her hands. "*This* happens. I've got the cartel breathing down my neck, one team member dead, and a warrantless IG investigation."

Sawyer settled back in his seat. "I'll give you that."

"So what's the Agency's plan to keep Layla safe from Mejía's people?" Hunter asked.

Sawyer arched an eyebrow. "We're working on it, along with the DEA." Then he looked at her. "And what exactly is Hunter's role here?"

She held back a laugh.

"What?" Hunter asked. "I don't have my own file?"

Sawyer's jaw twitched. "You're not one of ours." Then he paused. "Are you?"

"Most definitely not," Hunter said.

"Hunter has multiple roles. He's serving as my legal counsel, but he's also a PI, and we've known each other for years."

"That's how he knows what you do?" Sawyer asked.

"Exactly." These questions let Layla know an important fact—the file that Sawyer had on her omitted all information about her past with Hunter. "Let's get back to the topic of the cartel."

"We've got the new safe house set up. Ace and Dax will be leading your primary security detail, so you should be safe from the cartel threats for now. We've been briefed by the DEA and understand the threat matrix."

Layla realized she hadn't checked in on Zane and Cass yet. "Who have you spoken to at the DEA?"

"Mason," Sawyer answered.

"Do you know if the rest of the team is okay?"

"They're all right. Cass is accounted for at the DEA safe house."

"What about Zane?"

"I think he's staying with her."

Layla still thought it odd that Zane was somehow in the clear in all this, but there had to be a reasonable explanation.

They rode the rest of the way to the safe house in silence. This house was closer to Langley, and she figured that was by design. The CIA wanted to keep her nearby. They might have their suspicions about her, but this ordeal had also shown her that the Agency saw her as a vital asset, and she planned to use that to her strategic advantage.

They pulled up to the two-story Cape Cod–style home and parked. "Wait here while we do a sweep," Sawyer said.

The three men exited, leaving her with Hunter.

"Do you trust them?" he asked.

"Not exactly, but I do think they've been tasked with keeping me safe. Think about it, Hunter. The CIA needs me. Look at the great lengths they've gone to over the past few years to get me into the field. To groom me to take on big assignments. They can't turn a blind eye to those photos, but I think they're banking on me being clean and then pushing me as hard as they can to get into the field. Knowing them, it might even be a condition of an exoneration."

He groaned. "That's not what you want."

"I'll cross that bridge if and when we get to it, but I do have some confidence in their plan to protect me. It's like an insurance policy. If I'm innocent and they do nothing, they could lose someone they've put a lot of time and energy into.

And, of course, as you described, I'm unique. There aren't many people with my skill set."

Hunter smiled.

"What?"

"You're more than unique, Layla." He grabbed her hand. "You're very special. Especially to me."

Her breath caught as she looked into his ocean-blue eyes, and she wanted to block out the rest of the world and focus only on him. She remembered what it was like to kiss him, and she wondered if it would be different the second time around. She wanted nothing more than to lean into him and press her lips to his.

But the downside was too great. She didn't want to be interrupted by Sawyer and the others. It was a nice moment, but it would just have to wait. She squeezed Hunter's hand and hoped that he could still read her as well as he used to.

A knock on the window confirmed that she'd made the right move. The question was, What would her next move be?

CHAPTER
TWENTY

Izzy dreaded having this conversation, but it was one she had to have.

"Are you sure you're ready for this?" Aiden put the car in park.

"I think it's important to talk to my former colleagues. We can't talk to the detectives working the case at Arlington PD, but this is a concrete step we can take to look further into the sergeant's history. Alicia Thatcher used to work there. So she knew the sergeant pretty well. When I called her, she seemed open to talking to me, but I have no idea whether her relationship with him was good, bad, or indifferent."

Aiden nodded. "Do you know why she left Arlington PD?"

"No. But that's one of the things I want to find out. It looks like her condo is up there on the right." She pointed toward one of the buildings in the Alexandria neighborhood.

"Do you want me to come in with you?" Aiden asked.

RACHEL DYLAN

"No. I don't want to scare her off. She might think it's weird if you're there too."

"I completely understand. Just take your time. I'm in no rush. I brought plenty of work with me, so stay as long as you need to."

Izzy squeezed his arm. "Thank you again for everything." She gave him a kiss on the cheek and hopped out of the car. Then she made her way to the second floor of Alicia's building and rang the doorbell.

It was only a moment before Alicia answered. She was a tall, pretty blonde with green eyes, and she gave Izzy a big smile. "Izzy, it's so great to see you. Come on in."

"Thank you for having me." Izzy took in Alicia's stylish condo decorated in ivory and various blue hues.

"Come into the living room. I made us some coffee and tea. Which would you prefer?"

"Coffee would be amazing."

"Make yourself comfortable. I'll be right back."

Izzy was already glad that she'd come to visit Alicia, if for nothing more than to see an old friend and colleague. But she silently hoped that Alicia might have some information for her. Even though she knew it was a long shot.

After a few minutes, Alicia came back into the living room with coffee and some cookies.

"Oh my. Those smell fresh out of the oven." Izzy eyed the plate of chocolate chip cookies until her mouth started to water.

Alicia laughed. "Go ahead and dive in while they're still warm. I'll be right back." She returned armed with cream and sugar and a bowl of fresh fruit.

"Alicia, you didn't have to go through all this trouble for me."

Alicia shook her head. "It's no trouble at all. I'm always fiddling around in the kitchen." She took a sip of her coffee and then set down the lavender cup. "So, as much as I want to believe this is purely a social visit, catching up with a friend, I have a feeling there's something else going on."

"Have you seen the news?" The details of the sergeant's death had finally become public. While not everything was out there, it was enough that anyone who kept up with the news would have seen it.

"I think you're referring to the murder of Sergeant Tybee, right?"

The sound of his name made Izzy feel sick, but she pushed down the emotions that were becoming far too prevalent these days. "Yes. That's what I'm here about." She readied herself for the conversation. "I want to be fully transparent with you. You were always a good friend to me."

Alicia's eyes warmed. "I really appreciate that. Whatever it is, you can talk to me about it."

"Well, there's actually a couple of issues. First is that the detectives with Arlington PD identified me as a potential suspect in the murder."

Alicia's eyes widened, and she didn't say anything for a moment. "You can't be serious. How in the world would they come to that conclusion? How could you be a murder suspect?"

Here was where the conversation would start to get tough, but Izzy knew no way around it. At this point, she figured the truth would get out anyway and spread further than she could imagine because of events she had no control over. "They think I'm a suspect because the sergeant assaulted me."

"Izzy, I had no idea." Alicia took her hand. "Do you want to talk about it?"

Izzy bit her bottom lip as she considered how much detail to provide. "I never reported it. I know I should have, but at the time, I was so freaked out, ashamed, and totally naïve."

Alicia shook her head. "No way. Don't you dare put this on yourself. If he assaulted you, that's completely on him. Where did this happen? When did this happen? Was I still at Arlington PD?"

Izzy steeled herself as she recounted the story once again. It was becoming all too familiar. Memories that she'd boxed up and put away were now coming to the light of day. "That's how it all played out. Now you understand why I had to leave Arlington PD. There was no way I could work there with him after that. Just the thought of him even now makes me ill. He violated me and took away my choice, my power. I'm trying my best not to be a victim. I have moved on with my life. But, of course, there's *no* way I would have killed him, even if I would have liked to."

Alicia nodded. "You have every right to feel that way. What can I help you with now?"

"Here's the thing. Arlington PD zeroed in on me because evidently the sergeant had some type of shrine to me in his house."

Alicia raised an eyebrow. "That's creepy. Thank goodness you're okay."

"Yeah. The thinking right now is that he might have been killed in self-defense, but I'm not ruling anything out. I know you worked there for quite a few years. I'm hoping to see if you have any intel on potential enemies the sergeant might've had, or anything else you think might be helpful." Izzy paused, reluctant to ask but figuring she needed to. "And I also want to know if you had any negative experiences with him. I want to see if I was a one-off or if there's a pattern I can establish."

Alicia looked down and clasped her hands in her lap. "Nothing like what happened to you happened to me, but the sergeant was definitely highly inappropriate multiple times. Trying to ask me out or making comments about my body or what I was wearing. Sometimes I just blew it off as part of the world women have to face in male-dominated law enforcement. Like you, I never said anything about it to anyone. And now, hearing your story, I'm so sorry I kept quiet. Maybe if I had spoken up, he wouldn't have been in his position by the time he attacked you."

Izzy's mind felt jumbled as she put together this new information. "There's no way you could have known. And look at me—I didn't tell anyone either. I don't hold it against you. But the fact that something did happen to you makes me believe we are only the tip of the iceberg."

"And that means there are probably other women he assaulted or harassed. Maybe one of them is the killer, right?"

Izzy took a deep breath. "Yeah. I'm not looking to get any other woman in trouble, but I am trying to protect myself from prosecution. There are elements of this case that don't look good for me, so I want to defend myself the best way I can. We can at least bring up alternative theories and put some doubt in the detectives' minds. Even those questions and doubts would be helpful. Are you willing to talk to the detectives about what happened to you with the sergeant? I know it's a lot to ask, and I hate to do it, but I'm kind of in a desperate situation."

"Of course I'll help you. I stayed silent years ago when I shouldn't have, but I can do better now. I *will* do better. I'm happy to help you in any way that I can."

Izzy's heart warmed, and she looked into her friend's eyes. She wondered why they hadn't been closer while they were on the force, but they'd overlapped for such a short time period, and then Alicia had left. Which reminded Izzy of a lingering question. "Why did you leave Arlington PD?"

"When I was offered the chance to be an instructor at Quantico, it was an amazing opportunity and far too good to pass up. It really had nothing to do with what was going on at the force. At least, I didn't think it did, but now that you're bringing all this up, it makes me wonder whether subconsciously the culture there was part of my decision-making process." Alicia sighed and looked at her. "I'm really so, so sorry about what happened. I wonder if I had stuck around if there'd have been anything I could've done for you."

"Honestly, no one could've helped me at that point. I've had to go through a long process of counseling and grieving and trying to pull my life back together."

"How's that going?"

Izzy could answer this honestly, and it felt good to be able to say it. "I'm actually in a great place. I'm at NCIS, and I enjoy my work, although I'm still considering options for the future. In bigger personal news, I finally started to date again, and I'm completely head over heels. His name is Aiden. He works for Virginia State Patrol."

Alicia's eyes sparkled. "I can see by how you talk about him how much he means to you."

"It took me a while to be able to trust anyone. Especially another man. And to make it worse, another man in law enforcement. But Aiden couldn't be more different from the sergeant. He is loving, caring, and I trust him with my life."

"Sounds like he's the real deal. I'm very happy for you. Whatever you need from me, just let me know."

"I'll talk to the detectives and point them in your direction. I can't guarantee they'll want to talk to you, but I hope they will, especially since you're a former cop." Izzy considered her next question. "I'm pondering what my next career move should be. How do you like being an instructor?"

"It's really good. I like teaching. It suits my personality. Hey, once you have a few more years under your belt, I'd love to put in a rec for you. I think you could excel in that field."

Izzy would need a lot more time working in law enforcement before that was possible. Alicia had at least a decade of experience. "That's so generous of you. You're going to think I'm crazy, but I'm actually batting around the idea of going to law school."

"That's a great idea! You would make a wonderful attorney. You will be a fierce advocate. What type of law are you thinking about?"

Izzy wasn't sure how Alicia would react to her future career plans. "I want to be a prosecutor."

Alicia gave her a knowing look. "Now, that sounds like a plan. After all you've been through, it makes a lot of sense."

"A fresh start in my career could give me a new purpose. Putting scumbags like the sergeant behind bars would be fulfilling. Being able to seek justice in a different way. What I'm doing at NCIS is really important work, but I don't know that it's the long game for my career. Does that make sense?"

"Absolutely. I can see it in your eyes. If there's anything else I can do, let me know."

"You've already offered to do so much. And on that note, I'll get out of your hair."

"You don't have to run off. I've got more cookies."

Izzy looked down at the empty cookie plate and realized she'd eaten them all as they'd been talking. She laughed. "I might explode if I eat any more, but they were amazing. Just what I needed."

"You should stop by more often. It was so good to see you."

Izzy gave Alicia a tight hug, fighting back tears. She hoped this was the beginning of a massive break in the case. One that would ultimately get to the truth.

❖

Zane's mind was reeling from the interrogation he'd gone through that morning, still trying to figure out how he'd become a suspect in the DEA investigation. Someone thought he would be a convenient target, and it was his priority to figure out who was gunning for him. The cartel had more power and influence than most people could imagine. Unfortunately, their tentacles stretched wide and right into the belly of the DEA. The thought sickened him.

As a Marine, Zane could not imagine turning his back on his country and working for the cartel. And he was confident that once investigators looked closely at him and his background, they would realize that he could not be a traitor. He needed to figure out who could have the motive and the opportunity to set him up. But he also couldn't allow himself to be totally focused on those issues, because his partner still needed him.

He'd told Mason that Cass was solid, but he had his doubts. She had taken all of this very personally—which he understood, given that the attacks were highly personal. He sat beside her now on the sofa in the DEA safe house as she worked on her laptop. She had a serious look on her face, and a frown pulled down on her lips. He wondered what was going on in her head.

He tried to give her space to work and act as normal as possible under the circumstances, but he knew there was a huge cloud hanging over her—one of stinging fear. And he hated seeing her like that. The woman he had worked with for the past few years had always been tougher than most of the guys he knew. That had all changed when she became a prime target of the Mejía cartel.

"How's it going?" He figured that was a safe enough question to ask.

Cass stopped typing and looked at him. "Honestly, I'm just trying to finish some reports to keep my mind off the bigger issues. There's nothing like bureaucratic paper work for that." She gave him a slight smile. "What about you? You're the one just sitting there, staring off into space. Is it about being questioned today?"

He'd let Cass know what was going on because he needed someone he could trust on his side. "I have a lot on my mind. I know you do too. Today's questioning felt like a fishing expedition. If they really had the goods on me, I wouldn't be sitting here with you right now. It turned out those intercepts weren't fully vetted, and there's nothing concrete for them to bring against me. They weren't able to point to any other evidence either, other than the fact that I'm the only team member who hasn't been directly targeted by the cartel."

Cass frowned. "I'm so sorry they're putting you through this charade. They must be desperate if they have to point the finger at you."

"It's really nagging at me that someone would choose me as the person to finger as the traitor. Maybe it's because of my military history, but it hurts even worse because of that."

Cass nodded. "Zane, anyone who has ever dealt with you knows you operate with the highest level of integrity. You're completely loyal, honest, and though sometimes it drives me crazy, you always play by the book. I have no doubt that your name will be cleared, and they will find out who the real mole is." She looked up at him with her big brown eyes. "I know you don't want to hear this, but we still don't know one hundred percent that Mason is clean."

"I don't know, Cass. He seems about as unlikely a suspect as me. We have to dig deeper and assume there are darker forces at work here that don't follow the rules." Zane had found out the hard way that sometimes being a rule follower could get you in more trouble. But he also wanted to be able to sleep at night and know in his mind, in his heart, and in his soul that he'd done the right thing. That was the way he lived his life.

Cass put her laptop aside and turned to face him as she moved in a little closer. "I've been totally consumed with my own issues. I'm sorry I haven't been more in tune with what you've been facing."

"Don't give it a second thought. We're partners, right? That's what we do. We look out for each other no matter what problem or danger we're facing. I'm really glad you decided to come to the safe house. I sleep better at night knowing you're here."

"Yeah, about that." She paused. "I think *I* would sleep better if you were here. There's tons of extra rooms. And not just for my safety, although I selfishly have to admit that is top of my mind. We still don't know if the cartel has you in their sights. But if you stay here, we know you'll be safe."

Zane didn't know how to take Cass's comments. She'd been acting a bit strange lately. As far as their relationship went, what was once completely platonic, with not a dash of romance, had started to become a bit of something else.

And while Zane had to admit that he was attracted to her, he wasn't sure that getting involved with his partner was the best idea. Especially given the dangerous circumstances they found themselves in.

But the last thing he wanted to do was push her away, so he was trying to walk a fine line. And her idea did have some merit. He just had to make sure he kept strict boundaries in place. "Sure, if it makes you feel better. Like you said, this place has four bedrooms, so I'm sure we can stay out of each other's way. I want to make sure you have your privacy."

Cass laughed. "Since when do you care about that? This coming from the man who made me change outfits in the back of an SUV in Costa Rica."

Zane had completely forgotten about that. "That was out of necessity. And you know I wasn't watching."

"Of course you weren't. That's my Boy Scout." She placed her hand on top of his. "All joking aside, you really have been there for me, and that's something I'll never forget."

He tried not to think about how it felt to have her hand touching his, and instead tried to focus on coloring within the lines. He gave her fingers a pat with his other hand and then broke away from her. "Like I said, Cass, we're in this together." Anxious to change the subject to something more work-related, he said, "We've done a second run on everything. Everyone on our team, even the support guys, has come up clean. No connection to the cartel or to any organized crime. All background checks are clear."

"You didn't really think it was someone on our team anyway, did you?" she asked.

"No. But we had to check."

"We have to start looking at people working at headquarters. That's why I mentioned Mason. But there are other higher-ups we could consider. They could be playing both sides. It pains me to say it, but you know it's true. The more powerful these guys get, the more likely that they could be turned for a lot of reasons."

"Aren't you the cynical one?"

"I always am. It's one of my best qualities, right?" She smiled.

Zane wasn't born yesterday. Cass was definitely flirting with him. But what did he do about it? He hated facing that topic right now and would rather just keep shifting the conversation. "Have you talked to Layla?"

"Yeah. She's at an Agency safe house, but we've decided to keep the locations from each other for extra security. So she doesn't know where we are, and we don't know where she is."

Zane nodded. "That's a really good idea. I'm glad the Agency finally gave her some protection. Did she say anything about the IG?"

Cass shifted a bit closer to him. "Yeah. It didn't seem good at all. She didn't want to get into details on the phone, but it sounds like someone is trying to insinuate that she's working with Al-Nidal."

"That's even crazier than thinking I'm involved with the cartel. She's one of their brightest up-and-coming experts. Why would that make any sense?" He didn't like this development. The web of danger just kept expanding all around them.

"Beats me. But it shows that all of us are being targeted. Once the cartel has in its mind to screw up someone's life or kill them, we know how that plays out. Which is why I'm still worried that, in the end, Mason is going to push to have me put in WITSEC."

Zane shook his head. "That's extreme. Let's not cross

that bridge until we have to." He wanted to ask her about something else too. "I know you had your first counseling session this morning, but you didn't say how it went."

She tucked a strand of dark hair behind her ear. "It wasn't anything out of the ordinary. I don't know how much talking to psychologists you've done, but it's always the same questions. They wanted to make sure I'm not going to lose my mind or hurt myself or someone else, and that I am directly dealing with my feelings." Her voice rose with each word that came out of her mouth. "I *am* dealing with my feelings. I'm not one to lock my emotions up in a box. Just the opposite. She encouraged me to find someone I trust and talk to them. Which I guess, considering the only person I trust is you, would have to be you. So that's what you get for pushing me into it."

Zane felt himself falling deeper and deeper into this hole. But regardless of anything else that was going on, he wasn't going to turn his back on her. She'd been there for him a lot over the years, never questioning anything. So now he was going to be there for her. "Whatever you need, Cass, just name it."

She didn't respond quickly. Instead, she locked eyes with him as if she were trying to look deep within him. The next thing he knew, she had leaned in and her warm lips were pressed firmly against his. For a moment, his mind went completely blank. But he didn't freeze. He couldn't help himself. He kissed her back, blocking out any thoughts or consequences. There was definitely a spark between them. Even bigger than he'd expected.

But after a minute, when she tried to move in closer and deepen the kiss, he regained his senses and pulled away.

"Cass, we're both dealing with a lot of emotions right

now fueled by all of this, but our partnership is too important to risk by crossing any lines." He knew she wasn't going to like that response, and he prepared himself for her reaction.

She crossed her arms, starting to sulk. "You know, Zane, sometimes your goody-goody nature can be a real downer. I think you feel the same way about me as I feel about you, and have for a long time. We're both adults. I just think you're in denial, or playing like you are because it serves your purpose of keeping the moral high ground in our partnership."

That was more hurt and anger than he'd expected. He hesitantly took her hand. "Cass, I care about you more than you know. And because of that, I want to protect you at all cost. That includes protecting you from me. I would not be a good fit for you. Yes, we're good friends and great partners. But I am a crummy boyfriend. I don't do commitment, and you've heard enough about my personal life to know that what I'm saying is true."

"All right. Maybe we should just table this conversation until you're ready to face your feelings." She grabbed her laptop and opened it back up, starting to work again.

Zane figured this was his cue to exit. "Do you still want me to stay here?"

She let out a large sigh. "Do I want you to? Probably not. But do I need you to? Yes."

"Okay. I've got my go bag in the car. I'll get it and take a room at the other end of the hall from yours. If it will make you more comfortable, I can even stay down here on the couch."

Cass shook her head. "Don't be silly. There's no need for you to do that. It's not like I'm going to attack you in the middle of the night or something."

He knew she was attempting to be funny, but it didn't strike him that way. He felt badly about hurting her. But had she really had feelings for him for a long time? Could he have been that blind?

Maybe so.

CHAPTER
TWENTY-ONE

Layla waited anxiously for Hunter to return to the safe house that evening. He'd been doing some work at his office and was touching base with Mason. She'd busied herself reviewing some notes and trying to come up with an enemies list, as Scarlett had suggested. She put people on the list that she thought would never actually hurt her, but Scarlett's words echoed in her ears. She couldn't be naïve. She needed to take a brutally honest and objective approach, because her career was on the line. Her good name meant so much to her. It was becoming clear, though, that sometimes she saw the best in people when she should also see that they might be a threat.

As she stared at her list, she still found it hard to believe that anyone on it could have gone so far as to set her up with the Agency. In doing so, that person would know that her career could be forever in jeopardy. Or even worse, that she could be arrested and thrown in jail or locked away forever in a black site. This wasn't a small accusation, like she'd heard some other agents complain about. This wasn't an administrative mishap. No, this was major. Those pictures were devastating.

The one thing that gave her confidence was her faith. This wasn't up to her. God was in control, and she had to keep reminding herself of that. As those thoughts fluttered through her head, she replayed the discussion she'd had with Hunter and wondered how he could have had such a faith blowout. Yes, she'd had her struggles, too, but it had never resulted in the complete breakage Hunter seemed to be going through. If there was anything she could do to help, she planned on doing it. Especially now that she knew the full truth, something she was still trying to wrap her head around.

When she heard the voices of the security detail talking to Hunter, she set her notepad on the coffee table and looked up as he walked into the living room.

"Hey, glad you're back," she said.

Hunter took a seat beside her on the sofa. "How're you doing?"

"I'm fine." She picked up the notebook and held it in front of him. "I've been making a list of everyone I could think of who might be a possible suspect for framing me and starting the IG investigation."

Hunter took the notebook and ran his finger down the page. "Not a very long list, Layla. Are you sure this is everyone?"

She nodded. "Yeah, and it was difficult for me to come up with even these people."

"Don't beat yourself up over it. But keep an open mind. Especially about people you think might be your friends. Those are the ones you really have to worry about."

"How did it go with Mason?"

"All right. There's heat on Zane, but in my opinion that's the wrong play here."

Layla didn't think there was any way Zane was guilty. "I agree."

"The DEA isn't convinced Keith Hammond was working with the cartel. There's new chatter that the cartel took out one of the top CIA spies in Honduras."

Layla's worst fears were coming true. "I put a target on his back." She paused, letting that thought sink in. "I hate to think that my phone call got him killed, but it seems like that's precisely what happened."

"I'm sorry for what happened, but you can't take the blame. The cartel pulled the trigger. We have to find out who the real mole is and get them to flip and give us critical intel on Diego. That could be a game changer."

Layla could only hope and pray that was possible. She didn't know how long she could live like this. "If I'm being honest, it's not just the cartel that's bothering me, although obviously that's a concern. This whole mess with the Agency has really torn me up. Feeling like I can't trust anyone. Always looking over my shoulder. It's exactly the reason I don't want to be a field officer. I'm not cut out for such subterfuge. I love reading and analyzing and connecting the dots, but lying and presenting a false front and always being on the lookout for danger—that's just not me."

He took her hand. "You're a fighter, Layla. Much stronger than most people I know. While you might never want to be a field agent, you're more skilled than you want to believe. The Agency knows that. Think of all the testing you had to go through before they actually hired you. They know your strengths and weaknesses."

"They know everything, but that's what scares me. They know all of this, and yet they still keep pushing me down this other path. So what am I missing?"

"You underestimate yourself. While you might not want to do these things, you have the capacity to, and that's all the CIA cares about."

"That's why I'm worried that they're going to use this investigation to get the result they want. And the last thing I want to do right now is go back in the field. I feel like everything in my life right now is a field op. Just look at this." She lifted her hands, gesturing around them. "I'm in a safe house with a full-time security detail. I can't even go back to my own condo. We've been threatened in so many ways, and I don't see an end in sight. The only way to stop the threat to my life is a takedown of the cartel once and for all. And that's much easier said than done."

"Yeah, it's a tough order, but the good thing is that the entire DEA has a vested interest in bringing down the cartel. I can tell you from my conversations with Mason that it's all hands on deck over there. This isn't just about your team. I believe that when it's all said and done, they're going to be able to take down Diego. Once he's gone, the threat against the team's life is gone."

"Now who's the optimist? But you do have a point. I wish there was more I could do to help, but this isn't my specialty area."

"Well, thankfully it doesn't have to be, because the whole DEA is on top of it. What about Scarlett? Could she help us with your internal investigation?"

"She has a lot of connections, but unfortunately her hands are tied on the IG stuff. That's completely internal at the Agency, and the IG's office is walled off from everything else. Scarlett thinks I'm far too naïve and that I could make a good case officer if I just got over myself. She's much more hard-nosed than I'll ever be, but she's good for me. She balances me out." Layla paused for a second. "Kinda like you do." As the words came out of her mouth, she locked eyes with him. He still held her hand, and she gave it a squeeze. "I know we've been through more than most people, especially the craziness since we reconnected. But if I have to go through this, there's no one I'd rather have at my side than you, Hunter."

Silence hung between them for a moment.

"Layla, I feel the same way about you. I can't wash away all the hurt from the past, everything that happened and my role in it, but I can make you new promises for the future if you'll allow me."

"There's nothing I want more. But I have to be completely open with you, and I hope you can do the same with me. I don't want you to be misled and think I'm the exact same person I was in law school. Some of the things you find out about me might disappoint you."

"Well, I could say the same about me. But here's the thing: We don't have to live in the past and rehash everything that happened to us and how we handled it over the years. If there's something you want to tell me that you think I need to know or that you want me to know, then I'm all ears. But you should understand that there is no judgment as far as I'm concerned, and I know you'll do the same for me and my past. If you want to just make a fresh start, I'm completely open to that too. The thing that matters most to me is getting to know you again. The woman you are today, sitting here. The woman I fell in love with eight years ago during my first year of law school might have changed, but we can learn and grow together. I'm not crazy, though. I know you can't just flip a switch and act like all the pain and heartache you experienced because of me went away. Believe it or not, I can be patient, especially when it comes to you. Take all the time you want and need to work through it all. As long as I know that our past is not going to be a deal breaker in the end."

Her heart pounded. He had no idea how much she still felt for him today. An ever-growing connection by the moment. It seemed even more real than it was years ago, when she thought with her entire mind, heart, and soul that he was *the one*. "No, Hunter. I will not hold anything over your head. The truth has set me free in this instance. I understand you did what you did out of love for me. You're right that nothing can change the past heartache and pain, but I'm ready to move on. I'm ready for a new day. I'm ready to embrace the life in front of me right now for as long as God will give it to me, and I really hope that you can be a part of that."

"That's about the best news I've heard in a long time." He wrapped his arms around her, and she rested her head on his shoulder. "Having you back in my arms is the most amazing feeling in the world."

She moved back a little and looked right into his blue eyes. "It must've been really hard on you too. Of course I never thought of it like that, given what I thought went down, but you basically gave us up for me. And that act of complete self-sacrifice is something I don't even know how to comprehend. I'm sorry I never thought about how you must've handled all of this since you told me the truth. It seems incredibly self-centered of me."

He shook his head. "There's no need for you to apologize. I dropped the bomb on you that everything you thought was true wasn't, so it's natural that you haven't processed all the implications of what truly happened. And that's on top of all the threats to your life." He took a deep breath. "But you're right. It broke my heart to do that to you, and it was even worse to see you hurt and then to ultimately be alone. I'm not going to lie and say I haven't dated anyone since you, but there's been no one who could even begin to compare to you. You had my heart all those years, Layla, and you still have it completely."

She inhaled deeply as she took in his words. In her gut, she knew she was looking at the man she could spend the rest of her life with. In that moment together, it was just the two of them, opening up their hearts and revealing their true selves. The man and woman they were today—not ghosts of the past.

She scooted closer to him, and he took her cue. He put his hand gently behind her neck and drew her to him. They locked eyes once more before he kissed her. They had kissed a thousand times before, but this was like their first kiss all over again. The sparks flew between them, the attraction was undeniable, but this was so much deeper than that. This was a kiss that was not only healing old wounds but was also the promise of new beginnings together.

After a few moments, he broke away. As she stared into his eyes again, so many words were exchanged, but not one word was spoken. There was no doubt in her mind that she had never stopped loving Hunter, but today a fresh new love had been born.

CHAPTER
TWENTY-TWO

"You did what?" Aiden's brown eyes widened as he looked at her.

Izzy stood in his living room and thought about her response. "I know hiring a private investigator might seem a bit extreme, but after giving it more thought, I realized I needed help." She had not consulted Aiden before she made the decision to hire the PI because she knew he might push back against it, thinking the two of them could do it all on their own. But she figured it was best to outsource this to a professional if she really wanted to dig deep. "I'm sorry I didn't tell you sooner, but I was waiting to see if he actually turned up anything."

Aiden crossed his arms. "Well, I assume the fact that we're having this conversation means he did find something, right?"

She could tell he was a little ticked off at her, but he was so even-tempered that he didn't really show it. And for that she was appreciative. "Here's the deal. The PI examined the sergeant's entire social media presence and went even deeper than that, following up on all his connections and interactions. Even though the sergeant had a lot of privacy settings on some sites, some of his connections did not, which allowed the PI to get to them."

Aiden raised an eyebrow. "Don't leave me in suspense."

"The PI believes the sergeant had relationships with a couple of women who were quite a bit younger than he was. I've gotten both of their names, and I'm going to go talk to them."

Aiden's expression softened. "Izzy, has it occurred to you that you might not find the answers you want? Maybe these relationships were purely consensual."

Yes, she had thought about it, but she at least had to check it out. "We have to run down every lead. If it's as you say, then fine, I'll move on. But given the conversation I had with Alicia, I think there's going to be a pattern here. Powerful men like this don't normally have just one victim. If my hunch is right, there might be a whole host of people who had a motive to hurt the sergeant."

Aiden nodded. "Yeah, I guess you're right about that. What can I do to help?"

"This is something I need to do on my own. I'm actually going to meet one of the ladies in a few minutes. It'll be better if it's one-on-one, just like I did with Alicia."

He hung his head. "I feel so useless right now, but there's nothing I can do to help you."

That was the furthest thing from the truth. "Aiden, you just being you helps me more than you know. You're always there for me, and you're my rock during this difficult time."

"I just wish I could be more useful. Do you need a ride to wherever you're going?"

"No. I'm good. I'll give you a call when I'm done, and maybe we can meet up for dinner and talk about it. That sound like a plan?"

He pulled her into a big hug. "Sounds good to me."

She lingered for a moment in his arms, just enjoying being with him, but she needed to get her head in the game. The conversation she was about to have was going to be a tough one, and she didn't know any good way to lightly jump into the topic, especially with a total stranger. Talking to Alicia had been one thing, but they had common ground, and they knew each other. This woman might not even be willing to talk to her, but Izzy was going to try.

She gave Aiden a kiss good-bye and left to meet Kim Conway. After getting Kim's information from the PI, she'd had a quick introductory phone call with her, although she hadn't been completely forthcoming about the topic she wanted to discuss. When Izzy had said she was from NCIS, Kim didn't even give her a chance to explain before accepting the invitation. Izzy planned to make it clear from the beginning that this was not official NCIS business. She'd gotten her foot in the front door, but there was no way she was going to lie about the purpose of the meeting.

About half an hour later, she walked up to a bakery in Alexandria and saw the woman she thought was Kim sitting at one of the outside tables. She took a deep breath and then walked over to her.

"Kim?"

Kim stood up. She was below average height, with light brown hair and pretty brown eyes. Izzy guessed Kim was only a few years older than her. She also noted that Kim was small-framed like her. It made her wonder if the sergeant had a special thing for petite brunettes.

Izzy extended her hand. "Hi, I'm Isabella Cole. Thanks for meeting with me. Please have a seat."

"What can I do to help NCIS? The only time I ever hear anything about NCIS is from watching TV. I can't see how I could be involved in any of that."

Izzy prayed Kim wouldn't get up and walk out after she heard the truth. "Well, actually, while it's true that I'm an NCIS agent, what I want to talk to you about today is of a much more personal nature. It's not official NCIS business. Is that okay?"

Kim bit her bottom lip but nodded. "Yeah, I think so."

"I want to talk to you about a man named Henry Tybee."

Kim's demeanor instantly shifted. She gripped her coffee cup tightly in her hands. "Why are you asking about him?"

"Are you aware that the sergeant was murdered?"

Kim diverted her eyes before reconnecting. "I saw it on the local news, yes. What does that have to do with me?"

Izzy had to tread carefully. She didn't want Kim to scamper away. She needed this information, and Kim's initial reaction was already telling Izzy that she knew something. "You knew the sergeant, right?"

Kim nodded. "Yeah. We dated briefly."

"How did you meet him?"

"I worked part-time at a diner in Arlington during college. He came in almost every day. We struck up a conversation, and it just went from there. I knew he was a cop, so I was willing to take a chance on him, unlike the other random guys who hit on me."

And wasn't that a huge travesty. One of the things that bothered Izzy so much about what the sergeant had done was that he abused his position of power and authority. That was one of the reasons Izzy hadn't thought twice when he invited her to his office that night. She had trusted him completely.

Izzy was worried Kim might shut down, so she figured it was best to get right to the point. "I also knew the sergeant. I worked with him when I was at Arlington PD before I went to NCIS." She took a deep breath. "He sexually assaulted me."

Kim's eyes widened. "Are you serious?"

Izzy couldn't tell whether Kim was showing relief or confusion. "Yes. And the entire reason I'm here is to find out whether he hurt other women the same way he hurt me. Given that you said you dated briefly, I wanted to see what your experience was with him."

Kim didn't immediately respond. She looked away again and then took a sip of her drink. "I really would prefer not to talk about this."

Izzy understood that sentiment all too well. "Kim, I know if you had any experiences like I did, then you don't want to speak on this topic, but it's really important because the police are investigating the murder, and truthfully, they're looking at me as a suspect. I'm trying to show them that he had a pattern of abuse that is far and wide, and that his killer could've been anyone."

Kim leaned forward. "If what you're saying is true, then wouldn't it implicate me if I told you what he did to me?"

Exactly as Izzy had thought. Kim did have an unfortunate story to tell. "I'm not trying to implicate anyone specifically. I'm just trying to put the facts about his past behavior out there for all to see."

Kim shook her head. "No. It doesn't make any sense for me to talk, as far as I'm concerned. I don't want people knowing what happened to me and talking about it. I'm sorry about what you went through, but I can't help you."

Izzy only had one more chance to get to Kim. "I'm not pointing the finger at you by any means, but I am asking whether you'd be willing to speak to the detectives about your experiences with him. They need to understand the type of man he was. The whole picture. Not just the sanitized version of events they get from the rest of Arlington PD."

Kim looked away. "I don't think I can do that." Her eyes filled with tears.

Izzy took Kim's hand. She knew the pain the other woman felt. "I'm so sorry he hurt you too. I'm not going to push, but know that if you ever do need anyone to talk to about this, completely outside this case, I'm here for you. It took me a long time to get to a better place."

"You must be a lot stronger than I am, because I don't think I'll ever be in a better place as far as that topic is concerned. I'm sorry, but I need to go."

Kim grabbed her purse and quickly walked away before Izzy could say anything else.

Izzy put her head in her hands. She didn't think Kim had murdered the sergeant, but she definitely knew the sergeant had hurt Kim. Badly. And if that was the case, there were probably other women, and Izzy intended to find more evidence of his wrongdoing. If for nothing else, then to set the record straight about what kind of man Sergeant Henry Tybee really was.

A monster.

◆

Since yesterday, Cass had been giving him the cold shoulder, but Zane figured she just needed time to blow off steam. Hopefully they'd be able to get back to where they were. He racked his brain, trying to figure out when their relationship had taken a turn. They'd been solid as a rock for the past few years—and completely in the platonic sense.

Maybe he wasn't being sensitive enough to everything Cass had gone through. After all, he wasn't the one with a target on his back. He was going to try to be patient and give her the time and space she needed. But if they got through this mole investigation and things still weren't good between them, he couldn't see their partnership lasting, and that really bummed him out. But that was a battle for another day.

The team had been summoned to HQ for a meeting, and he and Cass waited in a conference room for everyone else to arrive. He hoped Mason had some good news for them.

Layla walked into the conference room by herself. He wasn't sure where Hunter was. He didn't know the full backstory between them, but it was obvious that there was something beyond business.

He noticed Layla had dark circles under her eyes. This case was wreaking havoc on them all.

Mason walked up to the front of the room and cleared his throat. "Thanks for everyone getting together so quickly."

Zane looked over at Cass, and they made eye contact before she quickly looked away. The cold shoulder continued. "Do you have something good for us?" he asked.

Mason ran his hand through his short dark hair. "Unfortunately, no. It's actually very bad news."

The room was eerily quiet. No one had been expecting this. Zane was sure everyone had been hoping for a break in the case.

"What is it?" Cass asked.

Mason looked at her. "Some of the cash seized from the op is missing."

"What?" Layla asked. "How is that possible? We did the

inventory checks ourselves, both in Honduras and once we got back stateside."

Mason sighed loudly. "That's precisely the problem. There's concern from the higher-ups that someone on this team is compromised."

"You think we took the money?" Zane didn't even try to stay calm. This was becoming completely ridiculous. "Every day it's a new accusation against us, and frankly, Mason, it's getting old. I've dealt with all the heat put on me, but it's out of hand to call into question the other members of the team. If there's evidence against any one of us, then by all means, bring it to the light of day, but all this speculation and innuendo is getting tiresome. Especially after everything each of us has done for the cause." He paused, hoping someone would jump in and back him up.

"Zane's right," Cass said. "If you really thought we stole that money, you'd fire us here and now."

Mason crossed his arms. "You all know I have your backs, but right now there's only so much I can do. I've been given my orders."

"And what are those?" Layla's tone wasn't much friendlier than Zane's had been a moment ago.

"Each one of you is going to be questioned. Zane, they're going to start with you."

Zane gritted his teeth. "Great. They've already convicted me. What, first I'm a traitor and now I'm a thief too?"

Mason's expression softened. "Man, I know this stinks. Just go in there, tell the truth, and we'll figure this out."

Zane wasn't convinced, but he'd been in the game long enough to know that sitting around and complaining wasn't going to solve anything. Better to get right to it. He stood up. "Where do I need to go?" No point in delaying the inevitable.

"I'll escort you." Mason turned to Cass and Layla. "Just sit tight."

Great, now he also needed a babysitter to watch him while he walked around HQ. The cartel had done a big number on him. This was a master setup if he'd ever seen one.

Zane followed Mason out the door, down the hall, up two flights of stairs, and finally into another empty conference room.

"They'll be here in a minute."

"What do you think is really going on here?" Zane asked him.

"I wish I knew, but I'm not going to lie to you, Zane. You need to be on guard and make sure you are being completely truthful, because if they catch you in any lie, even if it has nothing to do with this investigation, it could be real trouble. The higher-ups are getting nervous, and they want to make someone pay for this."

"You know me. You have to realize I couldn't have done any of this." Zane sounded more desperate than he'd intended, but it was becoming increasingly difficult to hide his feelings on this topic.

"I do, but the problem is that you don't have to convince me. You have to convince the powerful people above my pay grade, and to do that, you first have to win over the investigators."

As if on cue, the door opened and two people walked in—a short, stocky bald man and a younger redheaded woman. The man introduced himself as Palmer Sanchez, and the woman was Maddie O'Leary.

Mason excused himself, and then it was just Zane with the two suits. He couldn't imagine that either of them had seen any time in the field, but here they were, ready to pass judgment on him. Interestingly enough, these were not the people who had questioned him previously.

Sanchez opened a folder in front of him. "Your supervisor explained why the team was being questioned today, correct?"

"Yes," Zane said.

O'Leary leaned forward. "We've read your entire file, and we want to state up front that we are not here today to talk to you about the topic you've previously met with our team on, regarding the mole inside DEA. Is that clear?"

He wondered why they were so intent on drawing such a bright line, but he figured now wasn't the time to argue over an irrelevant point. He had bigger problems. "Yes, I understand."

"Great," O'Leary said. "We'll jump right in. You obviously recall retrieving funds from the Mejía safe house and bringing them back to the United States, right?"

"Yes."

"Were you ever alone with the cash?"

"I have absolutely no idea. I wasn't keeping tabs on things like that. My bigger concern was helping the team get in and out without one of us getting killed. That's the way it works in the field. None of us were taking the time to steal any money, since that's what you're getting at. And no, of course I didn't take any of the cash while in Honduras or back stateside. Is that clear?"

O'Leary smiled, and Zane wondered what he'd said to get that reaction out of her. "Agent Carter, we appreciate your zeal, but we're just trying to get to the facts. This isn't an inquisition."

He huffed. "Could've fooled me."

Sanchez rested his hands on the table. "It isn't. We really

are just trying to ferret out what actually went down in Honduras. Given everything that has happened since the team returned, this is just one more angle that we have to examine. You've been doing this for quite a few years. You're a Marine. You have the experience to see it too. Aren't there just one too many coincidences here?"

"You think this is an inside job and the person is on my team—or to take it further, you think it's me." Zane's anger bubbled right below the surface, and if he wasn't careful, he might explode. That would only make him look more guilty.

"Why isn't it you?" O'Leary's clear blue eyes questioned him.

"Because I'm a loyal patriot who serves my country. I'm not a thief, and I'm most certainly not a turncoat. I put my tail on the line all the time to fight for what I believe in. If I was that money hungry, why wouldn't I be in the private sector? Believe me, I get recruiters calling me all the time. But that's not me. It's not how I'm made. Never has been, and never will be."

"So if we dig into your finances, we're not going to see an influx of cash?" Sanchez asked.

A thought hit Zane. His family money. "You won't find an influx of cash, no, but you will find a substantial amount of funds. That money is from my family. I have it set aside and don't touch it because I don't like relying on things I didn't earn, and frankly, I don't have the best relationship with my father, and the money comes from his family business. If you look closely enough, you'll be able to confirm I'm telling the truth about that. All of that money is fully traceable."

As he watched their expressions remain unchanged, he realized they already knew all of this and were just testing him to see if he would tell the truth.

"Fair enough," Maddie said. "What about the rest of your team?"

That got his attention. "What do you mean?"

"Have you noticed any of their spending habits change?"

"You people are unbelievable. You want to talk about my team? Let's see. John Diaz was murdered. Cass and Layla have been attacked and are living at safe houses, and your concern is whether their spending habits have changed? This is beyond ridiculous." He paused for a moment. "But to answer your question directly, no. There have been no changes. People have been too concerned with staying alive."

Sanchez nodded. "How well do you know Layla Karam?"

Of course they would go after the Agency person. "I met her when we started preparing for this operation, but do I believe she could be involved in stealing from the cartel? Of course not."

"Don't you think that Agency operatives sometimes play outside the lines a bit?"

"Sure, but Layla isn't your typical spy."

O'Leary raised an eyebrow. "What do you mean?"

"Layla's an analyst, and that's what she wants to be. The only reason she went into the field is because they told her she had to. From what I got to know of her, there isn't a deceitful bone in her body, which makes being a spy pretty difficult. But she's brilliant. Her language skills are off the charts, and she was able to handle herself in the field, but that's not what she wants to do."

"You're confident she's clean?" Sanchez said.

"I'm confident my entire team is clean."

"Including Cass?" O'Leary asked.

"Yes. *All* of us. And Diaz as well." Zane didn't know how he could be any more clear about his feelings, but he had to speak his mind. "I don't know what you guys are really after here. Is it the truth? Because it doesn't seem like it. You seem hyperfocused on our team, but you need to start looking elsewhere, because the only thing you're going to find on my team are people trying their best to do their jobs and do them with integrity."

"Are you finished?" Sanchez asked.

"Yes." He could've said a lot more, but they didn't seem moved by any of his comments.

"One piece of advice," Sanchez said.

Zane tried not to seem too annoyed by Sanchez's arrogance.

"You have too much faith in people. Take off the blinders and look at things with fresh eyes. You might not like what you see."

"What is that supposed to mean?"

O'Leary looked at him. "What Palmer is trying to say is that you appear to see people's best attributes. In our line of work, we see the worst. Just make sure you're not going to be blindsided because of your loyalty."

"You don't have to worry about that. My team is solid. That's the end of the story."

O'Leary nodded. "I think we're done for now. You're free to go."

The last thing in the world he felt was free. There was something deeper going on here, but he had no idea who was setting up his team.

CHAPTER
TWENTY-THREE

After the inquisition yesterday at the DEA, Hunter had explained to Layla why he hadn't been included in the meeting—that he had been tasked to work on the theft. He'd been worried she would be upset, but she'd taken it in stride, saying she understood completely why he couldn't tell her.

He wasn't any closer to finding the traitor at DEA, but he had stumbled on something else that was giving him major anxiety. There was no reason to keep his findings from Layla now that the cat was out of the bag regarding the cash and she'd been officially cleared by the investigators after her interrogation yesterday.

He watched her stare intently at her laptop as she typed. He wondered if her mind was really in the game or if it was somewhere else.

"Layla."

She stopped typing. "Yeah?"

"We need to talk."

Those words got her attention, and she set her laptop on the coffee table. "What is it?"

"As I told you, I've been working on this money angle for a while now, and after I exhausted all the regular routes, I started going down some other paths to find answers."

She frowned. "This doesn't sound good. What did you find?"

He hated telling her this. "There are some weird things going on with Cass's money."

She groaned. "No. There has to be an innocent explanation."

Hunter moved closer to her. "How well do you really know this woman?" Before she could answer, he kept talking. "Let me show you what I found."

"Fair enough."

"First, it appears Cass has had some major financial struggles. She took out three loans from two different banks and cleared out her savings account."

"How much are we talking?"

"So far, from what I've been able to document, it totals over four hundred grand."

Layla's shoulders slumped. "Okay. But it's not a crime to have money problems."

"True, but that's not all."

"What else?"

This was where things started to get dicey. "Those transactions occurred a few months ago. But within the last month, there's been an influx of cash. Not in her regular accounts, though."

Her eyes narrowed. "Then where?"

"It wasn't easy, but I was finally able to track her financial activity to an offshore account."

"How much of an influx of cash are we talking?" Layla bit her bottom lip.

He knew exactly why she seemed distressed. "About five hundred thousand."

She sucked in a breath. "That's the amount they're claiming was taken from the cartel money."

"Bingo."

Layla shook her head. "You're telling me that Cass was able to steal *five hundred thousand* dollars right out from under all of us?"

"It could've happened once the money was back in the States. Maybe she had access to the vault on the op. Could there be some weak links there?"

She shrugged. "I don't know enough about DEA operations and how the transport and security works."

"Do you remember the denominations of the money?"

"Yes. Everything I saw was in hundreds."

"Then she could easily fit five hundred thousand into a standard briefcase. Do you remember her ever being alone with the money?"

Layla didn't immediately respond. "I'm thinking."

"Take all the time you need." For some reason, he couldn't help himself and took her hand in his. When she smiled, he squeezed her fingers.

"The answer is yes. Cass was alone with the money for a short time period while we were loading up the vehicles in Honduras. Only a few minutes, though."

"That is all it would take. I assume you all had standard gear, including large backpacks."

"Yes, but wouldn't that be bold, to stash the money in her gear?"

"Bold, yes, but given her stature on the team, maybe she thought no one would ever check. Although standard protocol for DEA on ops like this is a gear check back stateside."

"That didn't happen. We got back, and there were no searches or anything like that. It was a bit hectic, and we did do immediate debriefings, but if my belongings were searched, I didn't know it."

"Maybe she caught a break."

"This would rule her out as the mole, though, because I can tell you one thing, she wouldn't be stealing from the cartel if she were working for them."

Hunter nodded. "It might just mean that she got in some trouble, became desperate, and decided to take the cash. However, if she's vulnerable, that could make her a target for the cartel to blackmail into helping them."

"Yeah, but if she was on their payroll and stole from them, it would be over for her. What are you going to do with this?"

"I have to take it to Mason ASAP."

Layla nodded. "I know. I just hate it. I wonder what kind of trouble she got into."

"It has to be pretty substantial to need that kind of cash." He hated to say it, but he felt like he had to. "You know that if what I found pans out, she's going to be done at the DEA and will probably face criminal charges."

"You don't think there'll be any lenience?" she asked.

He doubted it. "I can't imagine they'd ever trust her to go into the field again. If they put her on desk duty, it would be a huge gift, but I think the most likely thing is that they will terminate her."

Layla gasped. "But what about her safety? Would they pull her out of the safe house?"

"I hope not, but I can't guarantee it."

She took his other hand. "They would be signing her death warrant if they do."

❖

Zane watched Cass as she poured them each a cup of coffee. He hated that there was still an uncomfortable tension between them, but he didn't know what to do other than try to act normal even if she was skittish.

What bothered him the most was losing their easy and open relationship. They had formed a strong bond over the past few years. He considered her one of his closest friends. And now he was going back over everything to try to determine when she had started having feelings for him, because he'd been oblivious to it.

He'd be lying to himself if he didn't admit he'd initially thought she was attractive, but once they were assigned as partners, he'd put up a mental wall that had been like a fortress, and it had worked. Until now.

"Why are you scowling?" Cass asked him.

He smiled. "I didn't realize I was."

"Good, because a scowl doesn't look good on you." She sat beside him at the kitchen table.

He couldn't help but say something. "Cass, can we talk?"

She sighed. "Yeah. I realize I was a bit of a jerk to you the other day. I won't lie, you hurt my ego."

"How?"

She laughed. "Isn't that obvious? You rejected me."

"It's so much more complicated than that, and you know it." Against his better judgment, he placed his hand on top of hers.

Her brown eyes locked onto his. "You can't have it both ways, Zane." She pulled away from him. "We're either setting some hard and fast boundaries, or we're going to explore if there's something more between us."

"You think I'm sending mixed signals?" he asked.

"Yes, and I've felt that way for a while."

He leaned back in his chair, trying to figure out how this had gone wrong. "Things have been crazy, and after you were attacked, I wanted nothing more than to protect you. If I made you think I was trying to make a move in the process, then I'm the one who needs to apologize."

"Oh, Zane. You're one of the good guys."

"Didn't you say just the opposite the other day?"

"I was mad and hurt. I said a lot of things I didn't mean."

He took her hand again. "Cass, I do care about you. More than is probably smart, but I also think we have a partnership that can't be easily replaced. And a friendship I value beyond anything in my life."

Tears filled her eyes. "I hear all of that, Zane. I really do. But . . ."

"But what?"

She took a deep breath. "I've fallen in love with you."

Talk about a punch to the gut. Before he could respond, he heard commotion coming from the front door, and after a moment, Mason walked into the kitchen.

"What is it?" Zane asked.

"I need to talk to Cass alone."

She shook her head. "Whatever you have to say to me, you can say it in front of Zane."

Mason raised an eyebrow. "Are you certain about that?"

"Yes," she answered quickly.

A wave of unease washed over Zane. Mason took a seat

at the table with them, and Zane prepared for bad news, which seemed to be the only kind of news they heard lately.

"What's this all about?" Zane asked.

Mason focused his attention completely on Cass. "There's something we have to talk about."

"Spit it out, Mason." There was no lightness in Cass's words. She was all business.

"As part of the ongoing investigation, some strange financial information about you has come to light."

Ah, Zane thought. Cass was going to have to give up her brother to explain those financial issues, but Zane was relieved that he already knew the truth.

"What exactly did you find?" she asked.

Zane didn't blame her for trying to feel this out a bit before she opened up.

Mason rubbed his chin. "Cass, it's not good. We know all about the three loans and the amount of debt you've accumulated. You know you should've disclosed that financial distress to me immediately."

She nodded.

"But it gets much worse than that. We have hard evidence of you depositing five hundred thousand dollars into an offshore account that you probably assumed was not traceable."

"What?" Zane asked. "That can't be right. Cass, tell him the truth. Tell him what's going on." He looked at her, but her eyes darkened, and she didn't immediately speak. "Cass? C'mon, tell him."

"Zane, what's your role in all of this?" Mason demanded.

"Zane doesn't have anything to do with this," Cass said. "Nothing."

"You both better start talking ASAP," Mason said.

Cass averted her eyes. "It's complicated."

"Can I have a moment alone with Cass?" Zane felt like he needed to intervene before this went completely off the rails.

Mason slammed his fist on the table. "Absolutely not. I don't think the two of you realize how much trouble you're in. I need some explanations right now before I have to call in reinforcements and haul you both off to a holding cell for a full interrogation."

Zane had never seen Mason lose his cool like this. "Let's just calm down. There's nothing criminal going on here."

"I beg to differ," Mason said.

"Enough!" Cass shouted.

Her words shut up both of the men.

"As I said before, Zane isn't involved in this." She turned from Mason and looked directly at him. "Zane, I'm sorry about everything."

"What are you talking about, Cass?" Zane asked.

Cass gripped her coffee cup. "I told you that my brother had a gambling problem and that is why I got into some dire financial trouble, because I was helping him. But that wasn't the extent of the problem."

"What else is there?"

"A lot." Her voice cracked.

Mason cleared his throat. "As touching as this moment is between the two of you, I need you to tell me the complete truth right now."

Cass didn't seem fazed by Mason's words. Instead, she put her hand on Zane's arm. "My brother got into even deeper trouble. Massive. They were threatening to kill him if he didn't pay up. He owed a lot of money. I feared they were actually going to carry out their threats."

Zane couldn't believe what she was saying. "Why didn't you tell me?"

"I didn't want to pull anyone else into this."

"So the five hundred thousand was to help bail out your brother?" Mason asked.

"Don't answer that," Zane said.

Cass's eyes widened, but she didn't say a word.

"Cass needs a lawyer," Zane insisted. "You're talking about some serious charges here."

Mason turned to him. "I'm trying to help her by not making this official yet."

"And I appreciate that, but you and I both know that if she admits to anything now, it can and will be used against her with both of us as potential witnesses, and I'm not going to stand by and let that happen."

"Don't I get a say in this?" Cass asked.

"Cass, please," Zane insisted.

Silence filled the room for a minute before she straightened in her chair. "I want a lawyer."

Zane blew out a sigh of relief.

Mason stood. "Fine. But this has now moved from informal to official. I'll give you two a minute, but then I'm taking you into custody, Cass. You'll be able to get an attorney, and we'll move on from there. Understood?"

She nodded, and Mason walked out of the room.

After a moment, Cass broke the silence. "I know you must hate me for keeping you in the dark."

"Of course I don't hate you."

"Things just got out of control. One thing led to another, and the next thing you know, my brother is in a dark, black hole that he can't get out of, and I was right there with him—I had to save him. He's the only family I have left. You know both my parents are gone. It's just me and him. He lost his way, and I felt this was my only option to help him."

"Is he in the clear now?"

She sighed. "For now, yes. Obviously, it was a big price to pay—both financially and emotionally, but he's trying his hardest to get his life back on track. I have to keep close tabs on him to make sure he doesn't fall back into bad habits." She swallowed. "Which will be a lot harder if I'm locked up. Anyway, I didn't want to drag you into my family mess."

And that was what hurt him the most, that Cass thought he wasn't to be trusted. That she couldn't come to him with her biggest and darkest secrets. "You could've told me."

"Could I, really? Zane, you're beyond reproach, and everyone knows it. A rule follower. I knew you would not approve of my actions even if they were to help my brother."

Was that really how she saw him? Yeah, she made jokes about him being too by the book, but this went much deeper. "I'd like to think, after all these years, that you'd see me as more complex than that."

She sighed. "You are. I'm not trying to argue with you. I'm just telling you how I felt. I didn't think I could tell you."

"Cass, you could've told me anything. You still can."

She hung her head. "I know that now, but at the time, I made the decision I thought was best in a difficult circumstance. I wasn't sure how I was going to help him, given I'd already maxed out everything I had. Then we went on the op. . . ."

He gripped her hand. "Don't tell me anything about the op, okay? Nothing. We'll get you an attorney and figure this out. But I can't be a witness here. Not against you. I care too much."

As tears started to roll down her cheeks, he couldn't help himself. He pulled her out of her seat and into his arms. The problem was that he wasn't just feeling the need to protect her. At that moment, he wondered if he'd fallen in love with her too.

CHAPTER
TWENTY-FOUR

On Saturday morning, Izzy prepared to meet Ann Marie Martinez, one of the other women the PI had identified from the sergeant's social media. Ann Marie had initially rebuffed her, but after Izzy pushed, she said that they could meet briefly at a downtown Arlington coffee shop.

Izzy walked into the shop and immediately saw her sitting by herself in the corner, working on her laptop with a deep frown on her face.

"Ann Marie?"

She looked up from her computer. "You must be Izzy."

It wasn't lost on Izzy that while she couldn't tell Ann Marie's exact height, she was definitely on the petite side, with dark hair. The pattern was holding. "That's me. Can I sit?"

"Yes, but as I said, I don't have long. I'm on deadline."

"You're a writer?"

"Yes, freelance," she said flatly.

So far so good. Given the time limitations and the frosty

reception, Izzy went for it. "I'll be as fast as I can, and I so appreciate the time. I wanted to talk to you about Sergeant Henry Tybee."

Ann Marie's expression remained neutral. "What about him?"

"You dated him?"

"Briefly."

"How did he treat you?'

Ann Marie arched an eyebrow. "Is that really any of your business?"

Maybe Izzy had pushed too hard. She needed to get information, not the stiff arm. This woman didn't know her at all. She needed to adjust her approach. "I'm sorry if this seems intrusive. I have a good reason for asking. The sergeant was murdered. Did you know that?"

Ann Marie's eyes widened. "No. What happened?"

"That's what the police are trying to find out. But in the meantime, I'm trying to determine if he had a pattern of abusive history with women."

Ann Marie leaned back. "Not with me."

"He treated you well?"

She nodded. "Yes, but we decided we weren't compatible, and that was that."

"Just like that? No hard feelings?"

Ann Marie shrugged. "None. I haven't really given him a second thought. I moved on with my life, and my focus is on my career."

Izzy might not have decades of experience under her belt, but she didn't need it to know Ann Marie wasn't telling her everything. "So no signs of abusive tendencies?"

"No. He was actually a bit too old and boring for my tastes. Too straight-laced."

Now Izzy really knew Ann Marie wasn't being forthcoming, but there was nothing more she could do about it right now. "Well, thank you for your time. I'll let you get back to work."

Ann Marie set down her tea. "You think he hurt other women?"

"I do."

"Well, obviously I'm sorry about that, but I don't have anything I can add from my personal experience."

"Understood." Izzy rose and thanked her again. As she walked away, she wondered what Ann Marie might be hiding.

◆

Layla awoke with a start. She must have been dreaming. There had been gunshots. But now, sitting up in bed, she didn't hear anything. The safe house seemed completely silent, as it should be in the middle of the night. Letting out a sigh of relief, she lay back down for a second.

A loud crash erupted nearby. She jumped out of bed and started to go for her gun on the nightstand, but she was tackled to the ground by a huge mass of a man. The breath was knocked out of her, but she willed herself to focus. She was under attack and had no idea where Hunter or the CIA security detail was. Then an awful thought struck her—what if they were all dead? What if those gunshots had killed them?

Those thoughts only made her angry, and she fought harder against the man pinning her to the floor. She was able to knee him in the groin, and he rolled off of her, groaning and muttering in a different language. Maybe Russian or something similar? She tried to get to her feet, but he caught her ankle in his large, meaty hand and pulled her back down to the floor. She hit with a thud and started kicking to try to break free, but he had regained his composure, and he punched her in the stomach.

As she tried to catch her breath, he punched her again, even harder. She rolled away, and he missed his next attempt.

She tried to scramble to her feet, hoping she could get to her side arm on the nightstand, but her attacker had other ideas. He lifted her off the ground and slammed her onto the floor. A scream escaped her lips as the pain radiated through her body.

Yelling again, she tried to gather the energy to keep fighting, but if this kept going much longer, she had no doubt she'd be dead soon.

She pushed to her feet and dodged another punch, but then he wrapped his hands around her neck and started squeezing. Stars flashed before her eyes as the breath started to leave her body, and she struggled not to lose consciousness.

As she started to say what she thought could be a final prayer, she found a burst of energy. She dropped low to the ground, startling her attacker, and his grip broke. That gave her the opening to kick him again in the groin, which brought him to his knees. She leapt for her nightstand, grabbed her gun, and aimed it at him.

"Don't move. Hands up!"

"Layla." Hunter rushed into the room, breathing heavily. His eyes widened. "Are you okay?"

She nodded, adrenaline surging through her body. "We need to secure him."

"I've got some zip ties in my duffel downstairs. Are you good here?"

"Yeah. What about Ace and Dax?"

He frowned and shook his head.

She knew that meant they were dead—but there was no time to focus on that. She stared into the light blue eyes of the man who had attacked her, unwilling to let him move an inch. "Hunter, how many other attackers?"

"Two. They're downstairs, dead."

Without looking at him, she said, "Okay. Go get the ties." He jogged out of the room.

"You won't shoot me," her attacker said in accented English.

"Try me. Who are you? Who do you work for?"

He didn't respond.

"You said something in Russian. Why is a Russian hit man working for the cartel?"

He smiled.

An odd response, but she kept pushing. "Tell me." She took a step closer to him.

"I work for the highest bidder. Doesn't matter to me. A job is a job."

So now the cartel was hiring professional hit men. Maybe Diego had expanded his horizons because the cartel members hadn't been able to seal the deal.

Hunter ran back into the room and fastened the hit man's wrists with the zip ties. The Russian grunted.

"I just started questioning him," Layla told Hunter.

"I'm not saying anything else."

"Yes, you are. If you want to live."

Hunter shot her a worried glance. Of course she wasn't going to kill the guy, but he didn't know that. She needed to play the bad cop right now, and she was the one holding the gun.

"I need answers. You start talking, and we'll see what we can do as far as a deal. You don't, and I'm going to blow out your kneecap."

The man's eyes widened.

"Layla, you can't do that," Hunter said.

It was actually to her advantage that Hunter didn't know she was bluffing. It made the act more convincing. "I can and I will."

She moved an inch closer and pointed the gun toward his knee.

He cracked. "Okay, okay. Yes. I'm working for Mejía. I don't know what you did, but Diego is out for blood. He will not stop until you are dead. You should've just let me kill you because the next person might not make it so easy for you. Being tortured by one of Diego's henchmen will be much worse."

Her breath caught, but she kept her hand steady on the gun. "What were your orders?"

"To kill everyone in the safe house."

"And how did you know the location?" Hunter asked.

He shrugged. "It was provided by the cartel contact. I'm not sure how they got it."

She glanced at Hunter. "We need to get out of here. Let's call this in, and then we need to move once backup gets here and can take this guy into custody."

She pulled out her burner phone and made contact. She only hoped she wouldn't be too late.

◆

Hunter couldn't believe this turn of events. They'd taken one of the Agency SUVs and were driving, but he had no idea where. He just wanted to put some distance between them and the safe house.

Layla said the Agency was working on a plan, but she'd been pretty quiet since they left.

One minute he'd been lying down, reading because he couldn't sleep, and the next, he'd heard the commotion in the other part of the house. A barrage of gunshots had made him jump into action. Layla's security detail had exchanged fire, killing one of the hit men, but unfortunately, both Ace and Dax were killed before Hunter had killed the second man. The CIA team's sacrifice had given him and Layla a fighting chance. When he'd pulled the trigger, it had been pure survival instinct kicking in, but he was trying not to think about it.

"You really did a number on that guy," he said to Layla. "He was huge."

"It was touch and go for a minute. He got the drop on me, and I had to fight a bit dirty, but when you're smaller, you have to fight differently."

"Another thing you learned at the Farm?"

"Yeah. I had some great teachers. Women my size who understood that we're never going to be able to take on a two-hundred-and-fifty-pound man using normal techniques."

"You weren't really going to shoot him, were you?"

"Of course not, but I needed him to think that I would and that I wouldn't hesitate. Sometimes half the battle is the mind game."

"It worked," he said softly. "Layla, I've never taken a life before. I've been on some dangerous jobs, but nothing like this."

"You had no choice, Hunter. You acted in self-defense. You heard that guy. Their orders were to take out everyone at the safe house. If you hadn't defended yourself, we would've all been dead."

He nodded. "Yeah, I get that. It just feels a bit strange, that's all."

She put her hand on his arm. "You did what you had to do. We're up against vicious enemies who will stop at nothing for revenge. They kill without any regard for human life."

"Have you ever taken a life?"

"Unfortunately, yes. On the Honduras op, I returned fire. I saw some of the men go down. I have no way of knowing if I'm the one who killed Diego's brother or if it was someone else on the team, but we were in a pretty hostile firefight, and we had to defend ourselves."

"How did you cope with that?"

"I asked for forgiveness for taking the lives, but I also know that the Lord understood the circumstances—that we were all fighting for our lives. I thought about those men and their families—who were probably completely innocent—and I cried for them and prayed for them. Experiences like this will test anyone. I wanted the analyst job so that I wouldn't have to make those life-and-death decisions, but here I am, making them anyway and trying to deal with the fallout the best way I can. And the only way I know how to handle it is to ask for God's help. I couldn't do it alone."

Maybe she had a point. "Thanks for that. Hearing your perspective on things helps me."

"Don't expect to process this overnight. You will need time. I know I did."

He nodded. "We need to figure out our next steps."

"I can't believe Ace and Dax are dead." She sniffed.

He knew she was not only in great pain, but also holding back her emotions over what had gone down. "I'm sorry. There was nothing I could do to save them."

"It's not your fault. I didn't mean it like that. I just hate feeling like I'm responsible. They were there to protect me."

He glanced at her. "They knew the dangers when they

signed up to be Agency security. We have to figure out how the Agency safe house got compromised."

"I know. I don't really want to believe that anyone on the inside would sell me out, but given the progression of events, I don't think we can turn a blind eye to that possibility."

"If that's true, though, maybe we shouldn't accept whatever they provide you next."

"You're forgetting that they still want to keep me under surveillance."

"Let them clean up the mess that just happened and see whether they want to put another security team in the line of fire."

"I don't want to put another team there, but I don't think I'm going to have much choice in the matter."

Hunter was uncomfortable with this entire setup. Something seemed incredibly wrong to him, but he couldn't figure out where the greatest threat was coming from, and that was essential to being able to keep Layla safe.

When her cell phone rang, it startled him, but he tried to play it cool.

"Yes," she answered, putting it on speaker.

"I'm getting reports from our people at the safe house now," Frank said. "What in the world happened? It's a complete bloodbath."

"We were ambushed," Hunter said. "We're fortunate to be alive. Those men were professionals and were not messing around."

"That's evident from the two dead bodies of my men," Frank shot back.

"With all due respect," Hunter said, "your men were doing their jobs, and their brave actions saved our lives."

"I know," Frank said. "We need to mitigate the risks as

much as we can, which is why I'm sending you to a different safe house with extremely limited access. I can guarantee you that it's not compromised."

"You still think I'm working with terrorists?" Layla asked.

Her timing surprised Hunter a bit, but he understood why she was so frustrated.

"I told you before, this has nothing to do with that. Yes, the cartel wants you dead. But that has nothing to do with your activities with Al-Nidal."

"There are *no* activities with Al-Nidal. The sooner you realize that, the better."

Hunter rarely heard Layla raise her voice like this.

"Why don't we focus on the immediate threat to your life?" Frank said.

Layla gave Hunter a frustrated glance, and he listened as she recounted their brief interrogation of the remaining attacker.

"We'll do a full work-up on him and see what else we can find, but the cartel starting to outsource only makes things more dangerous. I'm sending you coordinates to the new safe house. I'll have another team deploy and meet you there."

"Roger that." She ended the call and looked at Hunter. "What do you think?"

"Our choices are limited."

"I'm going to give Scarlett a call. Fill her in and see if she has any ideas."

"She's going to toe the party line. What other option does she have?"

"I wouldn't be so sure about that. She's stood by me through all the ups and downs at the Agency. If there's a way she can help, she will."

"Then I'm all for it."

For the next few minutes, Hunter soaked in the conversation between the two women. It was clear that they had each other's backs.

"Layla, I hate to say this," Scarlett said, "but I really think you need to go off the grid. I don't know if you can trust the Agency. Not after the safe house was compromised."

"But then I'll have the Agency after me too," Layla responded.

"Okay, let me think." Scarlett was silent for a minute. "You should go to the new safe house, but we'll also prepare a plan B in case things get dicey again. I'll make some calls and see what I can put together for you so you have an exit strategy if you need one."

"I don't want you to do anything that would put you in a bad position. I know how hard you've worked to climb the ladder."

"Don't you worry about me. I assume I can reach you on this number?" Scarlett asked.

"Yes, it's a burner."

"I'll be in touch soon."

The call ended.

"Well, I like how she thinks," Hunter said. "You were right. She's not afraid to rock the boat, huh?"

"You don't get to be in her position without taking risks."

"This is good. If she can find you a separate safe house not linked to the Agency, I'm all for it."

"I still can't believe the safe house got compromised. If not a CIA leak, then how?"

"Maybe they were able to track the Agency security detail somehow."

"I guess it's not crazy to think that the cartel could have someone on the Agency payroll." She blew out a breath.

He was more concerned about the fact that the cartel was implementing desperate measures by outsourcing their business to the Russians. Were they really that bent on revenge at all costs? It appeared that way.

"You're too quiet," Layla said.

"I'm sorry. I just hate you being in harm's way and me feeling so completely helpless to stop it."

"Hunter, what are you talking about? You did stop it. I'm probably only alive right now because of you taking out that other attacker, and I thank God He brought you back into my life."

There it was. Once again she believed God was at work here. The question was whether he did. His reconnection with Layla had caused a stirring inside of him about his faith. He was still trying to work through his issues, but there had been a change—even if he had been initially resistant to it.

"I think you may be right."

She smiled at him. "Worldly explanations only get you so far sometimes."

"True, but it's easy to focus on being rational and only seeing what's in front of you." He wondered how far he should open up. Considering the circumstances of the night, he decided to go for it. "Experiencing you in my life again has changed me, Layla. All for the good. It was like I was caught in this dark hole, just going about my life thinking that God had completely forgotten about me. But then everything started to have color and light again with you there. I don't know how to verbalize it any better than that, but your faith has helped give me strength through this."

"It isn't a one-way street, Hunter. I've been through dark days too. I've done things I wish I could change. But knowing that we've been given another chance—a fresh start—is just a glowing example of God's love and His perfect timing."

He hated that he was driving, because what he wanted to do more than anything was to pull her tightly into his arms and hold her. To tell her how much he still loved her and wanted to build a life together. But that would have to wait.

CHAPTER
TWENTY-FIVE

The next morning Izzy sat across from Detectives Stewart and Bryant again with Piper by her side.

"Agent Cole, we called you here because we have a concern," Detective Stewart said.

"We're listening," Piper responded.

Detective Stewart cleared her throat. "We believe Agent Cole has been conducting some sort of side investigation in regard to the sergeant's murder. Is that possible?"

Izzy should've known she'd get caught at some point, but she wasn't just going to roll over. "Last time I checked, there's nothing wrong with looking at the facts of a case."

"When you're the suspect, it's also called witness tampering," Detective Bryant chimed in.

Piper groaned. "C'mon, you two. You're better than this. You have a federal agent sitting in front of you, and you're baselessly accusing her of witness tampering."

"It's not baseless," Bryant said.

"Then, what do you have?" Piper asked. "I want to see hard evidence, not your wild-goose-chase assertions."

"We have the fact that Agent Cole hired a private investigator and has also been meeting with people she believes have relevant evidence to this case."

Piper frowned. "I need a minute to talk with my client."

"I bet you do," Detective Stewart said. "We'll leave you the room so you two can have some privacy."

Once it was just the two of them, Piper turned to Izzy, her blue eyes icy cold. "Please tell me they're wrong." When Izzy didn't immediately answer, Piper threw up her hands. "How in the world am I supposed to help you if you go rogue? What were you thinking?"

Izzy had known her attorney would be ticked, but she'd kept Piper in the dark for her own good. "I was thinking that I need to get to the truth." She wasn't going to pull any punches.

"And you don't think that's what they're trying to do?"

"I wasn't going to take that chance. We've talked about this before. The innocent aren't always vindicated. I couldn't take that risk. I had a feeling about the sergeant. Men like him are not onetime offenders, and I wanted to see who else he may have hurt."

Piper's eyes narrowed. "Let me guess. You found other women?"

Izzy nodded. "Yes. I should also tell you I spoke to a former officer at Arlington PD. Then the PI found two other women, and I'm fairly certain they were both abused by him."

"Exactly when did you plan on sharing this information with me? Your attorney! Didn't I tell you at the beginning that I would fight to the death for you, but that you had to be honest with me no matter what it was?"

Izzy forced herself to make eye contact. "I was still trying to figure out some things. I didn't want to bother you without something concrete."

"You can't hide critical information from me." Piper's tone had sharpened with each word out of her mouth.

"I'm sorry." What else could she say? She was clearly in the wrong.

"Where do you plan to go with all of this?" Piper asked.

"It's likely that one of the sergeant's victims or someone who knew about what he had done could be responsible for his murder. And while I'm not looking to get anyone else in trouble, I believe just the idea and the pattern of behavior is enough to muddy the waters, and that would provide reasonable doubt, if it ever came to that."

Piper threw up her hands. "You really are something. I should withdraw from this case."

Izzy leaned toward her, ready to plead, but Piper lifted her hand to stop her from talking.

"*But* I understand why you did what you did. From here on out, there can be no more secrets, and if I find out that you've been hiding something else from me, I will withdraw. Is that clear?"

"Thank you. I appreciate it. I'm sorry again." Piper was being more than understanding about the situation. "How do we handle this now?"

Piper gave her shoulder a reassuring pat. "It's going to be okay. I assume they've figured all of this out, so we just have you own up to it."

"I did ask the women I talked to if they would speak to the detectives. I think only one of them was game, my former colleague at Arlington PD, and I don't know if she ever reached out."

"Let's find out." Piper stood and opened the door for the detectives.

"Are you ready to talk now?" Detective Stewart asked as she and Bryant retook their seats.

Izzy looked at Piper.

"My client has done nothing wrong, detectives. I believe you've already discovered what she has done, and hopefully you've quickly followed up on the leads and information she uncovered that might be relevant to this case."

"And what would that be?" Detective Stewart asked.

Izzy jumped in before anyone else could speak. "If you haven't found out yet, it's only a matter of time before you determine, just like I did, that the sergeant had a pattern of abuse with women. I've only touched the tip of the iceberg, but I've seen enough to know that there are plenty of people who would've wanted him dead."

"Are you going to give us names?" Detective Bryant asked.

Izzy shook her head.

"Why not?" Detective Stewart asked. "Isn't that the whole point?"

"If they aren't comfortable coming forward, then I'm not going to be the one who calls them out. You would think, if I was able to locate these women, that Arlington PD wouldn't have any trouble." She probably shouldn't have added that last dig, but she couldn't help herself.

Detective Stewart drummed her fingers on the table. "I have to admit, Agent Cole, this is turning out to be quite the investigation."

"I want the truth, which is what I assume you want too, Detective." Izzy could feel Piper's glare about to cut through her, but she wanted to stand up for herself.

The detective nodded. "Of course."

Izzy leaned forward. "Then you need to look beyond me and the people in my life to find out the identity of the true killer."

"Agent Cole, we have hard evidence against one person so far in this case, and that person is you. You, by your own admission, wanted to kill the sergeant and sent him threatening text messages to that effect. He was clearly obsessed with you. Maybe he came after you again, and you snapped."

The scary part was that the scenario the detective laid out could have been true—except that it wasn't. "I'm telling you again, I didn't do this. You need to talk to others who could have critical information and stop solely focusing on me because I'm the most convenient target."

Detective Stewart opened a folder. "Well, we have actually spoken to one of the women you found."

"Who?" Izzy asked.

"Ann Marie Martinez."

That was surprising, given their conversation.

"You look stunned, Agent Cole," Detective Bryant said.

"I got the distinct impression from my conversation with her that she didn't want anything to do with this."

"You aren't the only one investigating here, Agent Cole. We tracked Ann Marie down ourselves, and she didn't have a lot of nice things to say about you. According to Ms. Martinez, you were harassing her about her relationship with the sergeant."

Izzy shook her head. "I handled her with kid gloves, and it was pretty clear from the start that she didn't want to talk about any of this. I did not push her in any way."

"Then why would she make that accusation?" Detective Bryant asked.

"Because I think she knows something and doesn't want

to talk about it. I believe digging deeper into everyone you're talking to is worthwhile."

Detective Stewart crossed her arms. "Does that include you too, Agent Cole?"

"Certainly. I don't have anything to hide."

"You have strong motive to have killed Sergeant Tybee," Detective Stewart said. "After everything he did to you, it would be natural to be struggling, and maybe one day it all became too much."

Piper lifted her hand. "I let you level that accusation once already, but a second time is too much. Now you're just badgering my client, and I won't allow it."

Piper's fiery response put Izzy more at ease. Piper was fighting for her. Izzy wasn't used to being in this position, but to know that Piper believed in her meant so much. Could she be a Piper one day? Could she advocate so passionately? She wasn't sure if she had it in her, but she certainly wanted to try.

"This interview is over." Piper stood.

"We'll be back in touch soon." Detective Stewart looked directly at Izzy. "Don't plan to leave town without letting us know, okay?"

Before she could answer, Piper spoke again.

"We'll cooperate, but it's just because we want this investigation put to bed." Piper grabbed Izzy's arm and led her out of the room.

Izzy could only hope that she hadn't just made things a lot worse for herself.

◆

Since Layla didn't have great options, she'd decided going to the safe house that Frank had set up was the best she and

Hunter could do while they waited to see if Scarlett could come up with something outside the system.

They'd gotten there late the night before—almost morning. The first twelve hours had been uneventful.

Frank had directed her to go radio silent with everyone—the DEA included—and she figured that might be the best course. They'd dumped their phones, and a CIA runner had delivered new phones without even seeing them.

She could tell by the tone of Frank's voice, however, that he was beginning to be on edge. She didn't think he really believed she was working with Al-Nidal. The fact that he'd been so helpful since she called him made her think that she was persuading him back to her side.

Hunter was working on his laptop, still intent on the DEA case for Mason. After Keith Hammond's death, they'd run into a lot of dead ends. Cass had pretty much been ruled out, given the theft, but there was still a big question mark over Zane's head, though she didn't think there should be.

When she heard a light knock on the door, Layla jumped up from the couch. Hunter lifted his hand to tell her to be quiet. He then pulled out his side arm, and she grabbed her gun from the coffee table beside her. No one should be at the safe house. Frank had notified her about the phone delivery earlier, and she hadn't heard from him since.

Layla and Hunter both moved slowly to the door, weapons drawn. Her pulse thumped loudly as she prayed this wasn't another attack.

She had almost reached the door when she heard a voice. "Layla, are you in there?"

She knew immediately who was outside. Hunter stopped her from moving any closer, but she was no longer afraid.

"Yes, I'm here." She looked through the peephole and

saw Nick on the other side. She opened the door, and he walked in.

"Are you all right?" Nick asked.

"Yes. What're you doing here? I thought this location was completely locked down." Or at least that was what Frank had promised.

Nick didn't answer, instead turning his attention to Hunter. "And you are?"

"Hunter McCoy." Hunter stood tall but didn't offer his hand to Nick.

Nick's blue eyes flashed with recognition. He frowned. "I didn't expect to see you here."

"We're working together right now," Layla said. "The more important question is why you're here. How did you find me?"

Nick looked at her. "Frank and I talked. I got him to reveal your location because I have some breaking intel you're going to want to know. I thought it best delivered face-to-face."

That got her attention. "What is it?"

"We know who set you up for the IG investigation."

"Who?" Her voice cracked.

"It was Bryce Wixom."

Her stomach dropped as a feeling of dread filled her body. "Are you sure Bryce betrayed me?" Even as she asked the question, she knew the answer wasn't going to exonerate her old friend. She couldn't afford to live in denial.

"We have a team bringing Bryce in as we speak."

"Would he really go to such elaborate lengths to set me up?"

"You did destroy his Agency career," Nick said flatly.

"And I was completely justified in doing so. He was the one playing fast and loose with the rules. Rules that were put in place to protect us all and make sure we don't become a bunch of lawless mercenaries willing to flip for the highest dollar."

Nick touched her shoulder. "I'm not saying you didn't do the right thing. I'm just speaking to Bryce's motivation." He dropped his hand. "We'll know a lot more after Bryce is questioned."

She nodded. "Is the direction from Langley for me to stay put?"

"It is," Nick said. "But can I speak with you privately?"

Hunter looked at her for permission.

"It's fine, Hunter."

"I'll just be upstairs." Hunter reluctantly walked away.

Once Hunter was gone, Nick moved closer to her.

"There's something else?" As if all of this wasn't enough.

"Something seems very off here, and I can't put my finger on it. Are you sure you can trust Hunter?"

"Yes," she answered with zero hesitation. "He saved my life. I wouldn't be standing here right now without him."

Nick touched her arm. "I know you have strong feelings for him. It was obvious when we were together that you still loved him, but I worry about you, and I want to make sure you're thinking clearly."

He seemed to be coming from a sincere place, and she saw his point of view. "It means a lot to me that you care enough to say those things, and I can see why you'd worry, but I can promise you that the threats coming at me are not from Hunter."

Nick looked down. "Where do you think they're coming from?"

She blew out a breath. "Besides the cartel, I'm not really sure. I'm worried about who I can trust at the Agency, if I'm being truthful. And then you add Bryce on top of that." She hesitated for a moment. "You know, I thought I had a real friendship with Bryce, but if he's behind the IG investigation, then that changes everything."

Kindness shone in Nick's eyes. "Bryce wanted to cross lines with you, and that only fueled the fire. I still believe you were justified, but it was a bold move to do to a friend."

She'd lost a lot of sleep over reporting him, but she'd felt compelled. "Do you think I should stay here?"

"I think you should be okay for now. Once we talk to Bryce, I'll have a much better read on the threat assessment." He looked at his watch. "Speaking of that, I should be going. I need to get back."

"*You're* going to be involved in questioning him?"

Nick nodded. "Yes. We didn't end on the best of terms, but I still think the world of you and your ability to contribute to the mission of the Agency. If Bryce has done something to threaten you, then it's my business to get to the bottom of that."

"Thank you. I really appreciate all you're doing to help me."

"You're special, Layla. I used to mean a lot of other things when I said that to you, but with the passage of time, I can say it to you in a completely platonic and professional way."

"I'm glad we're in a good place, despite the other circumstances." She believed that he'd gotten past her in the same way she'd moved on from him. Had their relationship ultimately been what she needed? No. But she could sure use his friendship.

After they said their good-byes, a few minutes went by before Hunter came back downstairs wearing a deep scowl.

"I don't like that guy," he said.

"I get it. But I actually think he's looking out for me, and given the circumstances, I'll take all the friends I can get."

"I know." He sighed. "I wish I weren't jealous, but I can't help it. It's one thing to know about people from our pasts, but to actually see them face-to-face makes it much more difficult."

She took his hands tightly in hers. "Hunter, what we have cuts through all of this. The lies, the past, the pain. What matters is where we are now."

He pulled her closer to him and wrapped his arms around her. Then he leaned down and whispered in her ear. "You know I'd lay down my life for you. To protect you. It's all I can think about."

Her breath caught. "You already have. Hunter, you don't have anything to prove to me."

"Don't I?" His voice cracked.

"No. I told you before. I know the truth. The past is the past. And I love you with all of my heart."

"Losing you again isn't something I can even begin to comprehend."

"Then let's not even think about that. Let's focus on moving forward with our lives together."

"Layla, if Bryce is behind this, you're going to have to keep me away from him."

"I don't think that's going to be an issue. If the Agency thinks he faked those photos, then there will be consequences." She placed her head on his chest and took a moment to calm herself.

He pulled back for a second and placed his hands on her face. "I love you, Layla. I don't know what else to say."

"That's all you need to say." Her heart felt like it might explode, because she knew he was all in, and in fact, he always had been.

CHAPTER
TWENTY-SIX

Zane entered a holding room at the DEA headquarters to meet with Cass, who sat at a small table, waiting for him. He got the sense that she'd been put through the wringer. Deep, dark circles hung under her pretty brown eyes. And yes, they were pretty. He was having a hard time getting back to where they'd been—the friend zone.

This bombshell she'd dropped on him had somehow brought them even closer. She'd hidden stuff from him, yes, but he got it. He had an awful relationship with his family. The fact that she was willing to lay everything on the line for her brother showed what kind of woman she was. He only wished she had come to him. He had more money than he knew what to do with and could have easily helped her. Although it occurred to him that he'd never told her about his money. They both had their family secrets.

All this Boy-Scout stuff had messed with his head. Did Cass really see him like that? He didn't see himself like that, but he wondered if somewhere along the way he'd given her the wrong impression. Yeah, he had a problem with perfectionism, but he was far from perfect. And he was beating himself up, because maybe that had caused her to do something that threatened not only her career but her freedom.

"Cass."

"I wouldn't have held it against you if you hadn't come. You still have your reputation to protect. You don't want to be known as the man who partnered with a thief."

He took her hand. "Don't talk like that. What are they saying?"

She looked at him. "My lawyer is working with them, trying to cut a deal."

That gave him a little hope. "What kind of deal?"

"One that avoids jail time, given my pristine record, but I won't be able to be a DEA agent anymore." Her voice sounded strained. "I have no idea what I'll do."

"Why don't we take it one step at a time?" Just the revelation that she wouldn't have to face jail time was huge and took a big burden off his shoulders. They could figure everything else out.

Her dark eyes widened. "*We?* You can't seriously act like you're going to stand by me through this. I've hidden things from you, and let's not even get into the other stuff I tried to pull."

"Yes, Cass. *We.* We're stronger than that. Yeah, you messed up, but that doesn't change our friendship. Our partnership." And whatever else there might be to come.

"It does, though. We'll never work together again. I'm done." Her voice got much louder.

"You might be done at the DEA. That's a harsh reality, but it doesn't mean your life is over. If you're able to take some sort of deal, you could start fresh. The DEA might be off the table, but there are other options."

"You mean in the private sector," she said.

"Yeah, totally, or there might be other agencies willing to overlook one lapse of judgment."

She raised an eyebrow. "You're talking CIA."

"You know I am." He couldn't help but smile.

She sighed. "Like you said, I'm not really in a position to make any plans right now. We can focus on one day at a time."

"Good."

She studied him for a moment. "Why, Zane? I don't get it. You had every right in the world never to speak to me again."

He took a deep breath, not sure what to say or how to say it. "You know, I'm not even sure myself. I just know that I really care about you."

"As a friend."

"For sure."

"As anything more?" she asked softly.

He stilled at her words. He didn't want to avoid the issue. That wasn't his style, but this was difficult. "Honestly, Cass, I'm not sure what I feel."

She nodded. "That's fair."

"We don't have to sort all of that out today, but I wanted you to know that I'm here for you."

Her eyes misted.

He couldn't believe he was seeing this from tough-as-nails Cass. That let him know she was really having a rough time, and seeing her in this weakened state broke his heart.

◆

After Layla's discussion with Nick, she realized she wanted to be a part of questioning Bryce. At first Nick had pushed back against the idea, but once she agreed not to be in the room, he had relented.

Hunter wasn't with her but was back at the safe house, working on the DEA investigation. He had been more than understanding about being left behind, given all the internal political issues this situation would cause within the Agency.

So now she found herself at Langley, watching from the surveillance room as Bryce's questioning began. Was she finally going to get answers to many of the questions that had been plaguing her?

True to his word, Nick appeared to be taking the lead and doing the questioning, along with Frank Gibson. In the surveillance room with her was the other, more junior investigator, Monty Hicks.

Bryce looked beaten down. He was normally completely put together, but tonight his hair was disheveled and his navy dress shirt was wrinkled.

Nick cleared his throat. "Bryce, this will go a lot easier if you don't play any games. We already know a lot. Your being forthcoming with us will go a long way in determining how this situation is going to be treated. If we feel like you're holding back or lying to us, I can personally guarantee we will push for the harshest penalty possible. Am I clear?"

Bryce didn't respond but didn't break eye contact with Nick either.

Layla's nerves were frayed as she waited to see how this was going to play out. She had no idea what Bryce was going to say.

Frank opened the thick manila folder sitting in front of him. "We want to talk to you about Layla Karam. You worked very closely with Layla while at the Agency, correct?"

"Yes, I did."

"How would you describe your relationship?" Frank asked.

"Before she betrayed me, you mean?" Bryce's nostrils flared.

This was going to be harder to watch than she'd expected. Bryce clearly held more animosity against her than she'd ever imagined.

"Let's start there," Frank said.

"Layla initially reported to me, but then she was promoted quickly. Way more quickly than anyone else I'd ever seen, by the way. We became peers and worked together on multiple projects, even though I'm a good ten years her senior. She was my go-to analyst and helped me get prepped for multiple missions."

Frank looked down at the papers in front of him. "I wasn't the person running the investigation that took place into your behavior and ultimately resulted in your expulsion from the Agency, but as I understand it, Layla, your friend, was the one who went to our office about what she believed you were doing. Am I right?"

"Yes." Bryce ran his hands through his hair, only making it messier.

Nick leaned forward. "Why don't we cut right to the chase, then? Did you retaliate against Layla because you were angry with her?"

Bryce averted his eyes and then reconnected. "You better believe I did."

Layla gasped at Bryce's forthright admission. He must have realized that they had him over a barrel, and he wanted to get out his version of the story. This could get really ugly. Fast.

"Tell us about it," Nick said.

"Layla was my friend. We had each other's backs. I watched out for her when people got mad about her climbing the ladder so fast. I could tell she was gifted, and I tried to show her the ropes. I stood up for her time and time again." His voice started to get loud. "And what did I get in return? A big, sharp knife right into my back."

She held her breath, waiting to hear what he was going to say next.

"Go on," Nick said. "What did you do, Bryce?"

Bryce straightened up in his seat. "I came up with a strategy to get Layla investigated. I wanted her to feel the heat just like I did. I wanted her to feel that kind of pain." Then he called her an awful name that made her sick.

"So you created these photos of Layla with Omar Assad?" Frank slid some photographs from the folder in front of Bryce.

He studied them for a moment. "Technically, I didn't create them, but I hired someone to. I'm good with photo manipulation but not nearly good enough to make it look completely legit like these do."

"So you wanted to get Layla in trouble?" Frank asked. "Really bad trouble, right? Because you would have known the consequences for this type of activity. If these pictures were true, then it could've been catastrophic. Much worse than the consequences for your conduct."

"After all she did to me? How she destroyed my CIA career? Absolutely."

"But that's not the worst of it, is it?" Nick asked. "It gets much worse than that, doesn't it?"

Bryce shifted in his seat. "When Layla came to me, asking if I was involved in the IG investigation, everything came flooding back. Her betrayal and the end of my Agency career. All those years of blood, sweat, and tears that I spent building up my reputation. And she just threw it all away like I was trash because of some moral high ground she *thought* she had. So, yeah, when she told me about the cartel attack, I thought I might have a golden opportunity."

"An opportunity to take her out. Kill her, you mean?" Nick asked.

Bryce's face turned bright red. "You're right. I wish the cartel had killed her."

Nick stood so quickly that his chair was knocked backward across the room. Layla sucked in a breath. She'd never seen Nick this angry.

"Maybe we should take a brief break," Frank said.

"No way." Nick walked around the table so he was on the same side as Bryce. He yanked Bryce up out of his chair and threw him against the wall. His hands closed around Bryce's throat.

Nick was going to kill him. Layla jumped up from her seat, but Monty touched her arm and pulled her back.

"Don't worry," he said. "They'll be okay. We have to let this play out."

Much to her surprise, Frank didn't do a single thing to try to stop Nick. Thankfully, after a few moments, Nick dropped Bryce from his viselike grip. "Tell me what you did."

"I used a friend here who owed me big-time to get Layla's safe house location, and then I reached out to an old cartel source and gave him the info."

Nick muttered some curses that made Layla's skin crawl. She really feared what would happen to Bryce, even if he had almost gotten her killed. She stared at Bryce. This cold, unwavering shell of a man was not the friend she'd once had. She didn't even recognize the person he'd become.

Nick's jaw twitched. "Because of what you did, a hit man killed two members of an Agency security detail and almost killed Layla. Their blood is on your hands."

Bryce looked defiantly at Nick, not showing any remorse. "I don't know what else you want me to say."

Nick walked out of the room and a moment later entered the surveillance room where she sat. "Can I talk to Layla alone?"

Monty nodded and exited.

"I thought you were going to hurt him," she said.

Nick groaned. "He deserves that and a lot more. What a sorry excuse for a man. I could've strangled him."

"You kind of did. Now what?"

"We'll get you completely cleared on the IG side of things, but the cartel is still seeking payback." He took her hand. "I'm sorry about all of this, but we'll get you through this and back to work. I give you my word."

"Thank you, Nick. Thanks for stepping up to the plate and fighting for me. What's going to happen to Bryce?"

Nick let out a low whistle. "I'll have to get the Agency lawyers involved, but if it were up to me, he'd be locked away in a cage for the rest of his miserable life."

"He does have rights."

"He sure didn't care about yours, did he? He gave you up, Layla. Even if he wasn't the one pulling the trigger, he killed those men on your security detail and tried to kill you."

She nodded. She knew he was speaking the truth.

"Hang tight in here for a few more minutes while we sort some things out."

Her heart broke at Bryce's betrayal, but she feared that all of this was far from over.

CHAPTER
TWENTY-SEVEN

While Layla was at the Agency, Hunter was spending his time on the DEA investigation. He had decided to take a different approach, so with DEA intel plus the help of one of his hacker friends, he had gotten into the texts of some of the actual cartel members.

If they found out he was messing around with their stuff, he'd be as good as dead. But he was confident in the firewall and all the extra protections they'd set up, thanks to an additional level of security from the CIA.

He didn't have Diego's or Roberto's texts, but he had messages from a variety of guys below them, and he was reading and trying to synthesize as fast as he could.

Currently, he was reviewing texts from Mateo Lopez. From everything he had gathered, Lopez was one of the direct reports to Diego. Most of the texts were operational in nature, and he had the feeling that if he stuck with it, he might get enough intel to provide the DEA with more leads on how to find Diego.

As he was reading the next string of messages, the tone suddenly changed. These weren't business texts. They were romantic. And very steamy, at that. He almost stopped reading because he didn't feel like it was right to invade these highly personal conversations. But the next word he saw on the screen made him freeze.

"What?" he said out loud. "No way."

He read the words again. *Scarlett, mi amor.*

His mind went into overdrive, and a sick feeling formed in the pit of his stomach. He was far from an expert on Latin America, but he felt fairly certain that Scarlett was not a common name in the region.

Could Layla's friend and mentor be working with a cartel deputy? He hadn't even considered the possibility that the mole could be at the State Department. But hadn't Layla said that Scarlett had worked at the DEA for years?

He scoured through the other texts, searching for references to Scarlett, but came up empty. It was highly possible that the one message had been a slipup. They probably never referenced each other by name for this exact reason.

How in the world was he going to break this news to Layla? She'd already been betrayed by Bryce, and now this. He had to be sure before he took this to her, but how could he be?

Immediately, he started researching Scarlett. He called his hacker friend and explained that he needed anything he could get on Scarlett ASAP.

Two hours later, he still didn't have a rock-solid case, but he had enough puzzle pieces that he couldn't hide this from Layla. There was far too much riding on this.

He had called her cell multiple times with no answer. It was so hard to be patient, but he knew that she would be safe as long as she was at the Agency.

He would just have to wait, and so he kept digging.

◆

Layla was on autopilot. There was too much hurt and betrayal for her to deal with her roller coaster of emotions. Bryce had not only threatened her career, he had wanted to take her life.

When Scarlett walked into the Agency conference room, Layla gave her a big hug.

"Man, I'm glad to see you," Layla said. "I'm sorry to have called you, but I needed to talk."

"I got a partial download from Nick." Scarlett squeezed her hand. "I am so sorry."

"Thanks." Layla held back the tears. "Can we get out of here?"

"Absolutely. Let's go to my place. We can get your security detail to follow us."

"Thank you."

Layla's hands were still shaking as they made the quick trip to Scarlett's house in McLean. She saw she'd missed calls from Hunter, but she'd call him back after she got done with Scarlett. She sent him a quick text telling him where she was going and then put her phone in her purse.

"Here we are," Scarlett said.

Layla had been to Scarlett's ranch home many times. She loved the house and felt comfortable there. Layla needed a place where she could decompress for a few minutes and shed some tears in a no-judgment zone.

She thanked the two-man security detail standing guard

on the premises. Knowing she had them and Scarlett, who was a highly trained operative, beside her, she felt safe—or as safe as she was going to feel.

They walked inside the house, and Layla let out a huge breath.

"Go put your feet up in the living room. I'll bring in some tea," Scarlett said.

"Thanks." Her phone buzzed in her purse, and she pulled it out. Hunter was being persistent in his texting. As she started reading his words, her heart dropped.

> Scarlett is the mole. Be careful. I'm on my way
> and have called in reinforcements. I'm so sorry.

She read the message again, but her brain didn't compute. This couldn't be right. Hunter had to be mistaken. Bryce was a traitor, but not Scarlett. Scarlett was her friend.

Scarlett walked in with the tea. "Layla, you're pale."

Layla put her phone back in her purse and looked up. "Yeah, I'm feeling a bit weak right now."

Scarlett sat down next to her and handed her the tea.

Layla picked up the cup but stopped short of taking a sip. She looked into Scarlett's eyes. "Do you have a weapon on you?"

"Not on me, but my gun is right over there on the table." Scarlett inclined her head in that direction.

"Do you mind if I take it? I'd feel safer with it."

"I don't know that you should be holding on to a firearm right now. Let's get you calmed down first. We have the Agency detail right outside the door, and I'm in here with you. You'll be fine. I promise."

As long as Scarlett didn't have the gun either, Layla was in good shape. She could block Scarlett's path if need be.

It also occurred to her that there could be something in the tea. Maybe she was being paranoid, but she couldn't risk it.

Layla placed the tea on the coffee table. "I think I'm in shock."

"What did Bryce say?"

"He was the one who set me up with the IG investigation. He also sold me out to the cartel by providing information on the safe house location. Can you imagine what that type of betrayal feels like? He was one of my friends." She purposely said that to gauge Scarlett's reaction. But there was nothing to show that Scarlett was flustered by it.

"I knew he was bad news, but good grief. He served you up to the cartel. I hope he's en route to a black site right now where he'll rot for years."

Layla shook her head. "No. They're doing this by the book. Lawyers and all." She paused. "I just didn't realize someone's thirst for revenge could be so great."

Scarlett took her hand, and it took all her willpower not to yank it away. "I've told you before, Layla, it's a harsh world out there. People you think are on your side can stab you in the back."

She squeezed Scarlett's hand before dropping it. "You'd know something about that, wouldn't you?"

Scarlett raised an eyebrow. "What do you mean?"

Layla jumped up and ran over to the table where the gun was. She picked it up and pointed it toward Scarlett. She wasn't messing around.

"Layla, what are you doing?" Scarlett asked.

"You betrayed me, Scarlett. You betrayed the DEA team. I want to know why. I deserve answers. You owe me that, at least."

"I have no idea what you're talking about. Put the gun

down and let's talk about this." Scarlett took a step forward.

"Don't move a single inch, or I will shoot."

"No, you won't. That's not your style."

"Oh, my style has changed greatly over the past twenty-four hours. Stinging betrayal has a way of putting things in a whole different light. So we're going to do this again. How long have you been working for the cartel?"

Scarlett's face reddened, and Layla knew, after looking into her eyes, that Hunter had been right. There was not going to be an innocent explanation.

"How did you find out?" Scarlett's voice wavered.

"That doesn't matter." She wasn't about to drag Hunter into this. "Talk to me. I need to know why."

Scarlett averted her eyes. "It has absolutely nothing to do with you. I tried to protect you."

"How is that possible?" Layla's voice rose. "The bombing, all the attacks? That's what you call protection?"

Scarlett looked back at her. "I had no choice but to give you up. It was my life or yours, and that was the only choice I could make. Diego saw you on the tape and demanded your name. I am responsible for making sure those tourists sat in your normal spot. I saved you, Layla. I did, whether you want to believe it or not."

"And you purposely tried to frame Zane to take the fall for your actions."

Scarlett nodded. "It was the most logical play I could make at the time."

"And Keith Hammond? What about him?"

Scarlett blew out a breath. "Keith was collateral damage. You brought him into it, and once I knew you were going to talk to him, I had to out him to the cartel as an Agency operative because I knew the cartel would be watching, and if I didn't give him up, then it would've come back on me. That was enough to get him killed, given how much of a warpath Diego is on."

The burning question was still there. "You still haven't told me why."

"When I was a field agent for the DEA, I started working a cartel member named Mateo Lopez. I was convinced he was going to become a top asset." She took a breath. "I thought I had him turned, but as we spent more and more time together, I ended up falling for him. And instead of me working him, he was working me."

"So you're not together?" She needed to get the facts.

"Not anymore. He played me. I thought it was real, but I was the stupid one. He might have cared about me at some point, but his aspirations got bigger than his feelings, and he had me locked in. I had no choice but to do their bidding, or they were going to expose the fact that I was once in a relationship with a top deputy in the cartel. My career would've been over. They had far too much leverage on me."

"What happened with the Honduras op?"

"Once Roberto was killed, Diego was beyond furious. He came to me for names. I gave them Diaz, Cass, you, and Zane but explained that I needed to keep Zane in play. Diego seemed to be okay with that, at least for the short term, although his ultimate goal was to take him out too. He wasn't messing around. His little brother had been killed, and he wanted revenge at any cost. I tried to help you as much as I could. Like I said, I saved you in the bombing. But at the end of the day, it was either you or me. I never wanted it to end up like this." She took a step. "But you're not going to kill me. You're going to let me go. I have passports. I can run. I can hide and get out of the country to safety."

"You know me well enough to realize I'd never let you go."

"It's because I know you so well that I think you will. I did my best to protect you each step of the way. Please return the favor. Once the cartel realizes I'm blown, they'll put a bullet through my head. All I'm asking for is a fighting chance to live. My life as I know it is over forever. Please show me mercy. *Please*."

Layla was torn. Was she just being played again? Did Scarlett actually care about her?

"Layla, you know I don't have any family. Everything I told you about my past is true. You're like my little sister."

"But when push came to shove, you still chose yourself over me. Just like Bryce. Two people I thought I could count on have sold me out and left a trail of destruction in their wake."

"But will my death do anything to solve all of that? It won't bring anyone back." Scarlett's bottom lip started to quiver. "We don't have time to debate this, Layla. Diego's men are probably on their way here right now. They've had a team stationed down the street since the Honduras op because Diego wanted to make sure I played by the rules. My house is under twenty-four-seven video surveillance."

"And you're just telling me this now?" Layla tried to think of the best way out of this. She didn't know what to do. Was Scarlett bluffing? Was the cartel really on their way to finish the job? She knew she wouldn't kill Scarlett, but would she detain her? That was the right thing to do, even though Layla was tempted to let her go. In the end, she had to go with her gut and follow the path that was right. They'd leave, but she wouldn't let Scarlett go. Her friend had made bad choices, and she had to be held accountable. "Scarlett, I'm so sorry."

Before Layla could say anything else, gunshots filled Scarlett's living room. Instinctively, she dove behind the couch and hit the floor, trying to protect herself from gunfire, her weapon at the ready.

The gunshots paused. She peered around the edge of the couch and saw that Scarlett had been shot in the head. Her body lay on the ground, and blood pooled around her skull. Her eyes were open but vacant.

Two men raced into the room. Layla raised her weapon to return fire, but behind them she saw Hunter with her security detail on his heels. One of the attackers fell to the ground. Hunter had shot him in the leg. Another round of gunshots and the other man was hit in the shoulder, and he collapsed.

Hunter rushed over to her. "Are you okay?"

"Yes, I'm fine." She looked at the men groaning in pain. "We need to secure them and then call reinforcements."

"I already made the call." Hunter jumped up and the security detail secured the attackers.

Layla walked over to Scarlett and crouched down beside her. She checked for a pulse even though she knew it was an act of futility. The tears fell freely as she stared at her friend's dead body. She couldn't begin to deal with how she felt, so she sat on the floor and prayed, because she didn't know what else she could do.

It wasn't long before the room was swarming with an alphabet soup of agents.

She stood in the corner with Hunter close by. "I can't believe this. I just can't."

"If I'd been only a second later . . ." Hunter said, his face still filled with fear for her.

"Don't even go there. You made it in time."

"They appeared on foot out of nowhere right when I pulled up. And I just knew I had to get inside and stop them."

She put her hands on his shoulders. "And that's exactly what you did."

"What happened with Scarlett?"

She quickly recounted their difficult conversation. She still couldn't believe that Scarlett was gone forever. "She was trying to convince me to let her go. She said that the cartel would kill her, and she was right."

Hunter nodded. "Scarlett made bad decisions."

Layla looked up at him, fighting back tears. "I did consider letting her go. Just for a minute. I wanted so desperately to believe that she was telling the truth. That she had tried to protect me as long as she could."

"And it's possible she was telling the truth. But when it came down to it, she put herself first."

"That's not true friendship."

He shook his head. "No, it's not. It's selfish, and she's the one who put you in harm's way. But you cared about her, and she cared about you."

Layla sighed. "I'm going to need some time to work through this."

He pulled her close. "I'm not going anywhere."

"Me neither." Their eyes locked, and even in this darkest of moments, the promise of the future hung between them.

◆

A knock on Izzy's door late Sunday night made Aiden jump up from the couch.

"We are both on edge right now," she said.

"This case is making us crazy," he responded.

"Let me see who it is." She walked over to the door and groaned when she saw Detective Stewart on the other side, but there was no use in hiding.

She opened the door. "Detective Stewart, what can I do for you?"

"Can I come in?"

"Sure." It wasn't like Izzy was going to slam the door in the detective's face. She led her into the kitchen, where Aiden was now standing. "Can I get you anything to drink?"

Detective Stewart shook her head. "No, thanks. I don't think this will take very long."

"More questions?" Izzy tried to keep her frustration in check. "We'll need to have Piper present."

Detective Stewart lifted her hand. "That won't be necessary. I'm not here to question you."

"Then what?"

"There's been a major development in the case."

Izzy's heartbeat thumped. "What happened?"

"Ann Marie Martinez confessed to killing Sergeant Tybee."

"What?" Ann Marie had been hiding something, but this was much worse than Izzy had expected.

"We questioned her pretty aggressively—the same way we questioned you. At first she stuck to her story, but after a while, she asked for a lawyer, and then we got a confession. Given the violent circumstances and the self-defense claim, the DA has worked out a plea deal."

"What were the circumstances?"

"It turns out that Ann Marie was viciously beaten and sexually assaulted by Sergeant Tybee a number of times. She was suffering from PTSD and experiencing severe psychological trauma. Even with all of that, she realized that she couldn't live with herself if she allowed you to take the fall. Given what had happened to her and Sergeant Tybee's pattern of abuse with other women, yourself included, the DA was willing to cut a generous deal. I wanted to let you know right away."

Aiden put his arm around Izzy's shoulders. "You owe Izzy an apology, Detective."

"No, that's not necessary," Izzy responded.

"Actually, it is. We pushed you hard, but we didn't want to be seen as showing favoritism to a former member of Arlington PD. But I am so sorry about what you had to go through. At least Tybee can't hurt anyone else."

"He'll never see his day in court," Izzy said. And that part bothered her.

Detective Stewart nodded. "That's true, but there's nothing we can do about it now. Can I have a moment alone with you before I go?"

"It's okay. You can say anything in front of Aiden. He knows everything about this ordeal."

The detective nodded. "All right. I was just going to encourage you to go back to counseling. I think you might need some help and time to handle the emotions that came with this investigation and Sergeant Tybee's murder."

She'd already had the same thought herself. "I appreciate that. It's a good idea."

"I'll be on my way. Never hesitate to reach out if you need anything."

After the detective left, Izzy turned to Aiden. "I've been thinking."

"Uh-oh. A new career idea?" He smiled.

"No. But this whole experience has given me lots to think about, and I've decided to do it."

"Law school?" His eyes brightened.

"Yes. I take the LSAT in a few months, and we'll see how I do, but I've already been researching schools. I'd love to go to Georgetown."

"Just like your friends."

She smiled. "Yeah, I can't wait to tell them."

He pulled her into a tight hug. "Izzy, I'm convinced you'll succeed in anything you set your mind to, and I know you'll make a great attorney. I hope you'll still want to hang out with a cop."

"Of course. If I'm a prosecutor, you never know how our paths will cross."

"I'm hoping they cross a lot more than that." He leaned in to kiss her, and she felt safe and loved.

CHAPTER
TWENTY-EIGHT

Zane couldn't believe the good news he had just received. Cass had been able to cut a deal that allowed her no jail time if she paid back all the money she took. It would take a long time for that to happen, but it was much better than facing hard time. If there was any way she would let him help her pay off the debt, he was going to do it. It hadn't been easy, but he'd opened up to her about his family life and the resources at his disposal.

"How did you pull that off?" Zane asked her, regarding her deal.

"It came at a price."

Uh-oh. "How high?"

"You know what you said about the Agency?"

"Yeah."

"Mason talked to some people there, and thanks to Layla's absolutely glowing recommendation, they're willing to take me on as a private contractor. I have a yearlong probationary period, and if I make the tiniest of missteps, the deal is off. But I'm thankful to have a job, considering the debt I have to pay back."

He took her hand. "You can do it, Cass. I'm here for whatever you need."

"You've been far too good to me."

He shook his head. "Don't talk like that."

"I'm just thankful you're still willing to be my friend."

He hesitated a moment. "Cass, I've been doing a lot of thinking."

"Me too," she said softly.

"And I wondered if you really meant what you said a while back about us."

She looked down and then right into his eyes. "I'm crazy about you, Zane, but after this, there's no way I'd push myself on you. I need your friendship."

"I want your friendship, too, but now you'll be working at a completely separate agency."

"Yeah."

"Let's give this thing a go, Cass."

Her dark eyes grew large. "You can't be serious. Not after all I've done."

He laughed. "Yeah, I'm totally serious."

She threw her arms around his neck.

"And I'm going to help you with your brother to make sure he gets the counseling and support he needs."

"I don't know how to thank you."

"No more secrets. Is that a deal?"

"No secrets." She lifted her chin and pressed her lips to his. They weren't perfect, but they were meant to be.

◆

"Home sweet home." The past week had flown by, but now Layla was finally returning to her neglected condo with Hunter close by her side.

She was still grieving Scarlett's death and betrayal, but the men they had apprehended had led the DEA to Diego's location. The DEA had wanted to capture Diego, but he was killed in a fierce firefight. The cartel was in complete disarray with its leader dead and no heir apparent, which meant the entire team was now safe from any threats of retaliation.

Bryce had negotiated a deal, but one that included a lengthy prison sentence. It gave her no joy to know he was locked up, but given how serious his offenses were, she knew the punishment fit the crime. Bryce had also given up his CIA source who had provided the safe house intel, and he was being punished as well.

Hunter looked at her. "Everything has been scrubbed to make sure there is nothing in here. No surveillance, no devices, nothing. And the CIA even threw in a top-to-bottom cleaning service, thanks to Nick."

She smiled. "So now you and Nick are friends, huh?" She was glad they'd been able to work together and put that past chapter behind them.

Hunter nodded. "Yeah, reluctantly, but he has really done right by you. And once I was convinced he wasn't trying to win you back, he and I got along a lot better."

"Being back home feels so strange." She looked around her condo.

"Well, get used to it, because things are going to go back to normal."

And that was part of the problem. "Yeah, about that."

"What's wrong?"

Her world was far from right. She was struggling with what path she wanted to take with her career. "I'm still having a lot of conflicting feelings about going back to work."

Hunter moved closer to her. "You don't have to make

any decisions right away. Take the time they're giving you. You have plenty of options. Even if you decide to leave the Agency, I can think of a million jobs that would be perfect for you—including actually practicing law, if you wanted to go that route. The ball will be in your court, and you can count on me no matter what decisions you make."

He was right, and knowing that he would stand by her meant everything. She might be unclear about her career, but she was certain about her feelings for Hunter. "I have no idea what I want to do. I don't know how I'll ever completely get over what they did to us. What they stole from us."

"I get that, but we're together now, and we have to believe that the Lord's plan is bigger than we can see."

Her heart warmed at his declaration. "You believe that?"

He took her hands. "Thanks to seeing you live your faith and actually watching firsthand how God has protected you and me. How through all of this messy maze of our lives, we were brought back together."

"I don't even want to worry about tomorrow and what it will hold. I want to embrace now and being here with you."

He squeezed her hand. "Then don't worry."

She smiled. "How about we go to the grocery store and then come back and cook a nice, normal dinner? How does that sound?"

"Only one thing would make that better."

"What?" she asked.

"If you'll kiss me first."

She grinned and fell into his warm embrace. Their road had been long and ever winding, but they had still ended up back in each other's arms.

EPILOGUE

Layla had taken the Agency up on a three-month sabbatical and was enjoying her last weekend before going back to work. Viv was hosting a dinner party, and they had just finished dessert, which included peach cobbler—Layla's favorite. She looked at Hunter seated across from her and smiled. He winked at her, and the butterflies still flew around her stomach like crazy.

They'd spent a ton of time together over the past three months, getting to know each other all over again. Yeah, they each had changed and matured, but surprisingly, they also found that many things about each other hadn't changed at all. Falling back into a natural rhythm in their relationship had been much easier than she had expected. Their vow to be completely truthful wouldn't always be easy, but it did ensure a level of trust between them.

She was going to be at a crossroads when she went back to work on Monday, and she was still deciding the ultimate direction she wanted for her career. One thing she had determined, though, was that she still believed in the CIA's mission. Hunter had told her that the Agency needed more people like her, and his words had resonated.

She helped clear the table and followed Viv into the kitchen, along with Bailey and Izzy.

"You shouldn't be cleaning. You went above and beyond for dinner." Layla took a bowl out of Viv's hands. "Let us do it."

"I'm just glad we could get together." Viv smiled brightly. "And we have something to celebrate."

"What?" Layla asked.

"Izzy got her LSAT scores!"

"Do tell," Bailey said.

Izzy's face beamed. "The number isn't that important, but it's good enough to be in the high range at Georgetown. I have a good shot of getting in! It's like a dream come true. I can't believe it."

Bailey gave her a hug. "You studied so hard."

"Thanks to you for all your help."

Bailey was a standardized testing genius and had tutored Izzy. Layla stayed far away from that. Those tests had never been her thing.

"It's good that we have things to celebrate now," Izzy said. "There have been so many battles over the past few months, I'm embracing this as a win."

"We all are," Layla said.

Viv gave Izzy a hug too. "Unfortunately, though, we probably won't see you as much now, especially your first year. You'll be locked in the law library, studying."

Izzy grinned. "I'll miss you ladies, but in the end, it will be worth it."

Layla loved seeing Izzy happy after everything she'd gone through. It finally felt like they were all in good places, and she hoped and prayed that would continue.

Hunter walked into the kitchen. "Can I steal Layla away for a minute?"

"Sure." Viv smiled. "We have the dishes under control."

Layla followed Hunter as he went out on the back porch. It was a cool day but not freezing.

"What's going on?" she asked.

Hunter turned to her. "I've been doing a lot of thinking."

Her stomach dropped, worrying that he had bad news.

He took her hands. "There's no need to frown. This isn't anything bad. I promise."

She let out a sigh of relief. "Good. Because it's been such a nice evening and a great way to decompress before going back to work."

Hunter took a breath. "Layla, since you came back into my life, we've faced some pretty awful things."

She was ready to move on to a new day. "But that's all behind us."

He nodded. "It is. And I'm so thankful that you're safe. But everything we experienced together has changed me—all in a good way. Before we reconnected, I was in such a dark place. I was completely numb and distant from God. I was just going through the motions in life but not really living it. The time we've spent together these past few months has been life changing. I never thought years ago that I could love you any more than I did then, but I was wrong about that. I love you even more now."

She looked into his blue eyes. "I love you, too, Hunter."

He smiled. "I know. I've never felt more loved. And our time together has taught me something else."

"What's that?" she asked.

"That life can literally change in a moment. I really do believe that God gave us a second chance. Not everyone gets another chance at love with the person who means the most to them in the world."

She moved closer to him. "This time nothing is going to tear us apart. Not the Agency, not anything. You have my word on that."

"Mine too, and I want to take it a step further." He took a breath. "I know we've only been in this new relationship a few months, but we had three years to build on. Three great years, if you cut out that last part."

"We agreed not to go back to that." She had put all of that squarely behind them.

He nodded. "This is a long and not very eloquent way of saying that, Layla, I don't want to waste another moment. We got derailed before, and I don't want that to happen again."

"Me neither."

"I was hoping you would say that." He dropped to one knee as he pulled a ring box out of his jacket pocket.

Her breath caught as she realized what he was about to do.

"We can have as long an engagement as you want, but I hope and pray that you'll want to be my wife. Layla, I love you with all my heart and soul. You're the light and goodness in my life. Your love has literally changed me, and your grace and forgiveness has shown me what real, true love is like. Layla, I love you. Will you marry me?"

She looked down at him holding the open ring box, displaying a princess-cut diamond ring. "What if I don't want to have a long engagement?"

He grinned. "Is that a yes?"

She nodded. "Yes."

He slid the ring on her finger, and it fit perfectly. Just like the two of them.

She pulled him up from his knee and gave him a kiss. "I love you so much, Hunter."

He kissed her again, and she heard the cheering.

She turned around and saw everyone peering out the living room window. "Did they all know?" she asked.

"Just Viv. I swore her to secrecy until we came out here. I told her to give us a few minutes before she told the others."

As she looked at the man she loved, her heart was so full. "I have never felt such happiness as what I feel right now."

He kissed her again. "And to think what we had to go through to get here."

Layla couldn't wait to see what their future held. She was convinced they could face anything together. And there was one more thing she was certain of.

"It was all worth it."

AUTHOR'S NOTE

They say that some books write themselves, and for me, *Backlash* was one of those books. I loved being able to bring a piece of myself into Layla's story. Layla and I have a lot of things in common. Like Layla, I am half-Lebanese from my father's side. I also have a degree in Middle Eastern studies and went to law school. And, like Layla, once upon a time I was recruited by intelligence agencies.

But that's where Layla and I diverge. I took a much different career path outside the government and became a lawyer in the corporate world. And while Layla was hesitant to become a CIA officer, she was still highly capable in the field—something I could have never been. It was super exciting to write a character that could do all the things I could never imagine doing. Sitting behind a desk is much more in my comfort zone than fending off attackers, taking shots from a speeding SUV, and dodging bullets!

This story is also special because I've always wanted to

write a leading character who was Lebanese, and I'm thankful for the opportunity to do so. I'm also thankful for the chance to share my faith through stories. My father was called to become a preacher many decades ago. As I write these words, I am about to mark the *seventh* year of his passing from this earth and into heaven. Oh, how I would have loved to call him up and tell him about this story! I have no doubt that he would have been fully intrigued and supportive, because that's the kind of father he always was. I know one day we will be reunited, and for that I am eternally grateful.

Thank you for taking this journey with me and allowing me to continue to share my faith and my stories with you—and a piece of my heart.

Rachel Dylan is an award-winning and bestselling author of legal thrillers and romantic suspense. She has practiced law for over a decade, including being a litigator at one of the nation's top law firms. The ATLANTA JUSTICE series features strong female attorneys in Atlanta. *Deadly Proof*, the first book in the ATLANTA JUSTICE series, is a CBA bestseller, an FHL Reader's Choice Award winner, a Daphne du Maurier finalist, and a HOLT Medallion finalist. *Lone Witness* is the winner of a HOLT Medallion and the Maggie Award and is a Selah finalist. Rachel lives in Michigan with her husband and five furkids—two dogs and three cats. She loves to connect with readers. You can find her at www.racheldylan.com.

Sign Up for Rachel's Newsletter

Keep up to date with Rachel's news on book releases and events by signing up for her email list at racheldylan.com.

More from Rachel Dylan

When elite members of the military are murdered on the streets of Washington, D.C., FBI Special Agent Bailey Ryan and NCIS Special Agent Marco Agostini must work together to bring the perpetrator to justice. As the stakes rise in a twisted conspiracy and allies turn to enemies, the biggest secret yet to be uncovered could be the end of them all.

End Game
CAPITAL INTRIGUE #1

You May Also Like . . .

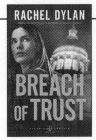

When corporate litigator Mia Shaw finds her colleague brutally murdered, she vows to make the killer pay. The accused is a friend of Noah Ramirez, who knows something doesn't add up. As Mia takes on a case of corporate espionage, Noah becomes her only ally. But can he convince her that the killer is still on the loose—and protect her from growing threats?

Breach of Trust by Rachel Dylan
ATLANTA JUSTICE #3
racheldylan.com

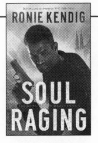

Done waiting for answers, former Navy SEAL Leif Metcalf seizes control and teams up with his greatest enemy—a move that comes with a deadly risk. Torn apart by opposing views on how to handle Leif's act of treachery, team Reaper hunts one of their own—agreeing only on starting, not stopping, the final battle prophesied in the Book of the Wars.

Soul Raging by Ronie Kendig
THE BOOK OF THE WARS #3
roniekendig.com

Terrorists have been smuggled in the country intent on unleashing a deadly attack, and FBI Agent Kiley Dawson and ICE Agent Evan Bowers are charged with taking it down—only, Kiley blames Evan for the death of her former partner and can't be in the same room as him. As threats ensue, the two are pushed to the breaking point in a race to save countless lives.

Minutes to Die by Susan Sleeman
HOMELAND HEROES #2
susansleeman.com

◊ BETHANYHOUSE

Printed in the United States
By Bookmasters